# SHERLOCK HOLMES

# *The Thinking Engine*

## Also Available from Titan Books

*Sherlock Holmes: Gods of War*
James Lovegrove

*Sherlock Holmes: The Stuff of Nightmares*
James Lovegrove

*Sherlock Holmes: The Spirit Box*
George Mann

*Sherlock Holmes: The Will of the Dead*
George Mann

*Sherlock Holmes: The Breath of God*
Guy Adams

*Sherlock Homes: The Army of Dr Moreau*
Guy Adams

## Coming Soon from Titan Books

*Sherlock Holmes: The Patchwork Devil* (April 2016)
Cavan Scott

*Sherlock Holmes: A Betrayal in Blood* (March 2017)
Mark Latham

# SHERLOCK HOLMES
# *The Thinking Engine*

JAMES LOVEGROVE

TITAN BOOKS

Sherlock Holmes: The Thinking Engine
Print edition ISBN: 9781783295036
Electronic edition ISBN: 9781783295043

Published by Titan Books
A division of Titan Publishing Group Ltd
144 Southwark Street, London SE1 0UP

First Titan Books edition: August 2015
2 4 6 8 10 9 7 5 3 1



A CIP catalogue record for this title is available from the British Library.

Printed and bound in the United States

# SHERLOCK HOLMES
# *The Thinking Engine*

# FOREWORD

In the account known as "The Adventure of the Three Students" I wrote that in the spring of 1895 "a combination of events, into which I need not enter, caused Mr Sherlock Holmes and myself to spend some weeks in one of our great university towns".

I realise that, with those few words, I may have sounded entirely dismissive of the circumstances that brought us to that place, as though the matter were of minor consequence.

I also somewhat mendaciously described Holmes as "pursuing some laborious researches in early English charters" at this unnamed seat of learning. That was, I confess now, misdirection. He was doing anything but.

The truth is that, at the time, I felt obliged to skate over what was one of the most challenging and intriguing investigations my friend undertook, not to mention one of the most hazardous. The "Three Students" case was merely a light, diverting interlude in a much darker and stranger symphony whose nature I was not prepared to divulge when the story appeared in *The Strand* in 1904. Now, however, nearly a quarter of a century on from the story's publication, I am ready to tackle the entirety of the affair in narrative form with as much frankness and honesty as I can muster. I am older, and the passage of years has given me perspective and distance.

Besides, I very much doubt I shall submit this account to my publishers and thus offer it for general consumption. It is likelier that it will add to the burgeoning number of manuscripts languishing in the tin dispatch box which I keep in the vaults at Cox & Co. Bank at Charing Cross.

The university town in question, then, was Oxford, and it is not without good reason that I was reticent about the month Holmes and I spent there during and after Hilary term of '95. For what transpired in the City of Dreaming Spires (to borrow Matthew Arnold's coinage from his poem "Thyrsis") brought us face to face with one of the strangest and most singular manifestations of evil we have ever encountered, and the world is better off not knowing the full facts.

Not only that, but so strenuous and punishing were the events involved that my companion was driven to breaking point, and indeed very nearly was broken. The same goes for our friendship, which was tested to its limits. These are not events which it pleases me to recall.

Much has been written about Charles Babbage and his remarkable steam-powered mechanical computers and calculating machines. Somewhat less is known about Professor Malcolm Quantock and his Thinking Engine – a device that seemed to possess the soul and intellect of a man…

John H. Watson, MD (retd.), 1927

# CHAPTER ONE

## The Rubenstein Collection Mummy

"Watson, old chap," said Sherlock Holmes, as the mummy of a four-thousand-year-old pharaoh came shuffling towards us in the Archaic Room at the British Museum, "I am prepared to concede, in this one instance, that a belief in the resurrection of the dead may not be wholly unfounded."

The mummy lurched across the darkened chamber with its arms outstretched. Loose ends of cerecloth dangled from wrist and elbow, twitching as it moved. Its feet dragged over the floorboards with a horrid, dry swishing sound reminiscent of old twigs and parchment. Its face had the very barest of features, shallow indentations for the eyes and mouth lurking beneath the brittle-looking bandages, which lent it a rudimentary, skull-like cast.

"I only said 'may', however," Holmes added. "That which appears to be perturbingly uncommon could, in the event, be quite commonplace."

My friend's *sangfroid* when presented with this all too tangible manifestation of the supernatural was impressive. I myself was in a state of some shock. I was rooted to the spot. A chill was going down my spine. The hairs on the back of my neck were standing up. I was experiencing all the clichés of terror, which at that moment felt freshly minted, in no way banal or tired, just all too appallingly true.

We found ourselves at the museum, at an hour when all right-minded folk should be tucked up in bed, owing to a visit by the Egyptologist Mr John Vansittart Smith, FRS, who had called on us in our rooms at 221B Baker Street the previous afternoon. At the request of this man, one of the pre-eminent practitioners in his field, Holmes had agreed to investigate a series of bizarre occurrences which had accompanied the Wallace Rubenstein Antiquities Collection on its year-long tour of Europe.

It had been alleged that the collection, which comprised several dozen priceless artefacts from around the globe, was in a very specific manner "haunted". Night watchmen at several of the venues where it halted on its peregrinations had reported hearing strange sounds emanating from the chamber in which it was exhibited. Some had even come face to face with an ambulatory creature that matched the description of the mummy of Pharaoh Djedhor – a 30th Dynasty monarch who had reigned during the 4th century BC – and had fled in fright from this apparition. Djedhor's preserved remains were the centrepiece of the collection, in no small part thanks to the large, ornately carved and painted sarcophagus that held them, a thing of considerable craftsmanship and beauty.

Although the watchmen's accounts of meeting the mummy while on their rounds were dismissed as nonsense by museum curators and directors, and on more than one occasion had resulted in a summary sacking, nonetheless the collection had begun to garner a reputation. Attendances had gone through the roof. Everywhere it went – the Kunsthistorisches Museum in Vienna, the Museo Arqueológico Nacional in Madrid, the *Ägyptisches* Museum und Papyrussammlung in Berlin – it drew crowds. People queued for hours to view it, lured by the glamour of otherworldly eeriness that now hung over it.

Several noted psychic mediums had declared that the Rubenstein Collection was thc locus of genuine unearthly activity, and found evidence to back up their claims, ranging from cold spots in the exhibition area to traces of ectoplasm on the floor, although the former could be ascribed simply to draughts while the latter usually turned out to be spillages of a somewhat more innocuous substance such as resin or wax.

Those in possession of more rational, scientific brains were of the opinion that the living-mummy rumours were just so much hogwash. A two-thousand-year-old corpse, most of whose vital organs had been removed upon death and stowed separately in Canopic jars, could not spontaneously come to life. Any who had witnessed the phenomenon were either drunkards, liars, or afflicted with mental debility.

The aforementioned Egyptologist, John Vansittart Smith, though definitely of the rational persuasion, nonetheless had an open mind. He admitted to us that not many months earlier, in the principal Eastern chamber of the Louvre in Paris, he had come across a living being whose comportment and conversation had left him in no doubt that he was in the presence of someone who had enjoyed a lifespan far in excess of man's usual allotted sum of years. This person, identifying himself as a priest of Osiris named Sosra who was born during the reign of Tuthmosis, had survived courtesy of an elixir of longevity he had concocted which vitiated disease and decay, thus all but conferring immortality on the user. Sosra, Smith said, had eventually perished in the arms of his beloved, a maiden called Atma who had been taken by plague and whose mummified remains he had pursued across the world over the course of many centuries with tragic doggedness.

Ever since his unnerving encounter, the Egyptologist had been convinced that the ancient Egyptians could lay claim to scientific and medical knowledge that far exceeded our own.

"What if," he said, "the stories about the Rubenstein Collection mummy are true? What if Pharaoh Djedhor languishes in some twilight state between life and death, kept that way by an infusion of herbs and chemicals introduced into his body during the embalming and mummification process? What if, from time to time, he rouses from this torpid state and staggers around briefly in a semblance of life? Mr Holmes, I implore you to look into this matter for me, so that I may know to my satisfaction whether my experience in France was a mere figment of my imagination or perhaps a hoax, or whether I really did spend an evening in the company of the oldest human being ever to have walked the Earth."

"I am no expert in archaeology or ancient history," replied my friend. "I can barely tell a Ming vase from a Qing vase. Surely it would be better if you yourself, Mr Smith, or one of your colleagues at the Royal Society or the Oriental Society, were to study the mummy and draw what conclusions you can from your analysis."

"Alas, that is not possible. Mr Rubenstein has stipulated that no items in his collection are open to scrutiny, not even by professionals such as myself. It is a crime against the advancement of knowledge, if you ask me, but he will not be swayed. He is very jealous of his property, it would seem, and fears it might be marred by careless hands. The mummy may not even be exposed to the open air, lest it suffer the ravages of our polluted city atmosphere."

"Intriguing. He allows the artefacts to go on tour, meaning they must be repeatedly packaged up, put in crates and transported from place to place, which entails no small risk of inadvertent damage; yet he is anxious that they should not be closely looked at, not even by those practised at handling such items."

"He is an American," said Smith, as though that explained much. "And very wealthy. A newspaper proprietor, I believe."

"Yes," said Holmes. "I have read about him. A former vaudevillian and theatre impresario who went into newspaper publishing and now has a string of dailies across the United States, the majority of them at the salacious and yellow end of the market. Yet himself a cultured man, it would appear, given his acquisition of some of the finest and most valuable of ancient treasures."

"It is possible to have refined tastes and peddle dross," I averred. "Often it is a mark of great intellect, the ability to create a product which appeals to the lowest common denominator."

"True, Watson, and such a talent has proved highly lucrative for some. I feel, however, that Mr Rubenstein would still like it to be known that he has a cultured side, hence his allowing his collection to be shown to the public on the Continent and in Britain. The publicity coup arising from the brouhaha about an animate mummy is, if nothing else, advantageous to his goal. Mr Smith? I would very much like to take this case on your behalf. I am interested in seeing this so-called living mummy with my own eyes, and to that end, Watson and I shall tonight install ourselves in the British Museum and lie in wait. With luck, Pharaoh Djedhor will oblige us by rising from his uneasy slumbers and embarking on one of his posthumous perambulations."

So it was that Holmes and I entered the museum shortly before closing time, just as the paying visitors were leaving. It was the very first day of the Rubenstein Collection's fortnight-long stay in London, and a great tide of people poured out of the Archaic Room, chattering excitedly, while the two of us shouldered against the flow, grim of purpose. We had obtained special permission to be on the premises after dark from no less a personage than Sir Edward Maunde Thompson, the museum's Principal Librarian and Director. Holmes had done Sir Edward a small service in the recent past, a matter concerning the theft of a gold Anglo-Saxon belt buckle. My friend was wont to dismiss the case as "a trivial diversion" but to my mind it involved some of his more ingenious examples of analytical reasoning, not least his deduction of the culprit's lack of a left eye based on nothing more than the angle on which a crowbar was deployed during the break-in. Sir Edward, at any rate, felt he owed Holmes a favour, and was returning it by granting us licence – contrary to regulations though it was – to roam the museum out of hours. He had some inkling of our reason for being there but stated that he would prefer not to be told explicitly, since he had no wish to be seen to be giving official credence to, in his words, "this absurd farrago of half-truths and wishful thinking".

We spent several long hours in the Archaic Room, hearing nothing but the whisper and sigh of the grand, venerable building around us and the clamour of pedestrians and road traffic on Great Russell Street outside the thick walls, all of which dwindled as the night wore on, leaving just the chilly, lonely rattle of the January wind. The only illumination came from moonlight slanting in through the high windows, which lent a phosphorescent silvery cast to the statues, pottery, swords, crowns, amphorae and other treasures that filled the room. The night watchmen had been instructed to give this particular corner of the museum a wide berth, an admonition which few of them minded heeding since at least half of them believed that Pharaoh Djedhor's eternal rest was more unquiet than it ought to have been and the remainder had no desire to have their scepticism put to the test.

"It is a most singular errand we are engaged on," Holmes murmured to me at one point during our vigil. "I would, of course, like to inspect the sarcophagus for myself, but I fear I cannot without disturbing its occupant and alerting him to our presence, which may have a deterrent effect. I would not care to inhibit friend Djedhor, should he elect to take the air this evening."

"Holmes, you're not telling me you think the mummy actually walks?"

"Do you suppose that it does not?"

Up until that moment I had been proceeding on the assumption that it was all hokum, a series of tall tales and misapprehensions which had grown with every stop on the collection's tour, gathering size and momentum like a snowball rolling downhill. Now, in light of Holmes's rhetorical question, I cast an uneasy eye towards the sarcophagus, which lay on a trestle some twenty feet from the glass-sided display cabinet behind which my friend and I had sequestered ourselves. It glimmered in the moon's glow, the features of its painted face suffused with a radiance that made them seem weirdly, I might even say preternaturally, alive. Its black-rimmed eyes seemed to sparkle with deep, long-held knowledge, and I could not help thinking of the withered effigy within, confined to that fig-wood coffin over three hundred years before the birth of Christ, a once all-powerful ruler of one of history's greatest and most enduring empires, worshipped as a god, considered a son of Ra, no less. Might he still be alive, fending off the approach of death via some arcane alchemical process lost to time? Might he, even now, be reaching for the underside of the sarcophagus's lid with bony, impossibly old fingers, to push it open and once again walk the earth as he did in the dim and distant past?

I won't deny that a chill descended upon me then and a knot of dread took up occupancy in my belly, so much so that when Holmes next addressed me, I started.

"Your service revolver is, I need not ask, to hand?"

"It... It is. Yes. In my pocket. But if we are about to confront the undead, what hope have we of stopping it with mere bullets? Are not such creatures impervious to harm by conventional means?"

"By repute they are," said Holmes, "and it is a pity we have not taken the precaution of investing in ammunition made of silver. It is surely better, though, to face them with some manner of weapon at the ready than none at all."

I could not fault his logic, but it did not comfort me. As the night wore on I became increasingly unsettled. The shadows in the room seemed to thicken, and I sensed the antiquities all around me as though they had an ineffable weight, as though their cumulative age was a force that made the atmosphere in the room heavy and oppressive. Time crawled, anchored by these many relics of long-gone civilisations in far-off yesteryears.

Shortly after the bells of St. George's, Bloomsbury struck midnight, we heard it – Holmes first, with his sharper ears. The merest of scraping sounds reached us, followed by the merest of creaks.

Before our very eyes, the sarcophagus of Pharaoh Djedhor began to open and the mummy slowly, stiffly clambered out.

# CHAPTER TWO

## The Bumptious American

"Now, Watson!" Holmes hissed. "Quick! We must move!"

I, though, was unable to, for I was still overcome by that surge of terror which had left my entire body paralysed. I could no more have moved at that moment than could the squat limestone figurine of a Mesopotamian fertility goddess which sat on a pedestal nearby.

The mummy lumbered towards us with a dire, implacable gait, seemingly aware of the horror its menacing appearance must strike in all who saw it.

All, that is, save Sherlock Holmes, who was not intimidated. Rather, he was energised, and leapt forward with a fierce glee, clamping a hand upon my arm and dragging me along with him. His touch had a galvanic effect, and though I was far from thrilled at being pulled bodily into the path of the oncoming revenant, I took heart from Holmes's intrepidity. If he was unafraid, should I not be also? My companion, after all, was far from being a fool. If he perceived no imminent danger in the situation, then no imminent danger there must be.

"Your pistol, old man," he urged me. "Take it out. Aim it."

I did as I was told, blindly compliant, cocking back the hammer with my thumb.

"You there!" Holmes said, speaking now to the mummy. "The jig is up. We have you at gunpoint. I would recommend you stand still and surrender, or face the consequences."

I did not believe for one instant that his barked command would have any effect. How could they on a creature whose mother tongue had not been uttered aloud in several centuries and who doubtless knew not one word of English? A creature, moreover, whose very existence mocked death.

But then a most remarkable thing happened.

The mummy obeyed.

It halted in its tracks, and its extended arms rose from horizontal to vertical.

"P-please," it stammered in an accent which sounded to my ears distinctly American. "Don't shoot. I give up."

Holmes gave vent to an arch laugh. "I knew it! The whole thing has been a charade, perpetrated by an associate of Rubenstein's from his theatre days. You are, are you not, sir, a vaudeville performer?"

"I am that, among other things," said the mummy, his tone somewhat crestfallen. "Kindly ask your companion to put away his pistol. I assure you I am no threat."

"Perhaps I should be the judge of that. Watson, keep your gun trained on him. Let us firmly establish the facts of the situation before we lower our guard."

"Watson?" said the mummy. "As in Dr John Watson? Then you, sir, must be Sherlock Holmes."

"None other. From your distinctive drawl I take you to be a native of one of the mid-western states of America – Wisconsin would be my guess, judging by a certain particular broadness of the vowels which derives from the many Norwegian settler communities there."

"That is true."

"Yet I discern the faintest tinges of a Slavic heritage too, in your rather choppy intonation. I suspect your parents are of European origin, immigrants. From Budapest, perhaps?"

"Now you are being truly uncanny," said the mummy, who was in no small way uncanny himself. "I was in fact born in that great city but we emigrated when I was very young."

"I confess that it is a hobby of mine, tracing a man's ancestry from his inherited speech patterns. It especially applies to your nation. Few Americans are just American. More often than not they betray the imprint of their forebears in their accents and vocabulary. I have composed a short monograph on the subject which is currently undergoing peer review by members of the Philological Society on its way to publication in their annual *Transactions*. Your origins, however, need not detain us, since it is your present activities with which we are concerned."

"Before you go any further," said the mummy, "may I at least remove some of these bandages? I have been bound up in them for nearly eighteen hours, and I find them constricting to say the least. Now that there is no further need to wear them, I may as well divest myself."

"By all means."

The impersonator of the dead Pharaoh Djedhor began carefully to unwind the cerecloths from around his head, to reveal a roughly triangular face with eyes set close together and eyebrows that canted towards each other at a very determined angle. His hair, wiry and dark, he combed with his fingers until it was somewhat neatened and given an approximate centre parting. Then he smiled sheepishly and stuck out a still cloth-wrapped hand. He could not have been more than twenty or twenty-one years of age, yet had the bearing of someone older and more worldly.

"It is an honour to meet you, Mr Holmes," he said. "Your fame has reached the shores of my homeland, and I must say, if I had to be apprehended by anyone in the commission of this little imposture, I'm glad it was you. To have been unmasked by a lesser man would have been humiliating, whereas to have fallen foul of the great Sherlock Holmes – well, I guess then we can call it quits."

I bristled at the sheer impertinence of the fellow. He evidently felt that he, a felon, was somehow the equal of my friend and that his capture *in flagrante delicto* was no more than the outcome of a contest, like a joust between two knights in which both were unhorsed. He could not, it seemed, have had a higher opinion of himself, his self-esteem excessive even by the standards of his own countrymen.

Holmes, for his part, was merely amused. "Whom do I have the pleasure of addressing?" he enquired, grasping the mummy's hand.

"I was born Erik Weisz," came the reply, "but I prefer to go by the stage name of Harry Houdini. Of the Brothers Houdini? The toast of Coney Island?"

"I regret your fame has not stretched as far this way across the Atlantic as mine has the other way."

The man who called himself Houdini looked disappointed, but not for long, his innate bumptiousness rapidly reasserting itself. "That state of affairs will unquestionably change. Soon the whole world will have heard of me, for with the assistance of my brother Theo I am developing a magic act which is wholly unique and which will one day be a marvel to all. Harry Houdini will become a household name to match yours, Mr Holmes. You mark my words."

"With such a force of vigour and passion behind it, I have no doubt your prediction will come true, sir."

"Holmes," I said with some surprise, "you are behaving very

amicably towards this man. Does the fact that he is a criminal mean nothing?"

My friend turned to me, head cocked. "A criminal, Watson? I am hard pressed to fathom what actual crime he has committed. Is donning the guise of a two-thousand-year-old Egyptian god-king against the law? I can't say I've seen that in any of the statute books."

"How about frightening museum watchmen after dark? Surely that is an offence? Trespass, too."

"But this is all just flimflam. Chicanery. Showmanship. Am I not right, Mr Houdini? You have been employed by Wallace Rubenstein as a cunning means of drumming up custom. He is paying you to rise from Djedhor's sarcophagus wreathed in cotton bandages and give your best impression of the walking dead, in order to generate interest in the exhibit and earn it a 'spooky' reputation. People's credulousness and word of mouth has done the rest. Rubenstein, despite his news publishing empire, remains a theatrical at heart. You can take the man out of vaudeville but you can't take vaudeville out of the man."

"Sensationalism is Wallace Rubenstein's middle name," Houdini admitted. "In his newspapers and in all aspects of his life. I did have my concerns that pretending to be a mummy would not work. Would the public fall for it? Yet there is something profoundly fascinating about a person seemingly rising from the grave. It touches a deep-seated nerve – our dread of death and our hope of an afterlife beyond it. This little stunt has power. I am convinced the same power will bolster my magic act and make it a roaring success, once it is fully developed. Apparent death, apparent rebirth – who will not pay to see that?"

Houdini managed to look both wistful and avaricious at the same time.

"Watson," said Holmes, "I believe it is safe for you to return your gun to your pocket."

I acceded to the request with some slight reluctance. Houdini watched me do it with no small relief.

"Mr Houdini," Holmes continued, "what impresses me most of all is the self-control you so clearly have in abundance."

Houdini offered a low, gratified bow. "It is one of my foremost qualities."

"To be entombed in that sarcophagus for so long a period – eighteen hours, did you say?"

"Since it was unloaded from the wagon just after six this morning and carried to this room. I am ostensibly part of the team of specialist removals men who are accompanying the collection on tour; that is my cover. Just before the sarcophagus is wheeled indoors, I sneak inside and ensconce myself. It is otherwise empty, by the way. Djedhor himself is waiting back at Rubenstein's mansion in Newport, Rhode Island, his body stored in a dry, well-ventilated basement room. Then, with great care, I strip out of my civilian clothing, bind myself up in bandages, and wait for the witching hour."

"Is it not claustrophobic?"

"I have ways of combating fear. The mind is a powerful tool, Mr Holmes, you know that as well as anyone. It can, provided it is subjected to the correct training and discipline, conquer all physical and emotional infirmities. I have studied the methods of Hindu fakirs and yogis, who are able to transcend the limitations of the flesh to a sometimes superhuman degree, and have applied them to my own work. I am now able to place myself in a kind of trance state, such that hours pass like minutes. I slow my breathing and lower my heart rate, even sometimes falling into a doze. Confined spaces with limited air supply hold no terror for me. I am as cosy in them as in my own bed."

"Remarkable. Would your magic act, then, involve entering into a confined space?"

"And then absconding from it. Dash and I – that is, my brother Theo and I – are also hoping to involve handcuffs, and possibly a straitjacket. The act is still very much in its infancy, hence I am obliged to take paid engagements of every description, however irregular, such as this one. Tell me, Mr Holmes, am I to be arrested? Handed over to your London bobbies? Is that your plan?"

"I am undecided," said Holmes. "No real misdemeanour has been perpetrated. No one has been hurt or materially disadvantaged."

I felt moved to point out that certain museum employees on the Continent had needlessly and unfairly lost their jobs.

"That is a fact," said my friend with a nod. "Perhaps then, Mr Houdini, we can come to some sort of arrangement. If you were to cable Mr Rubenstein and convince him to make suitable reparations to those people Watson has mentioned, the balance of justice will be righted and there will be no call to take matters further."

"That is most reasonable of you, sir. I should warn you, Mr Rubenstein may not like it. He is not fond of parting with money. Yet he will, if the only alternative is a public embarrassment. And in return, your and Dr Watson's complicity is assured?"

"I give you my word. I would advise, however, that in future you vary the timings of your excursions as Pharaoh Djedhor, for that is what first alerted me to the possibility that human rather than supernatural agency was involved here. Before I came to the museum this evening, while my friend Watson was tending to his patients at his practice, I made enquiries. I sent a number of telegrams and spoke at length with Sir Edward Maunde Thompson. I soon ascertained that Djedhor only ever made his presence known on the night after the Rubenstein Collection was installed in a new venue. Thereafter neither hide nor hair was seen of him until the collection proceeded to its next destination, whereupon he would immediately put in an appearance again. That was more than suggestive. It indicated a fixed pattern. It also indicated the involvement of a person of subtle courage and singular inner fortitude, just such a person as we have met tonight. I congratulate you, Mr Houdini, on your achievement, and salute you. Bravo."

Again Houdini bowed, this time from the waist with both arms stretched out to the side, as though receiving rapturous applause from an audience.

He and Holmes talked for some time afterward, their conversation focusing on the picking of locks – an area of mutual expertise – and various makes of handcuffs, particularly the Hiatt Darby and the notorious Bean Giant. Then we went our separate ways, Holmes and I to Baker Street, Houdini back to the sarcophagus, wherein he would change into his ordinary clothes and re-emerge at opening time to join the museum's first influx of visitors.

I myself had not taken to the arrogant, stocky little man at all. Holmes, on the other hand, was quite enamoured of him, and for the next few days sang his praises whenever possible.

"Harry Houdini is destined for a stellar career," Holmes said more than once. "You'll see, Watson."

And of course he was right. Houdini the Handcuff King became one of the most famous performing artistes on the planet, entertaining and enthralling millions with his death-defying escapological tricks, until his tragic premature demise in October of last year.

It is not with Houdini, however, that this narrative is concerned. Rather, it is with the events that occurred a couple of months after that night at the British Museum, by which time the Rubenstein Collection was securely back across the Atlantic and settled again in its owner's palatial summer home. Those events, not entirely unconnected with the mystery of the living mummy, were set in train on a cool spring morning in March, when Sherlock Holmes was perusing *The Times* over breakfast and abruptly let forth a shout that was half bemusement, half disgust.

# CHAPTER THREE

## An Insult and a Challenge

"Confound it all!" Holmes cried. "Have you read this, Watson?"

"I haven't yet taken the opportunity to look at the paper," I replied, setting down my teacup. "I have been attempting to finish this book, which so many of my patients have recommended to me, though for the life of me I can't think why."

"*The Sorrows of Satan* by Marie Corelli," said Holmes, eyeing the title embossed on the spine. "Improving stuff, I'm sure."

"The only thing it could possibly be said to improve, given its sales figures and the number of editions it has gone through, is the state of Miss Corelli's bank balance. I have never read such badly written tripe. This fellow Tempest, the protagonist – everyone keeps telling him that the aristocrat who is so interested in helping him dispose of his newfound inherited wealth, Prince Lucio Rimânez, is the Devil incarnate. Lucio! Might as well call himself Lucifer and have done with it. The situation is patently Faustian, yet Tempest remains oblivious. The fool doesn't deserve the money. And as for the author's chronic overuse of long dashes... Ugh. How rot like this ever gets published, let alone command such a wide readership, beggars belief."

"Professional envy, eh, Watson?"

"Hardly. By any objective reckoning I do respectably well from my sideline as an author."

"Not least because you have such sterling material to work with."

Holmes spoke wryly, with a deadpan expression, but he was preening, I could tell. I have already said elsewhere that I had never known the man be in better form, both mental and physical, than in the year 1895, and that his career as a consulting detective was at an acme of success, bringing him renown, acclaim and a handsome livelihood. With this, alas, came an air of ebullient satisfaction which occasionally bordered on conceitedness and was very hard to swallow, particularly at those times when my own temperament was of a more choleric disposition.

"If you dislike the book so much," he went on, "why are you so keen to finish it?"

"Because I want to know how it all turns out and discover what, if anything, Tempest learns from his fall from grace."

"Then Miss Corelli has done her job admirably, has she not? The purpose of a novel, after all, is to keep the reader spellbound and turning the pages all the way to the end, and I note you have been doing that with some avidity."

"Perhaps," I allowed. "Although I hate myself for it."

"If it's any consolation, I would be very surprised if the works of Marie Corelli and her ilk, that crowd of gushing romantics with their flock-wallpaper melodramatics, were still as popular a hundred years from now as they are today. Cultural tastes are fickle. Your chronicles of my exploits, by contrast, will in all likelihood continue to captivate future generations. That is a kind of immortality for both you and me – one, moreover, that does not require us to partake of a mystical Ancient Egyptian elixir like John Vansittart Smith's mysterious Sosra."

"Ah yes. Vansittart Smith. What do you make of his story of a seemingly centuries-old priest and his pursuit of the mortal remains of his lost love?"

"I am inclined to dismiss it as, at best, a misinterpretation of quite readily explicable events. Having looked him up in *Who's Who*, I know that in addition to Egyptology Vansittart Smith has studied botany, zoology and chemistry, becoming the proverbial jack of all trades and master of none. I suspect he is as easy to impress as he is to distract. One night in Paris a Middle Eastern fraudster told him a tall tale, which he swallowed whole, with the gullibility of the lifelong dilettante."

"That or he made the whole thing up himself."

"There is that possibility. His field of study attracts those who have a tendency to romanticise the distant past. Is Egyptology not more exciting when there is a whiff of mystery and enigma hanging over it? Would that not make Vansittart Smith appear more mysterious and enigmatic by association? For a scientist, he is something of a fantasist, and his spine-tingling little narrative may well be a genuine anecdote sprinkled with a great deal of imaginative spice. At any rate, it and he need not detain us any further."

I nodded in agreement, before returning to the topic from which we had allowed ourselves to become diverted.

"Do you really think, Holmes, that my writings will still be read a century or more hence?"

"I flatter myself that my name will be familiar to all long after I am gone from this world, thanks in no small part to you and your literary endeavours."

"You are too kind."

I set aside *The Sorrows of Satan*, having saved my page with a leather bookmark. In the event, I never did get round to finishing the novel, and I can't say my life is in any way diminished for that.

"I have brought a small smile to your face," said Holmes. "That is good to see. You have oftentimes been glum company of late. I understand why, of course. Your wife..."

My Mary had passed away the previous year while Holmes was still abroad, owing to complications arising during childbirth which had taken the lives of both mother and baby, and although I was over the worst part of my grieving, still I mourned her. The loss remained a gaping wound. It might take nothing more than the sight of a pretty young woman whose face reminded me of hers, or a whiff of a perfume similar to the rose-scented *eau de toilette* Mary had favoured, to renew the ache in my heart, as though only days had elapsed, not months, since she perished. Equally, I might find myself waking up of a morning in a dreadful funk and not knowing why, until I realised that it was because Mary was not there and I missed her.

Moving back into 221B with Holmes had been beneficial, in that it afforded me daily companionship and I was no longer rattling about at home on my own with sad mementoes of my time with Mary all around me. Holmes and the escapades he and I went on had proved a useful diversion from melancholy. Melancholy, nonetheless, crept up on me now and then like a venomous serpent and left me prone to sourness, as I was on that March morning.

"A small smile, yes, and with luck I shall be able to broaden it," Holmes continued. "This article on page ten has just caught my eye and piqued me. It is in the way of an insult and a challenge. May I read it out to you?"

"By all means."

Holmes cleared his throat and began.

"The headline runs, 'The Thinking Engine – A Computational Breakthrough?' The text beneath goes as follows. 'This last

Thursday, the 14th *inst.*, saw the unveiling of a computational device whose inventor pronounces it the equal of any human brain, even the greatest.'"

"A remarkable claim."

"'Professor Malcolm Quantock of Balliol College, Oxford, has built a device of such surpassing sophistication that, in his words, "it makes Mr Charles Babbage's Difference Engine seem a mewling infant by comparison". So profound is its analytical and calculating power, according to its creator, that it will not just resolve mathematical equations and tabulate polynomial functions but also' – brace yourself, Watson, here's the nub of it – 'solve crimes.'"

"What!" I ejaculated. "But that's preposterous."

"Is it?" said Holmes. "Well, we shall see. The article continues, 'The professor has christened his machine "The Thinking Engine", and it is presently installed in the new extension of Oxford's University Galleries, the museum on Beaumont Street which was established originally in the seventeenth century to house Elias Ashmole's and John Tradescant's combined collection of engravings, geological samples, zoological specimens and other curiosities.

"'The Thinking Engine is driven by a specially constructed five-horsepower petroleum-driven internal combustion motor which affords sufficient energy to operate an estimated one hundred thousand pinwheels and a similar number of sector gears. It is furthermore equipped with a printer to turn out answers in a typeset form on strips of paper.

"'Its most substantive quality, however, if Professor Quantock is to be believed, is its ability to interpret facts and data which are input by means of an alphabetic keyboard akin to that found on a common-or-garden typewriter. The professor declares that his device can and should be employed in the pursuit of justice by identifying the culprits of crimes whose solutions have thus far eluded the police. He vows to furnish conclusive proof of this by identifying beyond all reasonable doubt the person responsible for a recent terrible set of murders in the Jericho area of Oxford, and is poised to do so tomorrow, before an audience consisting of members of the public, academics, distinguished guests, and the gentlemen of the national press.

""“My Engine,” the professor is on record as saying, “is the superior of any policeman, from the lowliest constable to the highest ranking detective. I would go so far as to submit that it rivals in intelligence and deductive capacity even Mr Sherlock Holmes himself, the London consulting detective of some modest repute.”""

Holmes garnished these last three words with a snort of contempt.

“Some modest repute?” he echoed. “Said of the man who was charged by the Pope himself to enquire into the sudden death of Cardinal Tosca, and who investigated to everyone's satisfaction the shocking affair of the Duchess of Milnthorpe's missing toenail, not to mention the startling disappearance of Sir Edgar Beechworth MP halfway through a game of bezique, and the… the…”

My friend's indignation reached such a peak that he was momentarily at a loss for words. Now it was my turn to be the one who felt moved to bolster the other's spirits.

“The man is merely posturing, Holmes,” said I. “You should take it as a compliment that he has mentioned your name in the first place. ‘Even Mr Sherlock Holmes himself’ – implying that you are pinnacle to which all others aspire, the *ne plus ultra* in your profession.”

“I am the *only* one in my profession, Watson, and my accomplishments are anything but modest. It is that adjective which rankles so.”

“Perhaps you should calm yourself,” I suggested. “Here, let me pour you a fresh cup of tea. And that last slice of toast is yours, should you want it."

Holmes waved away my ministrations with a curt flap of the hand. He readdressed himself to *The Times* article, brandishing the paper with such a tight grasp that the newsprint puckered around his fingers.

"There is still more," he said. "It gets worse. 'Indeed, Professor Quantock has let it be known that, were Mr Holmes prepared to travel to Oxford, he would be willing to let his Thinking Engine match wits with that esteemed sleuth.'"

"There. See? 'Esteemed.'"

Holmes ignored my comment and carried on reading aloud. "'In this he has been backed up by the celebrated newspaper proprietor Lord Knaresfield, whose periodicals are widely distributed across the Midlands and the north of England. His lordship has offered a wager of five hundred pounds that no man who cares to pit his intellectual prowess against the Thinking Engine, Sherlock Holmes included, will be able to outsmart it.' And there the article concludes."

"Five hundred pounds." I let out a low whistle.

Holmes shrugged. "I have earned greater sums than that from a single case. All the same..."

"All the same, you consider that a gauntlet has been thrown down, one with very lucrative potential."

"Money has nothing to do with it, Watson. It is a matter of honour. This Professor Quantock has virtually sent me an invitation. Lord Knaresfield's wager merely adds a kind of vulgar glossy sheen to it. Doubtless his lordship expects to sell a few more newspapers on the back of his shabby act of opportunism. In that respect he reminds me of Wallace Rubenstein, the mummy charlatan. What is it about newspaper proprietors that they are so shameless and vain? They seem unable to stand idly by if presented with a chance to draw attention to themselves. Knaresfield has been ennobled, he is fabulously wealthy, but even that is not enough for him. He must make us notice him at all times."

"Come, come," I said. "Maybe to him it is all just entertainment, a harmless piece of fun."

"Harmless? That is open to debate. No, there is only one thing for it." Holmes slapped the paper down on the table so hard it made the breakfast things jump – and me too, for that matter. "My friend, we are travelling to Oxford forthwith."

"But, Holmes," I protested, "I have appointments. My midday rounds..."

"Cancel them."

"I can't do that."

"Then call in a locum. That Anglo-Indian fellow, what's his name?"

"Mukherjee."

"Yes. Him. You've told me your patients are fond of him, not least the female ones who praise his nice eyes and warm hands. You won't be missed for a day or so if Dr Mukherjee is there to take your place. Don't you fancy a spot of detective work?"

"But you have prior commitments of your own. The matter of the Austro-Hungarian ambassador's diamond tiepin."

"Solved. The housemaid has buried it near the bandstand in Hyde Park, where it awaits recovery by her merchant sailor fiancé when he next puts in at Tilbury. The clue is in the arrangement of the curtains in the windows of the embassy, which sends a coded message akin to the system of international maritime flag signals. I will send His Excellency a letter informing him as much."

"The anarchist cell in Ealing. What about that?"

"A farce. Amateur revolutionaries at best, completely incapable of making a bomb, let alone launching an insurrection. Inspector Lestrade is halfway to realising that, and his bovine brain will surely get him the rest of the way soon."

"That queer business of the skull-patterned butterflies in Dorset?"

"A problem for the lepidopterists of this world, not the consulting detectives. No, my slate is more or less clean, Watson. Clean enough that a trip to Oxford can easily be fitted in. You cannot deny that there's something intriguing about Professor Quantock's machine and what he asserts it can do."

"You certainly appear to think so. I'm withholding judgement. I don't see how a confection of cogs and sprockets can hope to emulate the infinitely complex workings of the human brain."

"My point precisely!" said Holmes, as he hurried off to his bedroom to begin packing a valise. "It is quite impossible. And you know how much I like to eliminate the impossible."

# CHAPTER FOUR

## The Head-in-the-Clouds Academic

So it was that, that very afternoon, we journeyed by train from Paddington to Oxford station, whence we made our way on foot the short distance to the Randolph Hotel, at which Holmes had booked us rooms. Directly opposite the hotel stood the University Galleries, a large, long, well-proportioned building designed in the classical style with a portico over the main entrance supported by lofty Ionic columns.

It was not to there that we then proceeded, however, but rather to the city's police station, which was situated some half a mile away down an alley behind a half-timbered Tudor house on the High Street. Holmes had arranged an appointment with an Inspector Eden Tomlinson. He proved to be a tall, lean, rather spare-looking man whose impressively luxuriant moustaches almost compensated for the lack of hair elsewhere on his head. As we entered his office he greeted us – Holmes especially – with a cordiality that was unfamiliar to us, given his profession. We were accustomed to frostiness, even scorn, from the policing fraternity, who as a rule resented Holmes, both because he was not an anointed officer of the law and because he was invariably better at the job of detection than they were. Tomlinson was refreshingly delighted to make our acquaintance.

"Mr Holmes," he said, "a pleasure to meet you in the flesh. You too, Dr Watson. Your chronicles of Mr Holmes's investigations have been inspirational to me. Inspirational!"

He spoke with a soft burr, indicative that he was a local man born and bred, for here is where the West Country begins, in my opinion – not at the borders of Somerset and Dorset but somewhat further east, in the hills and wide valleys of Oxfordshire and Gloucestershire. The Oxfordshire accent may not be as broad as that of Cornwall, say, nor the dialect as full of regional colloquialisms, but it has that drawn-out, curlicued quality which tells the traveller quite firmly that he is no longer in the true Home Counties. It is also very reassuring, redolent of hard work, integrity and steadfastness.

Tomlinson, it transpired, had for some while been in regular correspondence with Holmes. It had started when the policeman sent my friend a letter of admiration, saying he wished half the men on his force had even a small fraction of Holmes's insightfulness and acumen. This had developed into a prolonged, if sporadic, epistolary exchange during which Holmes had given Tomlinson tips on various cases that were baffling him, and the official had reciprocated by offering nuggets of inside information about police politics and proposed alterations to bylaws.

"May I say, I was more than a little upset by the news of your demise back in ninety-one," Tomlinson said, "and more than a little elated when you returned so miraculously from the dead just last year."

"There was no miracle about it," said Holmes. "It was simply a matter of removing myself temporarily from the field of play, in order to wrongfoot my enemies and protect myself and those nearest to me."

"Still, I wore a black armband and was properly distraught. You ask Mrs Tomlinson. 'A miserable moper', she called me, although she was not unsympathetic. Perhaps we shall one day learn the nature of your self-imposed exile and what you got up to during that time. Dr Watson? Will you be publishing an account of it?"

"When I am ready, and so is the world," I replied. "Not just yet."

"No indeed. It is, nonetheless, an honour to have you, both of you, visit our fair city. Although not, I might add, a complete surprise. Unless I am much mistaken, Mr Holmes, you have risen to the bait a certain Balliol professor of mathematics has dangled."

"It would have been remiss of me not to. The fellow is quite clearly keen to draw me into his orbit. How could I be so lacking in manners as to ignore him?"

"He's a queer sort, that Quantock. They almost all of them are, the dons round here. All that brain power clogging up their noggins, they quite forget how to behave like normal folk. But Quantock's amongst the worst for it. Strictly between the three of us…"

Tomlinson leaned across his desk and his voice took on a conspiratorial note.

"My men have had to pull him in more than once for odd behaviour. Nothing sinister or criminal, mind. Just odd."

"Oh? In what way?"

"Well, there was that time – I probably shouldn't be telling you this, Mr Holmes, not very ethical, but we are more or less in the same occupation, brothers in law as it were – when Quantock was caught wandering down the middle of St Giles' at three in the afternoon, weaving to and fro amongst the traffic. He was lucky not to get mown down by a passing carriage. We would have had him up on charges of drunk and disorderly, but there wasn't a whiff of alcohol about him. He excused himself by saying that he was performing mental arithmetic, calculating the frequency and trajectories of the vehicles around him, or some such. 'Testing the variables', he said. We cautioned him for reckless endangerment and let him go."

"The head-in-the-clouds academic," I said. "As blessed with intellect as he is devoid of common sense."

"Quite so, doctor. We see it a lot here, believe you me. On another occasion, he climbed the clock tower of St Mary's church, just across the road from us on the High." He was using the local abbreviation for Oxford's High Street. "There's narrow stairs all the way up the inside and public access to a terrace at the top. Views all across the city rooftops from there. He perched himself on the parapet, sitting with his legs hanging, like as though he was minded to cast himself off. Drew quite a gaggle of onlookers, he did, both Town and Gown. Several of the students, I'm afraid to say, were shouting up to him, encouraging him to jump. Students and their sense of humour..."

Tomlinson grimaced.

"They call them 'gentlemen', the undergraduates here, but the appellation is not always apt. At any rate, a sergeant of mine arrived on the scene, brave and conscientious sort, and went up to join Quantock. They had quite a friendly chat, by all accounts. The professor told my man he was listening to the peals of the many different bells that ring out across the city. You'll have heard them. Oxford is nothing if not a place for church and chapel bells. Quantock said he was looking for moments of overlap when the chimes created chords and, what's it called? The opposite. Dissonance."

"He has, it seems, an eye for patterns," said Holmes. "And an ear."

"That he does."

"And he was not in any obvious way suicidal?"

"Not as far as the sergeant could tell. He appeared distracted but not agitated or distraught. Eventually my man was able to coax him off the parapet and back down to earth, much to the disappointment of some in the crowd. But that's not the most outlandish thing Quantock has done."

"Do tell." Holmes steepled his fingers.

Tomlinson, in unconscious mimicry, mirrored the gesture.

"There was an incident between him and the Master of Balliol – a contretemps, you might call it. Normally such a thing would not have come to our notice. It took place in the grounds of the college, in the Garden Quadrangle, and what happens in an Oxford college tends to stay within its walls. We police have jurisdiction over the entire city, but the colleges prefer to regulate themselves wherever possible, with their Proctors and Bulldogs. They regard themselves as their own little fiefdoms, set apart from the rest of the world."

The inspector said this with a cluck of his tongue. I myself had attended the University of London, and while it was by no means as old or prestigious as Oxford or Cambridge, it was a similar kind of ivory tower, with its own idiosyncratic formalities and traditions.

"Quantock and the Master were arguing over some matter," said Tomlinson, "one which aroused such passion that they exchanged heated words and very nearly came to blows. In fact, Quantock did accuse the Master, Professor Caird, of laying hands on him. Caird denied it vehemently, but Quantock still wanted to prosecute. That's how we in the constabulary became involved, when Quantock stormed in to this very station demanding to make a statement. I gently persuaded him that there was nothing to be gained by bringing legal action against Caird. He is a man of great probity, for one thing."

"A moral philosopher, if I remember right," said Holmes. "I've read his book reconciling Hegelian rationalism with Christianity."

"I've yet to borrow that one from the library myself," said Tomlinson drolly. "He is a theologian, that much I do know. He is also Balliol's first lay Master, but I reckon him nonetheless as upright and unimpeachable as any bishop. I pointed out to Quantock that the act of taking such a man to court would surely rebound on him to his disadvantage. Besides, as I subsequently ascertained, eyewitnesses to the altercation, Fellows and Scholars amongst them, denied there had been any physical contact between the two men. Voices had been raised but not fists."

"Do you know what they were arguing about?"

"I interviewed Professor Caird at his lodgings as a matter of procedure. He insisted that he and Quantock had simply had a difference of opinion. It was to do with the line of research Quantock was pursuing and the amount of his time being taken up by pursuing it. At first Caird was none too amenable with me, seeming to feel it wasn't worth his while explaining high-flown intellectual matters to a mere policeman. I did some kowtowing, though, a bit of the old tugging the forelock, begging him to take pity on a poor rustic plod, and eventually he came clean. Nothing like flattering a man's intelligence to get him to open up. In that practice I was taking a leaf out of your book, Mr Holmes – the way you sometimes disguise yourself as humble folk in order to gather information and catch the villains out. Not that there's anything villainous about Professor Caird, I might add."

"The line of research in question was Quantock's Thinking Engine," said Holmes.

"It had become a preoccupation, Caird said, a fixation. Quantock was neglecting his lecturing and tutorial duties. Day and night he was working on the blessed thing, to the detriment of his students and possibly even his own mental equilibrium. But there was more to it, or so I divined – a deeper source of friction.

Reading between the lines, it seemed Quantock's contention that his machine can replicate the thought processes of any man sat ill with Caird's more spiritual inclinations. Caird, with his theologian's perspective, did not take kindly to the idea of a mechanical device capable of achieving the level of sentience which God has granted to just one species in all of Creation."

"I imagine you yourself haven't taken kindly to Quantock's insistence that his Engine is on a par with any police officer."

Tomlinson gave a grin that showed off gritted teeth. "It would be impolitic of me to furnish you with my heartfelt response to that particular remark. Let us say I disagree, and leave it at that."

"The occurrences you have described – am I to take it that Professor Quantock has been behaving in an erratic fashion and come to your attention only since he began developing the Engine?"

"I don't know the exact chronology of it. All I know is that until a year ago I had never heard of Malcolm Quantock. I would not have been able to pick him out from any of the other hundred mortar-boarded worthies of this town. But Professor Caird said that Quantock started work on his invention this time last year, more or less. So, putting two and two together, I think we can safely say there is a correlation."

"It is not uncommon," I said, "for people of an obsessive nature to become so consumed by their labours that they lose a few of their social graces."

I glanced sidelong at Holmes, who put on a thin-lipped smile but refused to return my gaze.

"I thank you for your confidences about Quantock," he said, addressing Inspector Tomlinson. "I shall share them with no one. Watson will do the same. There is one further item I would like to discuss, however."

"Let me guess. The Jericho murders."

"It is the case which the Thinking Engine is due to provide

a solution to, tomorrow. I should like to solve it myself, if I can, prior to that. At the very least I should like to be able to check that the answer this marvellous machine comes up with is the correct one, and if it proves to be in error and I know better, then I shall be able to say so."

"Not only that but, in the latter instance, you would be five hundred pounds richer."

Holmes sniffed indifferently. "The prize will be the victory, not the spoils."

"I wouldn't turn down five hundred quid."

"I never said I would turn it down. I will gladly take Lord Knaresfield's money, and spend it with an untroubled conscience. But, for me, what counts is defeating the Thinking Engine and repudiating Professor Quantock."

"I would not be unhappy to see that," said Inspector Tomlinson. "Here is all I know about the killings. I should warn you, however. It is a grim and grisly business."

# CHAPTER FIVE

## The Jericho Murders

Tomlinson's face was grave as he laid out the facts. A bricklayer by the name of Nahum Grainger was the chief suspect in the slaying of his wife Tabitha and their two daughters. Grainger had an unenviable reputation as a drunkard and a ruffian. He was forever getting into fistfights and, according to his neighbours, beat Mrs Grainger regularly and terrorised the children. When he imbibed too much, which was often, he was known to fly into a blind rage, knocking his wife about until she was black and blue while the girls cowered upstairs, quaking in fear. Sometimes he might take his belt to them as well, for good measure.

"What a charming individual," Holmes commented.

"Why ever did his family remain with him?" I wondered. "Surely the wife must have had some relative who would have offered aid and shelter?" I thought of my own dear Mary, and her seemingly unending supply of maiden aunts and distant cousins.

"It appears Mrs Grainger had no one she could turn to, her parents dead and her only living relations in Canada," Inspector Tomlinson said. "She had no employment, Mr Grainger being the sole provider. How would she have fed her children, they being only nine and seven years of age? Yet we have cause to believe that Tabitha Grainger did finally decide that enough was enough. A week ago she confided to a friend that she was going to tell her husband that she was leaving him and would take their children with her, even if it meant the workhouse. Two days later, all three of them were dead."

I shuddered. "The poor things. Grainger was responsible, no doubt."

"That's just it, doctor. Yes, one can easily imagine his anger, his pride in tatters. One can also imagine it festering within him until he could bear it no longer and resolved that his family were better off dead than free, the fire of such thoughts fuelled by gin and ale. He is the prime suspect. The trouble is, he couldn't have killed them."

"A-ha," said Holmes, angling forward in his chair. "And why not?"

"He has a watertight alibi. The three Grainger females were murdered at around four in the morning according to the sawbones, but Grainger himself was not at home. He was staying with a friend a few doors down. He had complained that his wife was making his life miserable and that he could not abide being in the same building as her."

"*She* was making life miserable for *him*!" I declared. "It is beyond irony."

"Now, the friend backs up Grainger's claim. This man – Tobias Judd by name – has said that Grainger was at his house all night and did not go out."

"Might we not assume Judd is lying?"

"We might, Mr Holmes. It would not be out of the question. He is a wheedling, craven sort who, like Grainger, treats his wife meanly. I have no doubt that Grainger could have browbeaten him sufficiently that he would agree to provide exculpatory testimony. The problem is not Judd himself but Judd's dog."

"Judd's dog?"

"A foul-tempered mongrel, huge and vicious. It barks at any and all who pass by the house and is liable to hurl itself on strangers. It can barely be restrained. In fact, the constable who called on the Judds to take their sworn statement nearly fell victim to the animal's savagery, and has the torn trouser cuff to prove it."

"The dog, you're saying, would have prevented Grainger from stealing out of the Judds' to go to his own house and kill his family?"

"Perhaps not physically, but had he attempted to do so the creature would have barked sufficient to awaken half the street and draw unwanted attention to his activities. It simply will not tolerate anyone coming in or leaving without putting up a racket. Even its own master is greeted as though he were an intruder rather than the householder."

I felt a surge of triumph. "Why then, surely that proves that Grainger was never in the house in the first place! If the dog was not heard when Grainger *entered* the Judd residence, we have no proof that he ever did so. The evidence of the dog is null and void!"

Inspector Tomlinson grimaced. "I myself had the same thought, Dr Watson. However, Grainger was seen entering the Judds' home at around eight. The elderly woman who lives opposite swears she saw him, and that damned dog surely did too, for the noise it made, according to the neighbours. We therefore have two witnesses, one at least I consider trustworthy, saying that Grainger entered that house and never left it."

I was a little put out but tried not to show it. "Perhaps you might have mentioned that earlier," I mumbled. "So the dog did nothing in the night-time?"

"We have encountered a similar curious incident before, have we not?" said Holmes.

"Don't tell me." Tomlinson raised a finger, frowning. "That hideous murder in Surrey, the stepfather who murdered his stepdaughter with a snake. He owned a menagerie of animals, as I recall. Was there a dog amongst them? I'm trying to remember the title... Ah yes, I have it. 'The Speckled Band.'"

"I'm afraid you're mistaken," I said. "Holmes was referring to the Silver Blaze affair."

"Silver Blaze! Of course." Tomlinson grimaced. "How daft of me. At any rate, the Judds' dog did nothing, least of all bark. The immediate neighbours on either side can attest to that, and they would have nothing to gain by lying. One of them told us the animal makes his life a torment with its din and he would willingly take a shotgun to it if the opportunity arose, yet he is adamant that on the night in question it was silent until six in the morning, when Judd leaves for work."

"Therefore Grainger must have stayed indoors all night, as Judd maintains."

"Just so, Mr Holmes. But that's not all. Tabitha Grainger and the two girls, Elsie and Flora, were stabbed to death, and from the shape and depth of the wounds we have been able to infer that a particular item was used as the murder weapon."

"Namely?"

"A boathook. Have you been to Oxford before?"

"I studied for a couple of years at Cambridge," replied Holmes, "albeit not to take a degree but simply to pursue some research of my own relating to chemistry and biology. Cambridge excels in those subjects and the sciences in general. My brother Mycroft, though, was an Oxford man, and has very fond memories of his time here, although they seem to consist largely of drinking and dining with certain exclusive and sometimes rowdy clubs."

"Alas, we have more than our fair share of those," said Tomlinson with feeling. "Gilded youth enthusiastically tarnishing themselves. I asked, however, mainly in order to establish if you know anything of the city's geography."

"Precious little."

"Jericho is an area to the west of the town, built on low-lying land hard by the canal. The canal is frequented by barges ferrying coal, stone, wool and agricultural produce down from the Midlands. It connects both the Grand Union Canal and the Coventry Canal with the Thames, which it joins here. Traffic to and fro is constant. It's one of Britain's busiest commercial waterways."

"I see. So a bargee might easily have been the culprit, as the boathook would seem to imply. Jericho's proximity to the canal makes it a plausible scenario."

"It's not beyond the realms of possibility that one such person might have sneaked into the Grainger house under cover of darkness and committed the wicked deed. There were no signs of a break-in, but then the back door had been inadvertently left unsecured that night. The streets in Jericho are arranged in a grid pattern, so the back gardens of the houses adjoin one another. The walls between are low, and on that particular street there is open access to them from one side where an alley runs down to the canal."

"In other words, this random, anonymous bargee made his way across a number of back gardens, armed with his boathook, with the intention of entering one or other of the houses – for what purpose?"

Tomlinson quirked one corner of his mouth. "Robbery, perhaps."

"Was anything taken from the Graingers'?"

"Not so far as we can ascertain. The family were not what you might call over-endowed with wealth, but such valuables and heirlooms as they had were still present when we inspected the place. We're considering the possibility that the bargee was surprised in the act by one or more members of the family and killed them in a fit of panic."

"It seems awfully coincidental," I said, "that this bargee should find his way onto the Graingers' property on the one night that the man of the house was absent and the back door unlocked. And, moreover, that he should take it upon himself to massacre them – a trio of defenceless females – rather than simply turn and flee."

"Dr Watson, please do not misconstrue my words. Nahum Grainger is the perpetrator. I know it as surely as I know my own name. The man is as guilty as sin. The damnable thing about the case is that we cannot prove it. This business with the boathook and the bargee is patently a tissue of lies, designed to lead us astray and have us chasing after some anonymous itinerant who never existed. Grainger had the motive. Yet we cannot find the murder weapon, nor can we make a dent in his alibi. He will get away with murder unless we can somehow prove that he returned to his house that night."

"Where is Grainger now? Do you have him in custody?" Holmes asked.

"Regrettably not. We had insufficient grounds on which to charge him and so were compelled to let him go. Subsequently he has gone to ground. The Judds claim not to know his whereabouts, and his employer says he hasn't reported for work in five days. My opinion is he won't stay hidden for long. The lure of the demon drink will draw him from his lair soon enough, and if we need to find him again, we have only to do the rounds of Oxford's seedier pubs and there he'll be – no doubt laughing aloud at the idiot coppers who've not been able to nail him. Of course, Mr Holmes," Tomlinson added, "now that you've arrived, there's a better than even chance we can finally bring the scoundrel to justice."

"Well, it's down to me and the Thinking Engine, inspector," said my friend. "I'd like to hope that one or other of us can oblige."

# CHAPTER SIX

## The Taint of Violent Death

Jericho consisted of little red-brick artisans' cottages arranged in terraced rows. It had been built to provide accommodation for employees of the Oxford University Press, that venerable publishing house situated on nearby Walton Street, and was mostly occupied by print workers and their families, although a number of people from other professions, like Grainger, also made their home there. Nobody was sure of the derivation of the area's name, but since it sat just outside the old city wall it was reckoned to have been christened in emulation of the Biblical term Jericho, which denotes a remote place.

This information was vouchsafed to us by Briggs, the constable whom Inspector Tomlinson had charged with escorting us to the scene of the crime and whom he had instructed to give us every conceivable form of co-operation. It was a novelty for Holmes and me to have the police unequivocally on our side, not impeding us but rather smoothing our path. It helped that Tomlinson was such an admirer of Holmes's work and methods, but coupled with that was his resentment of Professor Quantock's vaunting assertion that the Thinking Engine might one day do away with the need for police detectives altogether. Tomlinson had almost as much at stake, professionally speaking, as Holmes himself did. They were fellow travellers in more than one regard.

The day was drawing down, the sun low. There was a damp chill to the air that deepened the further we ventured into Jericho's warren of streets and the nearer we got to the canal. Oxford was palpably a degree or two colder than London. The gloaming of early evening had a dark golden hue which reminded me of twilight in the Scottish Highlands, yet the surroundings couldn't have been more different from that countryside with its wild, desolate beauty. Everything here was perfectly urban and ordinary.

Ordinary, too, would describe the Graingers' house, a classic two-up-two-down dwelling that was all but indistinguishable from any other in the street. That said, it bore an aura of desolation. I don't think that was just my imagination. It seemed to project emptiness and misery from every window, from every crack in the brickwork. One might have sensed that something awful had happened there even if one hadn't known.

Briggs let us in with the key, then left us to our own devices, confessing that he had "had enough of the wretched place" and did not wish to spend a minute longer within its four walls than he already had.

I could sympathise. The moment we crossed the threshold I became acquainted with a smell familiar to me not only from the numerous murder scenes Holmes and I had attended but from my time in Afghanistan, where it had been all too prevalent. There is a distinct difference between the odour of blood when it is spilled by accident or during the course of a medical procedure and when it is spilled through an act of malice. The latter kind, with its uniquely acrid tang, hung in the air here. Even five days after the murders, it was rank and unmistakable. Blood charged with fear.

Holmes began to explore the property with his usual questing, terrier-like intensity. He went from the cheaply furnished front parlour to the cramped back room which served as both dining area and kitchen, scrutinising a torn patch of wallpaper here, an ornament there. He tried the back door and found that it opened smoothly and quietly. Outside, in the untended garden, he scouted around, tramping through the overgrown grass and peering across the waist-high dividing walls. He concluded, without much surprise, that out here there was a dearth of useful evidence to be found. A recent heavy rainfall and the tread of countless policemen's boots had erased it all. Then he headed back indoors and up the uncarpeted stairs. I followed.

On the narrow landing we came upon the first bloodstains, dried to a dull black patina on the floorboards. Constable Briggs had told us that the body of the elder of the two Grainger daughters, Elsie, had been discovered sprawled on the landing. She had been in her nightdress. It was supposed that she had heard a sound and emerged from her bedroom to investigate. She had been the first to die.

In the front bedroom stood an iron-headed double bed. The covers carried a bloodstain too, this one more extensive than the one on the landing. Mrs Grainger had not awoken, it appeared, the depth of her slumber attested to by the half-empty bottle of Dalby's Carminative by the bedside. The murderer had slain her in her sleep.

Finally we entered the rear bedroom, which the two girls had shared. This presented such a pitiable sight that it very near unmanned me, for there were two narrow beds side by side and on each a stuffed toy: a cloth doll and a ragged-eared bear. Beside the bear was yet another dismal bloodstain. Spatters of blood also besmirched the adjacent wall.

I could not linger in that room more than a handful of

seconds. I excused myself and returned to the landing. Holmes reappeared not long after, and I could see that even his iron nerves had been affected. No matter the strength of one's constitution, the brutal killing of innocent children cannot be but shocking. One would not be human if one found it otherwise.

"Ghastly," Holmes said, his grey eyes reflecting the horror that must have been in mine too. "This is a squalid matter, Watson, however you look at it. Squalid and appalling. I shall be glad to see the culprit face the hangman's noose."

"I would willingly pull the lever if asked," I said. "Anyone who can do such a thing as this does not deserve to live."

With a nod, Holmes turned his attention to the ceiling behind me. He pushed past me wordlessly, and examined a trapdoor which had escaped my notice. Going on tiptoe, Holmes was just able to reach it and thrust it open. Then, stepping onto the banister that cordoned off the landing from the stairs, he hoisted himself through the aperture. His legs scissored like a swimmer's as he pulled himself up out of sight.

He was gone for quite some span of time, ten minutes at least. I heard the rasp of a match being struck and saw the beam of his pocket lantern flash around. Finally he rejoined me, descending in much the same manner as he had ascended. He brushed dust from his hands and the knees of his trousers.

"What did you find?" I asked.

"Not what I expected, and that in itself is telling."

"Pray elucidate."

"Terraced houses like these, built for the labouring classes, tend not to be the most structurally sophisticated. That is to say, corners are cut, amenities skimped on. For instance, there is quite commonly no partition between the attics, just a single continuous space beneath the roofs stretching from one end of the terrace to the other."

"My goodness. You mean that a person could crawl from the attic of any one house to the attic of another?"

"It would not be too taxing a proposition. You would need to squeeze around the chimney masonry of each house, which stands directly beneath the roof apex, but there is sufficient room. A determined man could manage it."

"A determined man such as Nahum Grainger."

"Yes. As long as Grainger took care to put his weight only on the wooden battens that surmount the ceilings so that he didn't break through the plaster, he could have used this route to travel from the Judds' to here and back without anyone realising."

"Not even the Judds' dog?"

"The dog, Inspector Tomlinson said, cannot tolerate anyone leaving the house or coming in without making a fuss about it. It defends what it regards as its domain. However, it would not have counted the attic trapdoor as an exit. The attic, to the dog, would still seem part of the house, its territory."

"Then you have solved the case, Holmes," I declared. "There was never any bargee. Grainger is the killer."

"Not so fast, old friend." Holmes pointed upward. "There are no gaps flanking next door's chimney breast. They have been bricked up."

"In such a way that they fully prevent access?"

"Fully. What is intriguing is that there is no similar obstruction that way." He gestured towards the next-door house on the other side. "The terrace runs north-south, and there are no partitions between here and its northern end, at least as far as I can see. Could the attics between this house and the southern end of the terrace all be properly partitioned, and the ones northward from here not? It seems unlikely. Let us go outside now. I don't need to see any more, and we have spent long enough in this miserable place."

I felt no small relief as we stepped out onto the street. The late afternoon air, though dank, smelled comparatively sweet, free from the taint of violent death.

"Constable Briggs?"

The policeman straightened to attention. "Mr Holmes?"

"Show us the Judds' house, would you?"

"Right this way."

It took no more than thirty paces in a southward direction to reach the home of Nahum Grainger's friend and alibi provider. Scarcely had we paused by the front door than the most tremendous barking began inside. The door shook in its frame as a beast of some considerable bulk threw itself against it. The barking continued, little muted by the thin barrier that separated us from its source.

I took an involuntary step backward. Since my experiences at Baskerville Hall, I have harboured no great fondness for the canine species.

A female voice within the house tried in vain to hush the dog. "Hercules, that's enough. I said that's enough. Hercules!" She soon gave up the attempt, and the wan, weary tone she used suggested that she hadn't been holding out much hope of success anyway.

Hercules the dog quietened down only after we had moved on, and at that, grudgingly.

"That was Mrs Judd we heard," said Briggs. "You don't want to speak to the lady? I could coax her outside, so that we need not have to deal with the dog."

"I see no call for it," said Holmes. "From what Inspector Tomlinson has told us of the Judds' marital relationship, I can't imagine Mrs Judd would tell us anything her husband wouldn't want her to. He himself isn't home, either, else she would have left chastising the dog to him. I would like to ask you, though, about the murder weapon. You and your colleagues are quite certain it was a boathook?"

"I know only what I've been told, Mr Holmes. The inspector himself observed that the wounds were not simple perforations. There was a peculiar bruising next to the point of entry. The coroner confirmed it during his post mortem examination. A boathook, as I'm sure you're aware, has a split head, with the hook part protruding at right angles to the spike and curving downward. Bit like a medieval pike, you know? Sometimes the spike can be blunt or knobbed, but bargees favour the sharp-tipped ones because they give a better grip when pushing off tunnel walls or the bank. The back of the hook left a mark on the victims' skin, showing amongst other things that the stabbing was done with some force."

"And no boathook has been discovered in the immediate vicinity?"

"We performed a thorough search, working on the assumption that the murderer might have discarded it as he left the scene, but we turned up nothing. If you ask me, it's at the bottom of the canal."

"Don't boathooks float?"

"They do thanks to the wooden shaft, but the head, if detached, will sink like any other lump of metal. If I were going to dispose of the evidence, that's what I'd do, take the head off and toss it into the canal. Then all you're left with is the shaft, which looks like any old pole, something no one would glance at twice, wherever you got rid of it."

"Of course, it may be that the bargee and his boathook are already halfway to Manchester by now."

"If there ever was a bargee," said Briggs. "Grainger did it. I know I oughtn't to say that. Innocent until proven guilty and so on. But I know he's our man, and somehow he's covering it up in such a way that we can't nab him, much as we'd like to. Cunning as the devil, he is."

"Perhaps not as cunning as all that," said Holmes.

Briggs raised hopeful eyebrows. "You reckon you've cracked it, sir?"

"It seems elementary to me, and I try not to use that word unadvisedly or profligately. I certainly don't say it as often as Watson here has me do in his writings."

"Would you care to fill us in, old man?" I said, unruffled. I was used to the barbs Holmes aimed my way about my portrayal of him on the page. He was forever finding fault with my depiction of his character and habits, unable to appreciate that we never see ourselves as others see us. Such was his vanity at times that he perceived as inaccuracy what was objective truth.

"Not until tomorrow," Holmes replied. "Let us see what the Thinking Engine comes up with before I hazard my own summation."

# CHAPTER SEVEN

## A Master Craftsman at Work

At noon the next day we left the Randolph and crossed over to the University Galleries. It was not without trepidation that I climbed the imposing steps and entered the building. My thoughts were of the Thinking Engine. What if it could do all that Professor Quantock said? What if its deductive powers compared with Holmes's? What if a machine had been created with an intellect to match that of one of the cleverest amongst us? What might that mean for mankind?

Beside me, Holmes seemed his usual confident self. His hands were thrust deep in his pockets and, if I don't misremember, he was whistling an air – a Schubert *lied*. His insouciance comforted me somewhat. I don't believe he thought for a moment that events that day would not go his way. At breakfast he had been amused when the hotel restaurant's maître d' sidled up to our table to apologise for the delay in the arrival of our order of poached eggs. The explanation had been that the new gas-fired range cooker in the kitchen, the first of its kind to be installed in all of Oxford, was misbehaving. "So do our inventions let us down," Holmes had responded sagely after the maître d' had glided away again. "Seldom as reliable as we would like. If I were a superstitious man, Watson, I might regard this instance of mechanical failure as a good omen. However, as I am, at this moment, a hungry man, I regard it merely as a deuced inconvenience."

Inspector Tomlinson was waiting for us in the museum's entrance hall and accompanied us down to the basement level. In a long, cross-vaulted room, a crowd of some forty or more souls stood chattering animatedly. One third of the room was cordoned off from floor to ceiling by a heavy black curtain.

The majority of those present were high-ranking members of various college faculties, dressed in their convocation habit of velvet caps and clerical-style gowns whose sleeves and hoods, through various permutations of colour, denoted academic discipline and level of degree. The university chancellor, Robert Gascoyne-Cecil, 3rd Marquess of Salisbury, was there, as was Oxford's lord mayor, John Seary, the former resplendent in gold-trimmed gown and gold-tasselled mortarboard, the latter likewise in ermine-trimmed gown and gold chain of office.

Also present were a few gentlemen of the press, most of them busy jotting shorthand notes. I recognised a *Times* journalist, author of the article which had brought Holmes and myself to the city, and a reporter from the *Illustrated London News*, Archie Slater. Slater was not well disposed towards Holmes, having first come to our attention when he wrote unflatteringly about him during the investigation into the affair of the Singed Antimacassars, a perplexing, even absurd case that I fully intend to enshrine in print one of these days. Since then, Slater had set himself up as something of a fourth-estate nemesis, using the *News* as a platform from which to launch broadsides at my friend whenever the opportunity presented itself.

Spying Holmes, Slater made a beeline for him. His somewhat

vulpine features were creased in a sneer. This expression was not reserved for Holmes in particular but rather was a permanent resident on his face, as though Slater harboured no emotion other than contempt.

"Mr Sherlock Holmes," he said, drawing out the words as one might a human hair from one's soup. "So you've shown up. The lads and I back at the office have been running a sweepstake as to whether you would."

"Doubtless you bet against me, Mr Slater."

"Oh no, on the contrary, sir. I was sure you would come and laid my money accordingly. I'm a couple of shillings to the good now, thanks to you." He gleefully rubbed thumb and forefinger together. "You, after all, would hardly turn down an opportunity to demonstrate to the world how brilliant you are, now would you? Not a man of your intellectual powers and, if I may say, overweening arrogance."

"You're quite right," said Holmes, as imperturbable as could be in the teeth of Slater's snidery. "It is never a chore for me to apply my deductive principles when I might find it rewarding. How is your mother, by the way?"

Slater blinked. "Beg pardon? My mother? What does she have to do with anything?"

"I should have thought her recent consignment to an asylum for the mentally infirm would be preying on your mind. Such a sad business, when the older generation's faculties start to dim and decay. No less sad is the fact that your bookmaker has been profiting so handsomely from you this past month or so. You really should consider getting your racing tips from a more reliable source than the stable hands at Epsom Downs. Those young men don't always know as much about horses as they pretend to."

"But… What goes on between me and my bookie is private."

"Naturally. Nevertheless, Mrs Slater must be wondering

about the shortfall in her housekeeping allowance and asking herself where the money is going. I hope she does not think you have been spending it on another woman, say, a young, up-and-coming West End actress? Were your wife to suspect a dalliance, my friend, I imagine it would not go well for you. Is her father not connected with the criminal underworld in numerous tangential but significant ways? Granted, he poses as a reputable Smithfield butcher, but no one can turn a blind eye to the less exalted circles in which he also moves. By dishonouring the nuptial vows you swore to the daughter of such a man, you are playing with fire."

Slater's sneer had almost entirely disappeared, to be replaced by the agog look of someone whose deepest, most intimate secrets had just been exposed – which of course they had.

"Still," Holmes continued, "your position at the *News* should be guaranteed, whatever else happens. That compromising information you have on the senior editor means you will never lack for gainful employment as long as he retains his position."

Inspector Tomlinson stood rapt throughout the foregoing exchange, his gaze travelling from Holmes to Slater and back again. His face evinced the delight of a journeyman watching a master craftsman at work.

Slater managed to recover his composure, and his eyes regained some of their habitual slyness. "You enjoy it, don't you?" he said. "Being able to pick a man apart at a glance. It gives you a thrill. Well, you may be a genius, sir, but I am a reporter, and for one of the capital's most widely circulated weeklies, what's more. My words are read by tens of thousands. You perceive the truth, Mr Holmes, but I *make* it. Never forget that." He poked a finger at Holmes's chest. "What I write is what *is*. I too can break people."

With that, he executed a sharp about-turn and went off to a corner to scribble in his notebook. At that moment he could not have more resembled a surly schoolboy, condemned by his teacher to write out lines as punishment.

"Bravo, Mr Holmes," said Tomlinson with a light hand-clap. "You made mincemeat of that insolent rascal."

"Personally," I said, "I think you could have handled him with more tact. Men like Slater do not make for good enemies. He is a scandalmonger of the first order."

"I do not fear him," Holmes replied.

"I didn't say you did. All the same, he could do your reputation irreparable harm with just a few strokes of his pen."

"He could try. I have the dirt on him, as I have just proved. If he made a concerted effort to traduce me in public, I could easily persuade him to recant. We are at stalemate, Mr Slater and I, and he knows it."

"Presumably you were able to extrapolate all those facts about him – the mother, the gambling losses, the actress, the blackmailed editor – simply from aspects of his appearance," said Tomlinson. "It baffles me how, though."

Holmes chuckled. "In this instance, inspector, I decided to make life easy for myself. For some time now I have had my network of young spies, my unofficial police force whom I like to call the Baker Street Irregulars, keep tabs on Mr Slater and his doings. One never can tell when such intelligence might come in handy."

Tomlinson was crestfallen. "Oh. You mean you cheated?"

"It is hardly cheating to keep oneself apprised about the activities of those who have shown themselves to be hostile towards one. It is prudence. Regardless, I would have known about Slater's mother, as would you have, inspector, if you had only taken the trouble to glance at his notebook. At the top of the page that lay open, he had written himself a reminder in shorthand: 'Visit M at Hanwell'. The initial 'M' must stand for 'Mother' – a man of Slater's limited charm has few friends – and Hanwell, as the good doctor here could tell you, is the location of the London County Asylum."

"Ah. I'm afraid I missed that."

"Well, be that as it may, the matter of Slater's losses at the bookmaker isn't at all difficult to work out either."

"Perhaps not to you, Mr Holmes, but I myself could see nothing about him that might suggest it."

"You heard him mention the office sweepstake and saw his elation as he described his winnings. That glint in his eye should have alerted you to the fact that he is an inveterate gambler. He was so pleased about securing a relatively trivial sum of money, a couple of shillings, it would not be hard to deduce that he has lately been on something of a losing streak and now considers that his luck has turned."

"The Epsom Downs stable hands?"

"A common source of tips, and notoriously a poor one. There is talk that some horse owners even bribe them to praise the horses of others, in order to lengthen the odds against their own. Thus, when the owners bet on their own steeds by proxy, the payout is better."

"All right then," said Tomlinson. "The actress. Your evidence for that must surely come from the Irregulars' observations alone."

"It could have come from your own observations, my dear inspector, had you been paying attention to Slater's attire."

Tomlinson stole a glance at Slater. "His clothing looks unremarkable enough to me. A touch shabby and threadbare, perhaps, but that isn't unusual for a man in his occupation."

"Shabby indeed, save for that smart-looking new silk tie. Have you not marked the pattern embroidered upon it? The Ancient Greek masks of comedy and tragedy, representing the two dramatic muses Thalia and Melpomene respectively. Incongruous on the person of a newspaperman, wouldn't you say? Therefore one might reason that it was a gift, and who would give such an item of apparel but a lover? A small token of affection that can be worn publicly, like a secret in plain sight, a code known only to the illicit couple."

"The theatre masks, then, led you to the lover's profession."

"They would have led you to it too, had you applied my methods. You pronounce yourself a devotee of my work, yet you seem incapable of emulating it."

Holmes said this with some asperity, but Tomlinson appeared not to mind. Perhaps that was an indicator of the level of his admiration.

"The reduction in the wife's housekeeping and her potential anger," the policeman said, "those would follow naturally from the gambling and the adultery. Slater is worried about the state of his marriage."

"More than worried," said Holmes. "His wedding band is not lodged fully at the base of his ring finger. There is a strip of lighter skin indicating where it would normally sit, and the band is lying just above that, out of place. That suggests he has been toying with it fretfully, wracked with apprehension. You may not have known, as I do, that Mrs Slater's father has some shady and unsavoury associates, but you might still have been able to tell that Slater is inordinately uneasy about the potential ramifications of his adultery. Since he does not strike me as the type who is prone to a guilty conscience, one must assume there is an element of fear at work, his own personal safety at stake. From whom might one most dread retaliation as a consequence of such an indiscretion? One's father-in-law."

"What about the compromising information about his senior editor?"

"As for that, inspector, you must ask yourself how a fellow as seedy and unscrupulous as Archie Slater, with so many private shortcomings, continues to hold down a post with a relatively prestigious organ such as the *Illustrated London News*. Few of us have a high opinion of Fleet Street, but the newspaper publishing industry does still have some standards when it comes to the conduct and deportment of its representatives. As it happens, the one fact I didn't know beforehand about Slater was that he was using blackmail to keep his position at the paper. It seemed so plausible, however, given the man's general character, that I felt it worth essaying. It was a stab in the dark which had a fairly good chance of hitting home."

"Which it did," I said, "to your great amusement."

"Pricking the balloons of blusterers and hypocrites does have its satisfactions, Watson."

"All the same —"

I never got to finish the sentence, for a stentorian voice rang out across the room, begging silence in a broad Yorkshire accent.

"Gentlemen, gentlemen."

The speaker was a glossily prosperous-looking fellow in late middle age whose florid complexion betokened a regular acquaintance with the bottle and whose abnormally black locks betokened a regular acquaintance with another kind of bottle, one which contained hair dye.

"Lord Knaresfield," Holmes muttered. "Sponsor of the wager."

Thumbs in the pockets of his waistcoat, fingers splayed over his fob watch chain, Lord Knaresfield proceeded to expatiate on his personal accomplishments at some length: how he had worked his way up from barrow boy to newspaper magnate; how he had been raised in a house with no running water and now lived in a Georgian mansion with fountains on the lawn; how as a child he had had to share a bedroom with seven siblings but as an adult owned more bedrooms than he could count.

"If I speak without humility," he said at one point during his peroration, "it is because I know what it is to be humble, and I did not like it. I am still at heart a working-class lad from the Dales, but I am also the millionaire you see before you who relishes the status and comforts his life's labours have brought him."

"I'm not sure how much more of this I can take," I said *sotto voce* to Holmes.

"Let him brag," came the reply. "It means it will be all the more entertaining when he has to hand over a lump sum of his hard-earned money to me."

"I do not back a cause lightly," Lord Knaresfield said. "But I believe Malcolm Quantock's invention to be one worth supporting. I'm all in favour of entrepreneurship. I'm also all in favour of great leaps in technology. The good professor appears to offer both, and if I can in any way help publicise his work through my involvement, it is so much better for all of us. Now, I see we have amongst us a guest whose presence is an ornament even in this illustrious company."

He gestured towards Holmes. All heads swivelled in our direction.

"None other than the great Sherlock Holmes himself, who has joined us from London and is doubtless as keen as we are to see the Thinking Engine in action."

"Your servant, sir," said Holmes with a bow which most would have deemed sincere but which I could tell contained a modicum of irony.

"I have it on good authority, Mr Holmes," said his lordship, "that you have taken the time and trouble to look into the tragic business over in Jericho."

"I have practised due diligence, yes."

"And have you arrived at a solution to the mystery?"

"I have."

"Pray do not reveal it yet. First we must set the Thinking Engine going. Professor?"

It wasn't until then that I noticed a small man loitering at one edge of the black curtain. He had chubby features and thick-lensed spectacles, with a somewhat distracted air about him. This, of course, was Professor Quantock. Unlike his fellow academics, he was dressed for the occasion in just a plain tweed suit. One hand fluttered like a moth as he responded to Lord Knaresfield's prompt.

"Y-yes," he stammered. "Absolutely. Set it g-g-going."

Quantock disappeared behind the curtain, and presently we heard the churn of a motor starting up. A smell of burning petroleum reached our nostrils as the noise of pistons pumping and drive belts whirring echoed around the enclosed space.

Then came another sound, a ripple of metallic clicks and ticks, like the workings of a thousand clocks operating at once. The curtain was drawn back, and there before us it stood: the Thinking Engine.

# CHAPTER EIGHT

## The Thinking Engine Thinks

I once saw one of Charles Babbage's Difference Engines on display at the Science Museum. I can recall marvelling at its complexity – all those regimented columns of rods, wheels and gears set within an oblong frame, intricate in the extreme – while finding myself not entirely capable of understanding just what it was supposed to do, no matter how many times I read the explanatory text on the card mounted next to the exhibit. It had calculating powers far in excess of any man's, that much I could glean. A piece of arithmetic which might take a human brain several hours to perform, it could complete in minutes.

Compared to that device, however, the Thinking Engine was of a whole order of magnitude greater, as like it as a whale is to a dolphin.

It filled the far end of the room, occupying hundreds of cubic feet. Its total dimensions were those of three or four omnibuses, I would say, and it comprised a cage-like structure packed solid with moving components. Everywhere one looked, there was a multiplicity of steel and brass parts, all slotting together with an uncanny, wondrous fitness. Wheels were spinning, cogs meshing, rods revolving, rising and falling. So much was happening at once, the eye could scarcely take it in. Sometimes the activity went in waves, like wind across a cornfield. At other times a substantial section of the Engine's innards would come to a standstill, while all around it continued in frenzy.

There were muted gasps from the audience of assembled dignitaries, and I saw the journalists, to a man, making frantic notes. Forgotten were the loud rumble of the motor and the Engine's clattering clamour. Forgotten too was the stench of fuel, the exhaust fumes of which were being funnelled up via a pipe to a fan-light window at street level and thence into the outside world, so as to avoid choking all and sundry in the room. Our focus was solely on the feat of engineering in front of us, that great block of machinery more complicated and convoluted than anything any of us had yet beheld, so full of interdependent pieces that it resembled in some strange way an organism or a forest in full leaf.

I aimed a sidelong glance at Holmes. His face was impassive but his eyes betrayed a scintilla of fascination. Inspector Tomlinson, for his part, was moved to mutter, "Well, blow me down."

A faint, belated patter of applause passed through the crowd. It was generous but guarded. People were impressed by the Thinking Engine itself but were reserving judgement. Now they wanted to know if it was as ingenious as it looked.

"Th-thank you," said Professor Quantock. His stammer, which I had initially ascribed to nervousness, turned out to be a permanent affliction, although it receded the longer he talked and the deeper he got into his subject. "What you are l-looking at is the f-fruit of a full year's work, days of concentrated toil, n-nights too. I have ad-adopted many of the p-principles devised by the late Mr Babbage, both for his D-Difference Engine and his proposed An-An-Analytical Engine. I b-believe I have improved on his work in ev-every respect, not least the addition of a motor to deliver operating propulsion rather than a crank handle.

"F-furthermore, I have increased the output level by some significant factor. The Difference Engine was designed to perform logarithmic and tr-trigonometric functions using sets of polynomial coefficients in order to produce tables of figures that are as acc-accurate as they are extensive. My Thinking Engine g-goes far beyond that. Its computational range encompasses values of twenty digits or more, and its speed of iteration is of a kind that Babbage could only have d-dreamed of.

"I have achieved this in part by switching from the decimal system to binary. My Engine utilises d-discrete packets of binary data working in c-concert so as to… so as to…"

His voice trailed off. He seemed to have lost his train of thought. He blinked owlishly at his audience through his spectacles, searching for what next to say.

Lord Knaresfield stepped in.

"What my learned associate is trying to tell you," said his lordship, "is that this contraption of his does not just look spectacular, it is spectacular. The proof of the pudding, as they say, is in the eating. Professor? Begin the practical demonstration."

"Y-yes. Of course. R-right." Quantock pulled up a stool and sat before a lectern-like unit which projected from the front of the Thinking Engine. He addressed himself to a spindly set of typewriter keys and started pecking at them with his fingertips. "I am providing the Thinking Engine with every scrap of information we have about the Jericho murders. Date, place, time, names. This the Engine c-converts into raw numbers, which it then interprets according to certain built-in protocols. I have previously installed comprehensive data r-relating to Oxford and its g-geography and people. Everything there is to know about the city is contained herein, accessible for retrieval. The Engine is a s-storehouse of local knowledge, as crammed as any encyclopaedia. When required, it will winnow through the statistics, sorting the wheat from the chaff, until it finds what it n-needs."

He tapped at the keys for several minutes, then thrust himself back from the machine and folded his arms.

"It shouldn't take l-long," he said, drumming fingers on forearm.

The Thinking Engine began to whir and rattle more agitatedly than before, some of its components flickering as fast as a hummingbird's wings. The volume of noise increased, until it seemed to drill right through to one's bones. Many present covered their ears. The floor vibrated underfoot. It was hard not to feel as though we were watching some chthonic force at play, a preternatural energy harnessed by man like the fictional "Vril" in Bulwer-Lytton's *The Coming Race*.

Gradually the racket diminished. The Thinking Engine grew calm, its movements slowing from their frenetic peak.

Then, with the onset of this relative tranquillity, a tongue of tickertape extruded from the machine not far from Quantock's typing station. He waited until it had finished spooling out before tearing it free from the slot.

"Would your l-lordship care to do the honours?"

"Happy to."

Lord Knaresfield took the length of tickertape from the professor, cast an eye over it and said, "The Thinking Engine has made its determination, as follows."

After a murmur of anticipation from the audience had run its course, he continued.

"It says here, plain as day, that the murderer is one Nahum Grainger."

"Hardly a surprise," grumbled Inspector Tomlinson under his breath. "After all this fuss, that's it? That's all the thing does? State the obvious?"

"The who of the case," said Holmes, "is of less pertinence than the how."

"Well, indeed. Yes."

"According to the Thinking Engine," said Lord Knaresfield, "Grainger used the communal attic space that links the houses in his street to travel from his neighbour's house to his own undetected."

"Can't have," said Tomlinson. "We checked up there. No way through."

"He disguised his passage through the attics..."

The flamboyant newspaper tycoon paused for dramatic effect.

"By bricking up the opening he used after he had used it."

Tomlinson slapped his forehead. "Curse me for an idiot. Of course! A bricklayer."

"The murder weapon, a boathook," said Lord Knaresfield, still reading, "was selected for the purpose of misdirecting the police by pointing the finger of suspicion at a non-existent bargee. And there we have it." He directed his gaze at Holmes. "How about it, Mr Holmes? Does the Thinking Engine's verdict jibe with your own?"

"In every degree," my friend said tightly. "The crime was no spur-of-the-moment deed. Grainger planned it out in advance, laying the groundwork carefully. He would have placed all the items he needed – bricks, Portland cement, trowel, bucket of water for mixing – in the attic above his house beforehand. Then, having gone to stay overnight with his friend Judd in order to give himself an apparently unimpeachable alibi, he crawled through to his house, descended from the attic trapdoor, and cold-bloodedly killed his family. After that he spent the next hour or so walling up the gaps on either side of the chimney. Quick work for one with his professional skills. The freshness of the mortar between the bricks suggested to me that the partition was relatively new. It had not been smoothly trowelled on the side facing the Graingers' house, indicating that the work must have been carried out from the *other* side. Grainger would then have left the Judds' the next morning carrying the tools of his trade, and no one would be any the wiser. May I examine that piece of tickertape, your lordship?"

"By all means."

Lord Knaresfield handed the strip of paper over and Holmes smoothed it out and perused the sentences that had been hammered into it by the Thinking Engine's letter wheel.

"Well?"

"I cannot gainsay anything I see here." Holmes's lips were pursed, his eyebrows knitted. "It does seem that the Thinking Engine has appraised the situation correctly in every regard."

Lord Knaresfield let out a laugh that was in part a roar. "So I did not venture my five hundred pounds recklessly. The Engine truly is a miracle of science."

Holmes's expression became even darker and more pained. "That would be the obvious conclusion to draw."

"Then it's settled. I thank you, sir, for participating in this most intriguing experiment of ours. Professor Quantock? Step forward, man. Take a bow. You have done the remarkable. You have built a machine that is every bit as intelligent as any of us."

The timid mathematician did as bidden, shuffling to the fore and blushing as loud applause broke out.

"R-really, it was nothing," he said. "It wasn't wholly m-m-my doing. I have only gone along paths laid out before me, following the lead of others."

His protestations were lost in the tumult of approbation. The journalists crowded round him, bombarding him with questions – all except Slater, who turned and stared at Holmes instead, gloating. He held up his notebook, poised his pencil over it, then brought the point forcibly down onto the page. That was all, a simple gesture, but there was no misconstruing its meaning.

A full stop.

In other words: *That's you done, Sherlock Holmes.*

# CHAPTER NINE

## A Monstrous Turn of Events

Holmes departed from the University Galleries in haste and with no observance of the niceties, no gracious words of congratulation for Quantock, no goodbyes for anyone. Tomlinson and I went with him, but we might as well have not been there for all the heed he paid us. He stalked across Beaumont Street and directly into the Randolph. I tried to waylay him in the lobby, but he shook off my hand with a peremptory grunt and hastened up to his room, taking the stairs three at a time.

"Best leave him be," Tomlinson advised. "The man clearly wishes to be alone."

"It's not like Holmes to be a sore loser," I said.

"Have you ever seen him lose before?"

"Not as such. There was that one occasion where an impressive young lady got the better of him, but he continues to count that as a victory, albeit a pyrrhic one."

"Then how would you know how well he handles losing?"

"I take your point. But even when a case is not going as he would like, or he is stymied, or a culprit has temporarily slipped through his grasp, he usually manages to remain stoical. Setbacks serve only to stiffen his resolve. This – this is something different."

"He has been embarrassed, doctor. That is what is different. Quantock's machine has mimicked the incredible deductive processes which Mr Holmes believed were his exclusive domain, until today. What must that do to his self-opinion? *I* am upset just thinking about it. To have been outshone, not even by any person, but by an agglomeration of cogs and such. Inconceivable…"

Holmes did not emerge from his room for the rest of that day. Several times I knocked on the door, either receiving no response at all or else a curt cry of "Whoever you are, go away!" I even tried the handle once, only to find the door locked.

"Holmes, old man," I said through the panels. "Let me in. We should talk."

He, however, seemed in no mood for discussion of anything. I was minded to beg the key off the duty manager and force an entry thus, but elected to give my friend the solitude he craved. If past experience had taught me anything, his funk would run its course eventually. Tomlinson was right in as much as Holmes had not been bested in quite this way before. The circumstances were unique, and the blow to his ego had to be devastating. I remained confident, nonetheless, that he would see reason soon enough. The world had not ended just because the Thinking Engine had arrived in it.

The next morning, Holmes came down to breakfast as though nothing untoward had happened. Helping himself to a generous portion of brawn slices and bacon-wrapped oysters, he engaged in airy conversation on such topics as the Dreyfus Affair and the critical reception for Oscar Wilde's latest play *The Importance of Being Earnest*, which most of the reviewers had deemed hilarious but heartless. I dared not raise the subject of the Thinking Engine lest it mar his mood. It seemed we were sweeping the whole episode under the carpet and moving on.

Then Inspector Tomlinson appeared.

"Ever so sorry to interrupt your meal, gents, but I felt I ought to bring you the news in person. I'd rather have you hear it from me than some other source."

"No apology necessary, inspector. Enlighten us."

"It's just that there's been a discovery, Mr Holmes. Down in Port Meadow. That's a patch of common land running between Jericho and Wolvercote, next to the river."

"A discovery?"

"In the water, snagged on reeds."

"Ah. A body. That of Nahum Grainger, I'll be bound."

"You don't seem surprised."

"He hardly ever is," I said, thinking that yesterday had been one of those rare occasions when he was.

"It was altogether too likely," Holmes said. "You would only have come to tell me about something, inspector, if it was connected with either the Jericho killings or the Thinking Engine or both. A leading player in the drama has not been seen for five days. Grainger turning up dead could not be discounted as a potential by-product of his crime."

"You reckon it is suicide, then? He was driven to kill himself through remorse?"

"I cannot say anything with any certainty unless I am permitted to view the body. Is it still *in situ*?"

"Just about. My men have dragged it up onto the bank and are awaiting a cart to come and take it to the mortuary."

"Then we must hurry."

Leaving our breakfast unfinished, we donned coats and boots and made our way north along Walton Street, past Jericho, thence cutting down across the railway line onto a broad spread of unploughed pastureland where several herds of cattle and a scattering of horses grazed somnolently. We waded shin-deep through grass, ragwort and plume thistle, following the meandering course of the river which, though the Thames, is known as the Isis where it flows through Oxford. Mist was still lifting off its turbid brown surface, like steam rising from milky tea. Geese and ducks dabbled, unconcerned.

Two uniformed policemen stood on the bank, at their feet a slumped heap of wet rags which proved to be the corpse. Nearby, an angler sat dazedly on his heels, clutching his fishing rod as though barely aware of it. He, it transpired, had spotted the body just as he was about to cast his first fly of the day. Having recovered from the shock sufficiently to fetch help, he had since lapsed back into a traumatised, uncommunicative state.

Holmes and I both knelt by Nahum Grainger's mortal remains.

"It is him?" Holmes asked. "Beyond doubt?"

Tomlinson confirmed it. "I'd recognise him anywhere, even if he were not so… disfigured."

The body was bloated, the face bulging until it had a froglike cast. The stench of putrefaction was strong, although it was accompanied by another sweeter smell, that of alcohol – gin, to be precise.

"How long, in your estimation, Watson, has he been in the water?" Holmes said.

I essayed an examination, gently touching the clammy wet skin of Grainger's cheeks and hands.

"The level of dermal maceration suggests two or three days," I said. "Likewise the distension of the belly. It usually isn't until at least forty-eight hours have passed before the build-up of intestinal gases is sufficient to buoy a drowned body back up to the surface. Prior to that, it will have lain on the river bed."

"As evidenced by the amount of silt adhering to the clothing."

"Also by the weed clutched in his hands. That shows cadaveric spasm. After death, his fingers involuntarily closed tight, seizing whatever happened to lie within their grasp."

"He had been drinking, by the smell of it."

"Which almost certainly contributed to his death. Even strong swimmers are liable to drown if heavily inebriated. Alcohol causes a rise in skin temperature, rendering the shock of immersion in cold water all the more intense."

"The Isis, at this time of year, is icy cold," Tomlinson offered.

"There could have been sudden cardiovascular collapse when he fell in. Death would have been instantaneous."

"A part of me wishes otherwise, doctor. For what he did, I would like him to have suffered. I'm not proud of that, and it's not professional of me to admit it, but it's true."

In a gingerly fashion, Holmes went through Grainger's pockets. The search yielded a single item beyond the usual paraphernalia of keys, loose change and handkerchief. He held it up for all to see.

It was the head of a boathook.

"Proof conclusive," he said. "Inspector, your murder weapon. Part of it, at any rate."

"The crucial part," said Tomlinson, taking it from him.

"I thank you for the courtesy you have shown us today," Holmes said, straightening up. "I can add little to what Watson has said already. It would appear that Grainger became very drunk two or three evenings ago and went for a walk by the river, no doubt unsteadily. He lost his footing and met with a grievous mishap. In that respect he has spared the Crown the trouble and expense of a trial, and done us all a favour. Watson!" He beckoned. "It is a pleasant enough morning and I could do with some fresh air and exercise. Would you accompany me?"

We traipsed alongside the river, tracing its course upstream.

Holmes was wrapped in silence, intently scrutinising the path we were on and the bank next to it. The policemen and angler were well out of sight when, all at once, he sank into a crouch with a cry of triumph. On hands and knees he examined a patch of disturbed earth, poring over it as one might a detailed illustration, his head cocking and canting like a bird's.

"What is it, old man?" I enquired after I had stood watching him for some ten or so minutes. "What have you found?"

"Evidence," came the reply. "I only wish it were more conclusive. You noted, of course, Grainger's hobnail boots. Specifically, the soles."

"Well, yes. And no. I saw that he had such footwear on."

"The hobnails in the soles formed a distinctive pattern. A few had fallen out, making that pattern in its way unique on each boot. Here is a corresponding imprint on the ground. Here too. And here. The placement indicates that Grainger paused at this very spot. And there, right at the lip of the bank, observe? Yet another imprint, that one smeared."

"This is where he slipped and fell in."

"We are perhaps three quarters of a mile upstream from where the body fetched up. The current could easily have carried it that far." Holmes stood, brushing mud from his palms. "Unfortunately, many other people have since trodden along this route, not to mention livestock, so I cannot construe a precise picture of what went on from foot impressions alone. It is like trying to read the original underlying text of a palimpsest. Nonetheless, I have seen enough to confirm my suspicions. All is not as it seems, Watson."

"Really?" I said. "I assumed the matter was over and done with. Grainger is guilty but dead. We can return to London confident that justice has been served, even if the law did not play its full part."

"Who said anything about returning to London?"

"I thought—"

"Thinking, Watson, does not always serve you well. Sometimes, indeed, it is your worst enemy."

"Dash it all, Holmes! That's unfair. I am far from being the blithering buffoon you often like to paint me as. Just because you are fond of playing your cards close to your chest, you should not mock the rest of us for not being able to see what hand you are holding."

He looked appropriately contrite. "Forgive me, my friend. You're right. Sometimes I do not make allowances. I forget that you haven't devoted quite as much time to mulling over this situation as I. As a matter of fact, I have been up half the night, deliberating. There are anomalies in recent events which bear further investigation."

"How so?"

"Consider, for one thing, the character of the late and not much lamented Nahum Grainger. A vile man, prone to anger and the liberal use of his fists, particularly against those least able to defend themselves. Intemperate in every respect. Yet when he commits a murder, it is done with guile and forethought. He did not kill his wife and daughters in a drink-fuelled fit of rage, as one might expect. He planned the deed coolly and rationally and executed it with some aplomb. The detail of the boathook – is that something you would think a mere bricklayer capable of? A manual labourer?"

"People are often more cunning than they appear, even manual labourers."

"No, no, Watson, it is quite incongruous. It points to a level of calculation and sophistication well beyond the reach of someone like Grainger. The same goes for bricking up the attic. A reasonably clever move, but also one as likely to draw suspicion as allay it. It is almost as if Grainger wanted to be caught – or rather someone else wanted him to be caught."

"He had help?"

"The penny drops, the drums spin, the winning combination appears. Grainger, I would submit, received advice and encouragement from a third party. He followed instructions – instructions which, unbeknownst to him, were designed to generate intrigue greater than the killings would otherwise have accrued by themselves. He was coerced into using a method which he believed would cover his tracks but which actually was leaving a spoor that the trained eye might readily follow."

"Then this is a conspiracy. A stitch-up, as the Americans might say."

"Grainger's subsequent demise would seem to confirm it. The moment he had done his bit, discharged his role, he became surplus to requirements and, moreover, a liability. He had to be got rid of. And how easily it might be accomplished. Ply him with gin all evening. Invite him to take a midnight stroll along an unfrequented patch of riverside. And then…"

Holmes seized me by the shoulder and made as though to push me in the water. I instinctively planted my heels and shoved back.

"Confound it, Holmes!" I remonstrated hotly. "Why did you do that? I nearly toppled in."

"See what a simple matter it would have been? Had you been in the throes of intoxication, you would not have resisted. You would have gone straight over the edge. An almost foolproof way of disposing of you, and few would suspect foul play. What this also tells us is that Grainger trusted whomever he was with that night, his aider and abettor. He was happy to accept the drinks he was offered and happy to walk beside the Isis with the other person positioned on the outside of him, so that he was between that person and the river. He thought he was with a friend and ally, and he was not. I almost pity him for that."

"This is a monstrous turn of events. If one is to see any bright side at all, it is that you have discovered an element to the case which the Thinking Engine, in all its wisdom, has not. That puts you ahead. The machine is not as infallible as we have been led to believe."

"I would not count it out just yet, Watson. I did not come to the conclusion that Grainger was a dupe until he turned up dead. Who's to say the Thinking Engine might not do the same, once apprised of the information?"

"What do you propose to do?"

"There is an unseen adversary at work here," Holmes said grimly. "Who he may be is at present a matter of conjecture, and I do not hold with conjecture. Facts are my deities; anything else, heresy. The only possible course of action is for me to prolong my stay in Oxford. For how long, I know not. All I do know is that this sombre business is not yet over and requires my continued attention."

# CHAPTER TEN

## The Three Letters

I myself did not remain in the city of Oxford, for I could not. My work commitments prevented it. I tendered my regrets to Holmes, who responded equably, saying my presence, though desirable, was not compulsory. He promised to keep me abreast of developments by telegram and to summon me if I was required. We took our leave of each other warmly and I travelled by train back to London.

On the following Saturday, Mrs Hudson drew my attention to an article in the latest edition of the *Illustrated London News*, a copy of which she had happened to purchase that morning. Written by none other than Archie Slater, it was an account of the first public demonstration of the Thinking Engine and was as biased and jaundiced a specimen of journalism as I have ever read. Slater painted a portrait of Holmes and his behaviour that day which was so inaccurate as to be justly termed a travesty. He averred that Holmes had "spluttered and frothed with indignation" when the Thinking Engine had pronounced on the case.

> It would be fair to say that Mr Sherlock Holmes exhibited neither grace nor forbearance as Professor Quantock's remarkable machine poured forth an accurate and credible solution. Rather, the venerable sleuth raged like an inmate of Bedlam, his high forehead agleam and the nostrils of his prominent, beak-like nose positively flaring. He then had the temerity to pretend that he too had arrived at the same solution, when it was obvious to everyone present that he had done no such thing and that this was a mere feint, a flagrant and desperate attempt to save face. The self-styled consulting detective had in truth been stumped, and his ignorance now stood revealed courtesy of a mechanical 'brain' that is clearly, in every way that counts, the superior of his.

I read on, my eyes widening in disgust and my jaw slackening in disbelief. Slater, not content with accusing Holmes of unruliness and imposture, stated that my friend had yelled caustic threats at Quantock and Lord Knaresfield before storming out. "His lack of self-restraint would seem to indicate a man at the end of his tether, who realises that his livelihood is now imperilled by the march of technology. Foolish would be the prospective client who entrusts his problems to Mr Holmes's care when the Thinking Engine is capable of performing the same task no less efficiently and *sans* displays of arrogance and emotionality of the kind we saw last Wednesday."

I immediately set to penning a letter of rebuttal, addressed to the newspaper's editor and disputing Slater's article point by point. I all but accused Slater of libel and implied that Holmes would have every right to institute legal proceedings against him. As I was sealing the envelope, however, Mrs Hudson brought up a telegram.

WATSON

BURN OUTRAGED LETTER TO ILN STOP NOTHING ACHIEVED BY SENDING IT STOP COME TO OXFORD AT FIRST OPPORTUNITY STOP

HOLMES

Again I availed myself of the service of my locum, Mukherjee, who joked that I was at risk of losing my patient list to him if I persisted in taking these leaves of absence. I also withdrew reluctantly from a rugby match scheduled for that afternoon. We, the Medics XV, were up against our arch rivals, the Silks XV, made up of barristers from the Inner Temple, but my team would just have to do without me and, despite the short notice, find another man to fill the Number Eight slot in the scrum. A higher duty called.

Holmes met me off the train at Oxford, and if he was at all discomfited by the way Slater had traduced him in print, he gave no sign. All he said, when I broached the subject, was that Slater was entitled to his interpretation of events and that the freedom of the press was sacrosanct.

"But not when it misrepresents the truth, surely," I said.

"For now, it is no more than a distraction. Slater's words will be forgotten soon enough."

I had my doubts, but said nothing.

Holmes had booked me into the Randolph again, and once I had deposited my belongings there, he led me straight out to a public house not far away, the Eagle and Child on St Giles'. It was a rambling, wood-panelled establishment, and we went through to an alcove at the back known as the Rabbit Room, which formed a cosy and very private space.

Here he introduced me to Dr Merriweather, a Classics don at Magdalen College whose handshake betrayed a detectable tremor and whose overall demeanour, down to his unkempt grey hair, was that of someone labouring under considerable strain.

"Dr Merriweather contacted me yesterday," Holmes said, "wishing to consult my advice on a personal matter of some delicacy."

"*Great* delicacy," said Merriweather. "Hence my proposal that we meet in a public place affording some level of anonymity, rather than in my rooms."

We were alone in the Rabbit Room, with the door between us and the rest of the pub shut. Even so, we spoke in lowered voices so as not to be overheard by eavesdroppers.

"I am," said the classicist, "currently the object of what I can only call a poison pen campaign. I have been receiving letters whose content is of the most scandalous nature. The sender accuses me of grievous professional misconduct and threatens to make these calumnies known to the college president, Sir Herbert Warren. That will not do at all."

"I take it, from your use of the word calumnies, that nothing the letters say is true," I said.

"Not one iota. The very idea! They are filled with baseless slurs only. Yet their progenitor has the power to harm me nonetheless."

"How?"

"For an academic at Oxford, Dr Watson, reputation is all. Careers rest, sometimes precariously, on the continuing respect of one's peers. Lose that and you lose everything. Common rooms are hotbeds of gossip, too, and college Fellows as prone to spreading scurrilous rumour as any charlady or parlourmaid. Once a whiff of impropriety adheres to one, it is hard to shake. One may as a result lose advancement, preferment, even one's post. All it would take is my persecutor dripping his venom in the right ears, and I would be done for."

"Who do you think it might be? A rival?"

"I do not know. It pains me to think that one of my colleagues would be so envious and resentful that he would subject me to such torment, but it is, I suppose, possible. There is always someone jockeying to take one's post and the benefits that go with it."

"The alternative is a disgruntled student."

"There have been pupils who have reacted badly when I give their work a low mark. One young man in particular, the Honourable Aubrey Bancroft, was unduly upset by my response to an essay he submitted on Homeric epithets earlier in the term. It was shoddy stuff, quite the laziest thing a student of mine has ever turned in, and I castigated him accordingly. He, in return, blamed my poor teaching. We had something of a row about it, I'm afraid, to the point where I felt moved to threaten him with rustication if he did not back down and recant."

"The Honourable," I said. "He hails from aristocracy?"

"The younger son of Charles, thirteenth Earl of Shiplea. Minor nobility, by all accounts."

"Minor or not, it seems young Bancroft does not take kindly to a mere commoner impugning the quality of his scholarship."

"A very disagreeable, stuck-up sort," Merriweather confirmed. "He was cowed, however, by the prospect of punishment, and I have not had any trouble from him since. He has, if anything, been more diligent than ever, and his work has markedly improved."

"He may still be the one responsible for the letters. Vengeance can lurk behind a chastened smile."

"That is all too sadly true."

I realised that I had been doing all the talking, while Holmes had been keeping his own counsel. I turned to him now and asked, "Is there anything you'd like to add?"

"You have been conducting the investigation in such a capital manner, Watson, I was loath to intrude. I should, though, like to see the offending letters. You have of course brought them along, Dr Merriweather?"

"Of course."

Merriweather delved into his inner jacket pocket to produce three small envelopes, which he handled in a gingerly fashion, placing them on the table in front of us as though they were as unstable as nitroglycerine.

"They were slipped under my oak in the night," he said. By "oak" I knew him to mean the outer of the two doors of his rooms; it is a university expression, and to "sport one's oak" means to keep that door shut as a sign to discourage unwanted visitors. "The first appeared a fortnight ago, the second ten days after that, the third the day before yesterday. I don't know if the timings are a useful detail."

"No details are useless," said Holmes. "Some are less relevant than others, that is all."

"I live on a staircase on Magdalen's Great Quad – ground-floor accommodation, as is customary for dons. The staircase entrances line the cloisters and are accessible to anyone, so at night-time, under cover of darkness, the culprit would have been able to dart in, deliver the letter and dart out with little risk of being spotted."

"Unless he lived on the same staircase himself, meaning he would only have to creep down and back and it is even less likely that anyone would have seen him."

"That is so, yet I do not share the staircase with any of my own pupils. The students who live on the two floors above count no Classics men amongst their number."

"That does not necessarily preclude them from guilt. And Bancroft?"

"His rooms are also on the quad, on the opposite side from mine."

"Very well. Now then, let's see what we have here." Holmes

took the topmost of the envelopes and fished out the letter from inside. "This is the first of them, I presume?"

Merriweather nodded.

"Generic notepaper," Holmes said. "Twenty-pound bond. Cotton content. Cockle finish." He held it up to the window. "Conqueror watermark. Manufactured by Wiggins Teape. All of which tells us nothing, alas. It could have been purchased at just about any high-street stationers."

He applied himself to examining the letter's short piece of handwritten text. I read it over his shoulder.

MERRIWEATHER, YOU PIFLLING PERNACIOUS FOP, YOU DO NOT DESERVE THE EASE AND BARM THAT LIFE HAS BROUGHT YOU. YOUR DOCTORATE WAS OBTAENED BY FRAWD, YOUR THESIS AN ACT OF PLAGIARIZM. I WILL EXPOSE YOU.

"This cannot be the handiwork of an educated man," I averred. "The numerous misspellings suggest poor schooling and literacy. That surely rules out any Oxford man, doctor – students, your fellow academics, Bancroft himself."

"So I assumed," said Merriweather. "Yet it has occurred to me that that could be precisely what the sender wishes me to think. He is feigning a low level of mentality in order to deflect suspicion."

"Holmes? Your view? Any inklings?"

But Holmes was already engrossed with the second letter.

REFLEKT ON YOUR MANY FEILINGS, MERRIWEATHER. YOU HAVE NOT EANNED YOUR PUSITION ON MERIT. I AM TAUKING OF YOOR PROPENSITY FOR BLATANT BLANDICHMENT AND BOOT-LICKING.

"Our letter writer has a penchant for alliteration, I'll give him that," I said. "What does his use of capitalisation signify, I wonder."

I was prompting Holmes for an opinion, but he offered none. Instead, having perused the second letter for some minutes, he turned his attention to the third, which was the longest of them all.

> YOU ARE IMFAMOUS FOR TREETING SOME OF YOUR PUPILS MORE FORGIFINGLY THAN OTHERS. YOU HAVE SUPPLYED THEM CONCISTENTLY WITH HIGH MARKS WHICH INCREASE THE MORE THEY COMBLIMENT AND FLATTER YOU. YOU HAVE FOREWARNED THEM OF THE QUESTIONS THEY WILL BE FOWCED TO CONFRONT IN THEIR EXOMS. THE PARSIALITY AND FAVOORITISM YOU SHOW ARE ENBARRASINGLY OBVIOUS. DO YOU KNOW WHO I AM NOW? OF THE MANY EXCEPTIONAL CHARACTERS THAT STAND BEFORE YOU, MINE SHOULD NOT BE TOO DIFFICULT TO SINGLE OUT CORRECTLY.

"He has grown in confidence with this one," I said. "He is taunting you in a whole new way, Dr Merriweather. Not content with insulting and denigrating, he is inviting you to guess his identity. Clearly he is familiar to you, an acquaintance of some sort. The final sentence admits it. 'Of the many exceptional characters that stand before you…' He is someone who has been in your presence more than once."

"I have drawn a similar conclusion," said Merriweather. "But a goodly number of people, exceptional or otherwise, might be said to 'stand before' me in the normal course of my duties. Stand in my rooms awaiting my assessment of an essay. Stand in the dining hall as I and the other faculty members walk past in procession to reach the high table. Stand in the college chapel for the singing of hymns at Sunday service. Magdalen comprises a student body of some two hundred. Faculty and ancillary staff add a few dozen to that total. Far from narrowing down the list of suspects, the 'characters' reference would seem to widen it to include just about the entire college."

"Do any of the accusations hit home? I'm not suggesting that they're true, but do any of them strike you as the sort of opinion one particular individual might hold about you?"

Merriweather shook his head vehemently. "I cannot believe I have given anyone grounds even to suspect me of such actions. I have always endeavoured to comport myself with dignity and integrity in every aspect of my life. I have never plagiarised. I have licked no one's boots – vile expression. I have never consciously shown favouritism, nor would I ever facilitate cheating in an exam. I prize *virtus* above everything. Do you know what that is? It is the Ancient Roman concept of virtue, encompassing the attributes of courage, honesty and worth. These should apply not just in one's private practices but in one's public dealings. For the Romans, *virtus* was gained through both illustrious deeds and proper conduct. I have written a paper on it, focusing on the writings of Sallust and Cicero, both of whom expounded on it at great length, and it is a philosophy that has, I hope, shaped my own nature."

"It is almost as though your epistolary abuser knows that and is using it against you."

"He could not wound me better than by aiming his malicious arrows at the values I hold dearest."

Holmes, who had been busy going over all the three letters once again, at last looked up and spoke.

"You are both of you missing what lies plainly before you," said he. "The culprit has identified himself by name in these letters."

"He has?" said Merriweather and I in unison.

"Moreover, in a manner specifically designed for you to interpret, Dr Merriweather."

"I am at a loss to see how."

Holmes's grey eyes danced with delight. "Allow me to illuminate."

# CHAPTER ELEVEN

## A Signature in a Dead Tongue

"The misspellings," Holmes said, "give the superficial impression that the sender of the letters is not a cultured, erudite man. Yet that impression is patently erroneous. Would an illiterate employ words such as 'pernicious' and 'plagiarism'? Regardless of how inaccurately he has spelled them, they are long and complex words. Similarly, the syntax of the sentences is anything but straightforward.

"Further to that, the misspellings themselves are inconsistent. Our poison pen friend gets 'your' right every time except once in the second letter when he uses two *o*'s in place of *o-u*. A simple monosyllable is normally no problem for him but defeats him on one occasion? I find that hard to swallow.

"And who would write 'earned' as 'eanned'? It is not as though the latter sounds like the former when said aloud. The same goes for 'fowced'. Misspellings tend to be phonetic. He would far more likely write 'forced' with an *s* instead of the *c* or perhaps with a *u* inserted between the *o* and the *r*.

"In all, it seems rather contrived, does it not? As if the misspellings are there to serve some specific, deliberate function.

That was the view I took, at any rate, as I read through the letters, and the closing sentence of the third confirmed it for me. The word 'characters', after all, does not simply mean people or personalities. It also, in a more literal sense, refers to a letter of the alphabet or symbol, written or printed. Many such *exceptional* characters stand before us on these pages. If, as instructed, we single them out correctly – by which I mean extract the letter which should appear in each misspelled word were that word spelled as it ought to be – we derive a series of characters."

"You're saying the letters have some sort of cryptic cipher embedded in them?" I said.

"That is exactly what I am saying." Holmes produced a fountain pen and a small notebook and began to write. "It should be an *f* rather than an *l* to make 'piffling'. 'Pernicious' has an *i* as its second vowel, not an *a*. 'Balm' is spelled with an *l*."

He continued in this fashion until he had written down a line of letters:

FILIUSCAROLUSNAVISPRATUM

This he divided up into four separate words using diagonal strokes:

FILIUS/CAROLUS/NAVIS/PRATUM

"Now then, Dr Merriweather," he said. "That looks like Latin to me, but my schoolboy knowledge of the language is a tad rusty. Would you be so good as to translate?"

"*Filius* means son," said Merriweather. "*Carolus* – that's medieval Latin for Charles. *Navis* is ship, *partum* meadow. My God!"

"Yes. The letters' author has named himself. The son of Charles, Earl of Shiplea. Lea and meadow are synonymous, of course."

"Bancroft," I said. "He is the guilty party after all."

"The impertinent whelp!" Merriweather exclaimed.

"It is quite a clever trick," said Holmes. "The first word is concealed within the first letter, the second within the second, and the last two words, which effectively make up a single word, within the third. Together they form a signature in a dead tongue with which you, Dr Merriweather, are intimately familiar."

"As though he is further mocking me."

"The use of capitals is an authentic touch, since that is how the Romans themselves wrote their texts."

"And yet the grammar is deficient. *Carolus*, *navis* and *partum* are all in the nominative case but ought to be in the genitive: 'the son *of*…' That is typical of Bancroft. He is hopeless on his declensions. I am forever marking him down in his Latin compositions, and his Greek, on that front. To be honest, Bancroft is one of the worst students I have ever had the misfortune to teach. He barely scraped a Third in his Honour Moderations and I do not expect big things from him in his Greats either."

"How does he come to have a place at Oxford at all?" I said.

"That is one of the mysteries of life – although it may have something to do with the generous sum his father, himself a Magdalen alumnus, has pledged towards the refurbishment of the library roof. I was rather prevailed upon by my head of department to accept the son for matriculation, when his Oxbridge entrance exam papers suggested he has no great aptitude for Classics nor the kind of first-class brain we look for here. Money, alas, so often trumps ability."

"Now, at least, Bancroft has sabotaged himself. He surely cannot stay on at Oxford after this. You need only present your President with the evidence which Holmes has revealed, and Bancroft will be sent down in disgrace."

Merriweather looked very satisfied at the prospect. "I should not be sad to see him go."

Holmes held up a hand. "Let us not be too hasty. I think it only right that we confront Bancroft first before condemning him. Who is to say that the coded signature isn't itself a piece of misdirection?"

"Someone else sent the letters," said Merriweather, "and is trying to pin the blame on Bancroft?"

"It is a possibility that should not be discounted. I doubt your fractious relationship with him is a secret within the college. Who better to make a scapegoat for this malfeasance than a pupil of yours with a known antipathy towards you? Watson, you and I shall pursue this further at Magdalen. Dr Merriweather, I suggest you do not come with us. To be seen at the college in the company of Sherlock Holmes may lead people there to wonder why you might need me, and that runs the risk of exposing a problem you would rather did not become common knowledge. I shall do all I can to preserve your anonymity. With luck, we shall manage to resolve this matter in such a way that your *virtus* remains intact."

# CHAPTER TWELVE

## The Honourable Aubrey Bancroft

Magdalen College proved to be one of the most beautiful places I have encountered, more like a stately home than a seat of learning. It was a symphony of battlemented walls, Gothic and medieval architecture, and long sweeping elevations, all built of warm Cotswold stone and set within extensive grounds through which the River Cherwell, a tributary of the Isis, ran in several divergent channels like the marbling of fat in a side of fine beef. It boasted an imposing bell tower, tree-lined walks, and even a deer park whose expanses of grass were empurpled by spring fritillaries and being nibbled by a small herd of fallow deer.

Getting into this academic Arcadia was, perhaps predictably, not easy. At the Porters' Lodge, the college's main entrance on the High Street, Holmes and I were soundly rebuffed. In no uncertain terms the porter told us that as we were neither Fellows nor students, we were not permitted onto the property, not without express invitation, preferably a letter of introduction. In the absence of that, we could not take one step further, and if we tried he would summon a Bulldog, a member of the university's private police force, and have us forcibly evicted.

Holmes took the setback in good spirit. "There is more than one way to skin this cat, Watson," he said as we beat our retreat. "I have spent much of the time since we last saw one another familiarising myself with the layout of the city by means of long exploratory walks. I am aware that I am out of my customary milieu, and it pays to know the local terrain. The majority of the colleges in Oxford are like castles, walled and gated, their entry points manned, but Magdalen's borders are somewhat more porous. Be warned, however. We are going to get our feet wet."

And so we did, taking a convoluted route that entailed trudging through damp swampy meadows and a shallow stream until finally we emerged in a gardened area somewhere at the back of the college. It was then a relatively simple matter to navigate our way to the Great Quad. Holmes insisted that while on the college property we must act as though we belonged, so as not to arouse suspicion and draw attention to the fact that we were trespassers, and to that end he affected a confident, strutting air which I did my best to emulate. My squelching shoes and sodden trouser cuffs made it more difficult than one might suppose. We did attract inquisitive glances from some of the people we passed, but Holmes simply touched a finger to the brim of his hat and bade them good day in such a charming and disarming fashion that their curiosity was assuaged.

"The key to duplicity," he confided to me, "is not to act furtively in any way, and the means to achieving that is to adopt a role and believe in it. Right now, for instance, I am a visiting ecclesiologist, here to study fifteenth-century liturgical texts kept at the Bodleian Library. If confronted, I shall say precisely that, and quote such titles as *The Whetenal Psalter* and *The Closworth Missal*. My tone will be polite but pious, like that of a rural vicar. I doubt anyone will argue."

"And what if you are recognised as Sherlock Holmes?"

"Then my fame, such as it is, will be my armour."

In the event, he was not called upon either to deploy his thespian skills or to exploit his celebrity, and we reached our destination unchallenged. The Great Quad's ivy-wreathed cloisters circumvallated a large, immaculate lawn. Atop the buttresses perched a series of stone figures which ranged from the representational – a hippopotamus, a greyhound, a jester – to the grotesque, the latter category including gargoyles and miscellaneous unclassifiable monsters. Holmes informed me that these statues were known at Magdalen as "hieroglyphicals" and were alleged to represent the virtues which students should seek to embody and the vices they should strive to avoid.

"So now we shall ascertain whether or not Aubrey Bancroft has absorbed a moral lesson from his surroundings," he said.

Names painted on boards outside the entrance to each staircase identified the residents therein. The young aristocrat was at home and opened the door to Holmes's knock with alacrity. A bottle of champagne hung from his hand, and his face was flushed.

"About time you turned up with that extra booze. This one's nearly... Oh. Who are you?"

"I am—" Holmes began.

"Don't care," said Bancroft. "Stopped caring three seconds ago. Goodbye."

He swung the door shut, only to find Holmes's foot interposed between it and the jamb.

"What the devil? How dare you. Remove your foot at once, sir, or you will answer for it."

"I would advise you, young man, to listen closely to what I have to say and heed it well," Holmes intoned in a voice that brooked no demurral. "A great deal depends on what you tell me during the next few minutes, not least your future at Oxford.

There is also a fair chance that your life is in danger."

"Is that a threat? Do you know who I am?"

"I am not threatening you and I am not your enemy. If, however, you are in cahoots with someone, a person who has inveigled you into committing a misdemeanour against your tutor Dr Merriweather, then it is possible you may not live to rue your involvement in his schemes. Do I have your attention now?"

The inebriated Bancroft sobered up somewhat at that. "You're serious."

"Deadly so."

"You had better come in then."

His lodgings were disorderly. Sundry items of clothing and sports equipment were strewn on the floor, books were stacked in teetering piles, and empty bottles cluttered up corners. I found myself thinking that we were in the presence of someone no less dissolute than Nahum Grainger but, unlike that menial, so cushioned by family wealth that such a lifestyle was readily sustainable and even carried a weird sort of glamorousness. He could afford, in every sense, to fritter his days away in indolence and debauchery. As the younger son of the Earl of Shiplea, he would not even have to shoulder the responsibilities of the hereditary title upon his father's death. Those would fall to his older brother. His own future was a horizon of hazy, cloudless blue.

Catching my disapproving gaze, he said, "Bit of a mess, I appreciate. My 'scout' despairs of me. I pay him extra not to bother tidying up. It's such a nuisance to have someone busybodying around during the day when I am trying to work or… other things." He smirked, as though the "other things" referred to were clearly pursuits of more importance to him than any intellectual labour. "So what are your names, gents? And to what do I owe the honour of your visit? What is so important that you have come barging in on a man when he's making the most of an idle Saturday afternoon?"

Holmes introduced us, and Bancroft affected disdain.

"Ah yes, the detective fellow and his doctor friend. I've heard of you. Pals of mine follow your adventures avidly. Me, I prefer a bit more derring-do in a story. Kipling – now he can spin a yarn. And the Raffles tales by that Hornung chap, they're jolly fun."

"Those are fiction," I pointed out. "I trade in reportage."

"Highly fictionalised reportage," Holmes interjected.

"Reportage sprinkled with a dressing of fictionality," I rejoined, "to make it more easily palatable."

Bancroft gave a rather odd twitch of the head, then swigged from the neck of the champagne bottle, upending it to shake the last few drops down his gullet. "So, am I to feature in one of your next offerings, Dr Watson? I daresay I would buy that issue of *The Strand*, in order to see my name in print."

"You realise you are in some considerable trouble, don't you?" Holmes said, holding up the three letters in their envelopes, which Merriweather had permitted him to take with him.

"For those things? The letters I sent to mimsy old Merriweather? I don't think so. Just a spot of harmless fun. The silly beggar had it coming. Rusticate me? *Me*?" Bancroft twitched his head again – some kind of involuntary spasm, as it seemed to my eyes. Perhaps an idiosyncratic reaction to alcohol, I thought. "Never happen. Pater would never allow it. Does Magdalen want its library roof fixed or not?"

"You could well be sent down for what you've done. Disgraced."

"Poppycock. I am going to graduate, come what may. My father's donation is conditional on that. No MA Oxon, no cash, it's that simple. I can't believe Merriweather didn't take it all in the spirit in which it was intended, as a prank. What a stick-in-the-mud he is."

"Did you not anticipate that you might be found out?"

"It was a possibility, I suppose," Bancroft replied with a shrug. "I tried hard to disguise my handwriting. Using capitals helped."

"And the Latin cipher pointing to your identity?"

The young aristocrat blinked. "Beg pardon? Latin cipher?"

"The misspelled words."

"Oh, those. It was meant to look like the letters were from some ignorant dullard. Throw the foxhounds off the scent, as it were."

"You're unaware that the misspellings served a subsidiary purpose?"

"I have no idea what you're talking about." Bancroft moved to a chair, which he cleared of detritus before sitting down heavily in it. "Sorry, feeling a bit queer all of a sudden." He inspected the champagne bottle. "Think I've managed to drain this one all by myself. Normally I have a good head for champers. Must be stronger stuff than I thought." His neck tightened briefly in a kind of rictus. That was when I began to grow concerned.

"Holmes..." I said.

"Just a moment, Watson. Allow me to go out on a limb here, Mr Bancroft, and assert that you yourself did not come up with the content of the letters. Rather, they were dictated to you by a third party."

"Maybe. What of it?"

"You copied out verbatim a text you were given for each one."

"Why not? It read so well."

"Who was it? Who put you up to the deed? Is it by any chance the same person you were expecting to see when Watson and I arrived? The one who'd gone out to fetch, as you put it, 'extra booze'? Have you and he been celebrating together? Toasting your collaboration?"

"Me toasting it, not him. Doesn't drink, does he? Teetotal, temperate, whatever it's called. Happy to open a bottle but not to touch a drop. How can someone not like alcohol?"

"Would you describe him to us?" Holmes persisted. "Name him, even? Can you do that for us?"

"More questions," said Bancroft, beginning to slur his words. "You make my brain very noisy with your questions. Make lights flash in front of my eyes as well."

That clinched it. "Holmes," I said firmly, "unless I am very much mistaken, this man has been—"

Before I could complete the sentence, Bancroft lurched from the chair. His limbs shook as though he were afflicted with St Vitus's dance, and then he collapsed supine on the floor, the bottle slipping from his grasp and rolling away.

I sprang to his side, giving him a quick but thorough examination.

"What's wrong with him, Watson? This isn't mere drunkenness."

"No," I said. "He has been poisoned. Strychnine, if I don't miss my guess."

# CHAPTER THIRTEEN

## The Distance of Care

As if to prove the accuracy of my diagnosis, Bancroft started to go into convulsions. His back arched, while his lips pulled back into a terrible grimace and his eyes rolled up until only the whites showed. His heels drummed on the floor.

"Damn it," Holmes said. "Of course! The head and neck movements. Those are the early signs of strychnine poisoning. Fool that I am for not recognising it. Tend to him, Watson. What must be done to save him?"

"Ideally, a dose of bromide of potassium and chloral, or else tannic acid, administered orally. But as I have none of those to hand, we must induce emesis – get him to vomit up the poison. A salt water solution should do the trick."

Holmes searched the rooms for salt. Finding none, he hurried off at full tilt for the college kitchens. I, meanwhile, made Bancroft as comfortable as I could, placing a bundled-up sweater under his head for a pillow. The convulsions grew steadily more violent, his body bending backwards in an opisthotonus so severe that I could swear I heard tendons creak. His jaw locked open in trismus, and moans issued forth from his gaping mouth that sounded like the agonies of a soul in Hell.

After several minutes with still no sign of Holmes, I realised that Bancroft was at risk of causing himself permanent muscular damage if he continued to contort and hyperextend in this way; he might possibly even shatter vertebrae. In the absence of an ingestible emetic substance, I had no alternative but to force him to vomit manually. I plunged the index and middle fingers of my right hand into his throat, pressing down on the tongue and prodding the uvula. I braced myself for the rush of regurgitation, which when it came was copious and noxious. Most of it sprayed up my sleeve and into my lap, although some also found its way onto my face.

I knelt by Bancroft; he lay shuddering before me, both of us covered with the contents of his stomach, I more liberally than he. Little by little his convulsions subsided. His moans abated. I felt close to vomiting myself, but my years of medical experience had taught me how to control my gag reflex. There is a kind of detachment that descends over one when presented with human effluvia in all its glutinous and often vile-smelling glory. A good doctor can switch off his body's natural responses by focusing his mind on the suffering and wellbeing of the patient. I call it the distance of care.

Bancroft was stable and calm by the time Holmes returned with a shaker of salt. Holmes, by contrast, was panting hard, and his hat was gone, his jacket lapel torn, and his tie wrenched askew.

Before I could ask why he had taken so long and looked so dishevelled, a couple of bowler-hatted men burst in behind him and grabbed him by the elbows.

"Got you!" one of them cried. "You won't escape from us again, chum."

Holmes tossed the salt shaker to me underarm, and I caught it.

That action drew his pursuers' notice to Bancroft and myself and our respective states of vomit-besmirched prostration and genuflection.

"What's all this? Is that Mr Bancroft? What in God's name have you done to him?"

"I?" I said. "Nothing much. Merely saved his life – although he is still in jeopardy and must be got to a hospital forthwith. He needs an oral application of an activated charcoal infusion to soak up any strychnine still in his digestive tract, and thereafter round-the-clock observation. There remains the danger of lung paralysis and death by asphyxiation, and also of brain damage. Well? What are you waiting for? Don't just stand there gawping. Fetch transportation. Hop to it!"

The bowler-hatted men, whom I understood to be Bulldogs, exchanged looks. Neither seemed to know what to do. Eventually they agreed that one of them should go to flag down a passing cart or cab while the other stayed to keep Holmes in custody.

"Well done, Watson," my friend said. "Good work."

"Shut up, you," said the remaining Bulldog. "I don't know what's going on here, but Mr Bancroft looks in a bad way, and if you've had anything to do with it…"

"I assure you I have not," said Holmes. "I too was attempting to save him when you and your colleague apprehended me. Had you but listened to my protestations then, instead of belabouring me with your fists, I would have got back here sooner and perhaps spared Watson his unfortunate showering."

"Yes, well, you shouldn't have resisted arrest. Fetched me a couple of decent blows, you did. That didn't incline me to give you the benefit of the doubt, if you catch my drift."

"I had to escape your clutches somehow. Trust me, if I had really wanted to hurt you, I would have. I tend not to unleash the full panoply of my baritsu skills on those whose job it is to uphold law and order. I could have utterly incapacitated the pair of you, but instead I let you off easy."

"My aching ribs say otherwise."

"It seems I needn't have bothered, however. Watson had the matter well in hand. Look at the state of you, poor chap. Mrs Hudson will not be happy about taking that suit in hand."

"I fear this suit is beyond salvage and destined for the dustbin," I said, glumly eyeing my soiled garments. "Did you not try your ecclesiologist persona when accosted? Did it fail you?"

Holmes chuckled mirthlessly. "Alas, neither this fine representative of the university police nor his cohort gave me time to. As I left the kitchens, they were upon me in a flash. It is almost as though they were lying in wait for me." He turned to the Bulldog. "Is that the case?"

"We had a tip-off," the man said. "Someone told us there was an intruder on the premises, and furnished us with your description and the location where he'd spotted you."

"How fascinating. And what did this someone look like?"

"Not that it's any of your business, but it was one of the dons. Can't say I recognised him, but he was wearing the clobber – robe, mortar board. Biggish chap. Moustache. Red hood on his gown. That's about all I can tell you. Didn't stop and talk to us for more than ten seconds. Me and Coggins hurried off soon as he was done, and when I chanced to look back over my shoulder, he was gone."

"Did that not strike you as peculiar?"

"When it comes to dons, peculiar is par for the course. So, no. Anyway, that's enough of that. You're the suspicious character here. Your friend too. It's you two who should be giving explanations, not me."

"Once the Honourable Aubrey Bancroft is safely on his way to hospital, I shall answer any questions you have. I shall also avail myself, if I may, of the opportunity to summon Inspector Eden Tomlinson of the Oxfordshire Constabulary. He will vouch for the bona fides of both Watson and myself, and with his assistance I am sure we can unpick this knotty predicament."

# CHAPTER FOURTEEN

## JUST ANOTHER JOBBING INTELLECTUAL

By the time Tomlinson arrived, Bancroft was on his way to the Radcliffe Infirmary on Woodstock Road. At a hospital of such repute, I had no doubt he would receive top-notch care. The next twenty-four hours would be critical. If he survived those, he stood to make a full recovery.

"What's all this then, gents? Got ourselves into a spot of bother, have we?"

Holmes outlined the situation, illustrating his account by showing Tomlinson the poison pen letters and demonstrating how the cipher worked, to the inspector's intense fascination. He also drew Tomlinson's attention to the discarded champagne bottle whose contents had poisoned the wielder of the poison pen, saying it was a crucial piece of evidence.

"Have your forensics man use Mandelin's reagent on whatever liquid remains inside," he said. "I'm sure the results will test positive for strychnine."

All this took place under the glowering gaze of the two Bulldogs, who seemed to resent the presence of a police officer on the college grounds but also had no choice but to accept it. The university might be a self-governing body but even it must bow before the law of the land.

"What a pretty pickle," Tomlinson said. "It doesn't look good for you and Dr Watson, Mr Holmes, on the face of it. A person might readily assume that the pair of you were the culprits. You were caught in a room with a poisoned man. It's at least plausible that you administered the dose yourselves."

"It is not!" I expostulated. "It's absurd. If not for us, Aubrey Bancroft would be lying dead. What would we have to gain from killing him anyway? And why would we do it in so self-incriminating a manner, loitering at the scene to watch him die? It would be as though we were begging to be caught red-handed."

"Please calm yourself, doctor. I don't think for one moment that you are guilty, either of you. I was going to say that that would be the inference of a complete idiot."

The last three words were aimed with some acerbity at Coggins and the other Bulldog, whose name we had ascertained was Stanway.

"Likewise only a complete idiot," Tomlinson continued, "would apprehend a gentleman who insisted, as Mr Holmes did, that he was undertaking an errand of mercy."

"He'd stolen a silver salt shaker from the kitchens," Coggins protested.

"Borrowed it," Holmes said.

"It looked like thievery," said Stanway. "We weren't to know."

"Besides, he oughtn't to be here," said Coggins. "The other fellow neither. They haven't permission. They're interlopers, like."

"That is true," Holmes allowed. "I hold my hand up and admit it unreservedly. Watson and I did gain access to the college by illicit means."

"There. See?"

"There was no alternative. It was essential that we pay a call on Bancroft at the earliest opportunity, and in the event it is just as well that we did. Now, if the President of Magdalen wishes us to make reparation somehow, I'm sure we can come to some arrangement. Perhaps a donation towards the upkeep of the library roof? I fear the Earl of Shiplea's promised funding for the repairs may not, after all, be forthcoming."

Thus was the matter smoothed over, and Holmes and I were given leave to depart. Tomlinson accompanied us to the Randolph, where I gratefully bathed and changed into a spare suit of clothes. I came downstairs to find Holmes and the inspector taking afternoon tea together in the hotel lounge, and I joined them, gladly wolfing down finger sandwiches and scones.

"Amazed you can eat at all, doctor," said Tomlinson, "after what you've just gone through."

"Loss of appetite has never been a problem for Watson," said Holmes. "His rotundity should attest to that."

"Military service and my surgical residency at Netley," I said, aiming a sharp look of rebuke at my friend, "taught me the imperative of filling my stomach whenever I could, whatever the situation, however hungry I was. One could not be sure when or where one's next mealtime might be. It is a habit which has stayed with me ever since and which has only been broken on occasion, under extenuating circumstances."

One of those occasions had been in the wake of Holmes's supposed death, when for a spell my grief almost completely suppressed the instinctive desire for sustenance; similarly following Mary's death, when all food tasted like ashes to me and I wasted away to a skeleton of myself. It was only since the new year, in fact, that my capacity for dining had returned to its former level and I had begun to put on weight again. I would not have described myself as "rotund", however. I may have been carrying an extra pound or two around the midriff, but I was, thanks to my rugby playing, in fairly respectable shape for a man in his mid-forties.

"We were just discussing one or two of Mr Holmes's cases before you appeared, doctor," Tomlinson said. "In particular I'm intrigued by this Moriarty individual, this 'Napoleon of crime'. An academic gone bad – fair chills the blood, it does. I'm only relieved that he occupied the mathematical chair at one of Britain's minor universities and not, say, here. To think, if that had happened, I might have bumped into him on my rounds as a constable. Such a monstrous force for evil roaming these very streets…"

"He was not yet a fully fledged criminal mastermind while he was pursuing his studies into asteroid dynamics and the binomial theorem," Holmes said. "I doubt he would have stood out amongst his peers at all back then. It was only after he was compelled to resign from his post and decamped to London that he began putting his mental powers to their darkest, most heinous use. Up until then, the odd disturbing rumour aside, he would have passed as just another jobbing intellectual."

"It's surprising he hasn't cropped up in more of your tales, doctor."

"He could, inspector. He yet may," I said. "I have notes relating to at least half a dozen cases in which Professor Moriarty's hand is detectable, and it is likely I shall get around to chronicling at least some of them. I feel safe doing so, now that he is dead and his chief of staff, Colonel Sebastian Moran, in jail. At least, Moran *was* in jail, although alas that is no longer the case."

Holmes nodded gravely. "His escape from custody last September was a thing of brutal beauty, I must say. You heard about it, Tomlinson?"

"Afraid I didn't."

"He overwhelmed the two policemen guarding him in the back

of the Black Maria that was taking him from Pentonville to the Old Bailey, simultaneously strangling one with the manacles around his wrists and the other with the chain of the shackles around his ankles. He then kicked the door open while the carriage was still in motion, leapt out onto the street on High Holborn, and hobbled away. He was gone in a flash, lost amid the milling West End crowds. I suspect a confederate was waiting for him nearby in a hansom, the whole thing prearranged – location, timing, the lot. That wild, wily old shikari."

"Shikari?"

"It is Urdu for 'big game hunter'. As deadly as the tigers he used to shoot in Bengal, Moran is, and as averse to captivity. And yet, without Moriarty to guide him, he is no menace. If he has any sense, he will be lying low, far away from here, perhaps back in his spiritual home, the jungles of the subcontinent."

"I did not know of Moran's existence when I was writing 'The Final Problem' two years back," I said. "I was unaware that Moriarty had had a primary accomplice or that Moran had tried to kill Holmes after Moriarty failed, pelting him with rocks while he made his way back along the Aare Gorge from the Reichenbach Falls. As far as I knew, Moriarty was gone and his evil empire utterly destroyed, thanks to Holmes's Herculean efforts. All the same, while I was working on the story I was glancing constantly over my shoulder, and even when I submitted the manuscript to Newnes at *The Strand*, it was not without some trepidation. Such was the extent of Moriarty's organisation and influence that I half expected his spider-like grasp might somehow reach out from beyond the grave and touch me. I would have abandoned the undertaking, had I not felt the overwhelming need to set the record straight and defend Holmes from certain attackers, not least Moriarty's brother."

"Gad, there's another of them!" Tomlinson exclaimed.

"As far as I'm aware, Colonel Moriarty – there is also an excess of colonels in this tale – is no more than he appears to be, a former soldier now gainfully employed as station master at one of the busier railway hubs in the west of England, Bristol Temple Meads I believe. He has engaged in no criminal activity that we know of. However, he published a letter keenly avowing that his sibling was innocent of the offences he had been credited with and moreover that he was nothing more than the victim of rank vilification from certain quarters. He did not mention Holmes by name, or me, but it was clear whom he meant. What he wrote was an absolute perversion of the facts, yet it gained some currency, not least through the auspices of Archie Slater."

"Yes, the redoubtable Mr Slater of the *Illustrated London News*," said Holmes. "He it was who took up cudgels on Colonel Moriarty's behalf and penned a couple of articles which, had I not been 'dead' at the time, would have been actionable. He took Colonel Moriarty at his word and gave his scurrilous insinuations about me a veneer of credibility. He even conducted an interview with the man and reproduced his assertions unquestioningly as though they were fact. I am content to ascribe it all to an outpouring of grief and shame, the minor Moriarty driven half mad by the opprobrium attaching to his late brother and, by association, him. Hence it is forgivable. At any rate, he has gone quiet since my return. Perhaps wisely, he has sensed that it will not profit him to continue venting his spleen, now that I am around to respond in person."

"How is it there are so many who are so eager to revile you, sir?" said Tomlinson. "It baffles me. You are quite obviously a paladin of truth and justice, yet even amongst the ranks of the police some find you beyond the pale."

The inspector's description of Holmes's virtue caused me to inhale a goodly mouthful of tea, a vision of my friend astride a white horse like a knight of old in my mind's eye.

"If I may answer that," I said, recovering my composure, "it has always been true that those who routinely and energetically do good are considered suspect, their motivations questioned. Such is human nature, to regard altruistic behaviour as though it were a disease or a mental disorder. It is also true that possession of an acute intellect is an attribute many find intimidating. Holmes does himself no favours in that regard, since he tends to have little patience with anyone less cerebrally gifted than himself, which is to say everyone. The average person does not care to be reminded of his averageness and hence looks askance on the above-average person and views with deep mistrust and even hostility the exceptionally above-average."

"You are too kind," said Holmes with a touch of wryness.

"Mind you," said Tomlinson, "gents like Professor Moriarty do give brainboxes a bad name."

"Granted," I said. "There can be little worse than a brilliant mind allied to a wicked soul, dedicating itself to deeds that harm others and benefit no one but its owner. I have often wondered what the world would be like had you, Holmes, elected to pursue self-interest rather than dedicating your life to the detection of crime and the unmasking of villains."

"I rather imagine I should have ended up like Mycroft."

"Yet your brother, for all his propensity for personal indulgence, helps safeguard queen and country against malign outside forces. I meant what if you had followed the same path as Professor Moriarty?"

"Were I to have done so, neither you nor Tomlinson nor anyone, not even Mycroft, would know about it," said my friend. "I would remain as invisible and incognito as Moriarty did in his pomp. I would pose as a gentleman of good standing and background, without stain or blemish on my name, conducting my nefarious schemes in secret all the while. I might even anoint myself a consulting detective. Would that not be a delicious and most ironic cover identity? Publicly foiling the crimes of others while covertly committing my own."

"Can I quote you on that?"

The interrogative came from Archie Slater, no less, who unbeknownst to us had sidled up to our table while we were in the thick of conversation. He had his notebook out, and now licked the tip of his pencil as though fully prepared to jot down anything we said. This was his idea of a joke, but no one smiled save him.

"Speak of the devil," Holmes said. "I was just regaling the inspector here with an account of your involvement in Colonel Moriarty's ill-advised and rather regrettable assault on me. You encouraged him in his advocacy of his brother's innocence."

"So what if I did? The man had a right for his voice to be heard."

"You seem to me," said Tomlinson, "a more than usually obnoxious specimen, even by the standards of your profession."

"I have a job to do and I do it, same as any of you," Slater retorted. "You might as well criticise a lion for bringing down gazelles or a shark for eating fish. Whatever it takes to make a living."

"The difference between you and a lion or a shark, Slater," I said, "is that you have a choice about the damage you inflict on others; those beasts don't. I would rather take my chances with a wild predator, who may or may not attack me from the front, than an unscrupulous journalist who will almost certainly stab me in the back."

"Oh, well put, doctor. Very witty. Odd how some critics accuse you of not being able to string together a decent sentence on the page, when you're quite the Shakespeare in person."

Before I could deliver a suitable riposte, Slater continued, "But I didn't come to trade quips, however much fun it is. I came for a comment from you, Mr Holmes."

"A comment on what?"

"Ah, didn't you know?" Slater said with disingenuous puzzlement. "That is amazing. Not ten minutes gone, the Thinking Engine has begun tackling another case. Something to do with a Professor Merriweather, I think his name is, and the son of a peer of the realm."

"What!" I exclaimed.

"Rum affair, it is. Somehow Professor Quantock got wind of it, either from the Magdalen College porter or one of the university Bulldogs, not sure which. There's an undergraduate lying in a bed at the Radcliffe Infirmary, poisoned if the reports are true, his condition very poorly indeed. Quantock is busy informing the Thinking Engine about it all. You should come across and see."

# CHAPTER FIFTEEN

## THE GREATER GLORY OF LORD KNARESFIELD

Accordingly we trooped over to Beaumont Street and entered the Galleries.

In the cellar chamber, the Thinking Engine hummed and chattered busily. Professor Quantock was seated before it, typing. Lord Knaresfield was also present, along with a clutch of journalists. The newspaper proprietor had a beaming, munificent look on his face.

"Mr Sherlock Holmes!" he cried as we entered. "Back for more, eh? Thought you might have learned your lesson the last time."

"I come merely as an interested observer, your lordship. It would be wrong of me not to declare, though, that I have already resolved the Merriweather case to my satisfaction."

"Well, sir, then the five-hundred-pound wager still stands. If the Thinking Engine makes a muck of it, I shall write you a cheque on the spot. Did you get that, all of you?" Knaresfield was now addressing the journalists. "The contest is on again, Sherlock Holmes versus the Thinking Engine. Make note. Mark it well for posterity. That's an order, straight from your paymaster."

"Do these gentlemen all work for your newspapers?" Holmes enquired.

"All but that Slater. Does it matter? I assure you they are quite impartial, if that's what's troubling you. I do not interfere with editorial policy, unlike some other press barons I could mention. My staff and freelancers are allowed to speak for themselves in whatever way they see fit. As long as nothing they publish gives offence, oversteps the bounds of decency or, most important of all, harms sales, then I leave them well alone. That said," he added, "when a story such as this comes along, one in which I am personally involved, I do like it to be reported, if you know what I mean. What's the use of owning national newspapers if they can't make room for a few column inches about one's escapades every once in a while? It'd be like having a yacht and never sailing in her."

My friend ignored the man's insufferable bluster. "I am still somewhat unclear why you have taken such an interest in Quantock and his machine."

"Simple," said Lord Knaresfield. "Look at the thing. Such sophistication, such beauty. Imagine a world where Thinking Engines are commonplace. Every city, every town has one. Every major newspaper office, too. Imagine what journalists could achieve with so powerful a resource. All that information at their fingertips. As a research tool it would be invaluable, and as a method of verifying stories. That's what I'm seeing when I see the Thinking Engine at work: something that can aid my employees and enable them to do their jobs quickly, efficiently and accurately."

He looked over at the vast, industrious computational machine, and his expression was that of a father watching his child grow, the future taking shape before his eyes.

"I fancy myself a bit of a visionary, Mr Holmes," he continued.

"I've no doubt you do."

"Yes, always ready to adopt new methods, new processes,

anything to speed up the rate at which I can supply product to the masses and make it better and more attractive. When it comes to printing, for instance, I am not content with the usual rotary presses or linotype matrices. Those are old hat. I am currently investing in new kinds of presses that incorporate pneumatic sheet feed and delivery, and have ambitions to import the Lanston Monotype caster that the American papers have started using, a typesetter which makes justification, amongst other things, infinitely more precise. The Americans also have the halftone rotogravure reproduction system which I covet. Crystal-sharp photographs duplicated on newsprint at high speed – I'm looking to introduce that in Britain very soon. My papers will carry the best pictures, and others will look on in envy. Speaking of which… Smile!"

A journalist had produced a portable wooden Kodak box camera, which he proceeded to aim at Lord Knaresfield and Holmes. The former assumed a chest-puffing posture and extended a hand to the latter, who looked taken aback and, disregarding the proffered paw, bent aside so that his face was not in shot. There was sufficient daylight in the room for the photograph to have turned out decently had Holmes not shied away at the crucial moment, just as the journalist depressed the button on the side of the camera to trigger an exposure.

The journalist ventured to make a second attempt, but Lord Knaresfield waved him off.

"Mr Holmes obviously does not want his picture taken. We must respect his wishes."

"Thank you, your lordship," said Holmes. "I am not wholly averse to publicity but neither am I wholly comfortable with it, certainly not to the extent that you are. I have a high enough profile as it is without my face appearing in the papers."

"We see it regularly in *The Strand*."

"That is different. Mr Paget's illustrations convey the idea of me rather than an accurate likeness. It is an acceptable compromise. I would prefer that the criminal fraternity not know exactly what I look like, if it can be avoided."

"A lesser man might regard that as a poor excuse." Lord Knaresfield's habitual joviality hardened just a little, his voice gathering a rime of frost. "He might presume that you simply did not wish to be seen with him."

"If I am to be honest, I should not like it to appear as though I was to some extent condoning the Thinking Engine and your zeal for it, and the two of us together shaking hands with the device prominent in the background would do just that."

"Would that be so bad?"

"When the Engine has been set up as a direct opponent to me? I think so, yes. I think, too, that for all your fine talk of technology and the latest advances, Lord Knaresfield, what drives you in this particular instance isn't any of that. It isn't even the increase in circulation of your newspapers, such as it is, that you are deriving from this story. Doubtless there is some curiosity about Quantock's machine amongst your readership but not enough to warrant the time and effort you have been putting into promoting it. You do not live in Oxford, yet you have been here since last week, away from home and hearth, away from your business. I know this because you, too, are a guest at the Randolph – in its grandest suite – and your private landau has been parked on St Giles' all this time. The golden 'K' monogram on the doors is a nice touch, by the way. Not ostentatious at all. No, something else is impelling you to stay and supervise press coverage of the Thinking Engine, some other motive."

"And what might that be?" Knaresfield said, an eyebrow arched.

"At present I am unsure," replied Holmes. "But I intend to find out."

With that, he spun on his heel and re-joined Tomlinson and myself. Lord Knaresfield fixed him with a hard stare, which Holmes studiously ignored until at last the press baron uttered a loud, affronted harrumph and paced across the room to Professor Quantock's side.

"All done?" he demanded.

"N-not quite," replied Quantock, still pecking at the typewriter keys. "Nearly."

"Well, get a move on, man. Time's wasting."

"Don't badger me. I'm con-concentrating. One can't r-rush the inputting procedure."

"You didn't make a friend there, did you, Mr Holmes?" said Tomlinson.

"I didn't intend to. I resent Knaresfield using me as a puppet in his sideshow. I am under no illusion that Slater came over to the Randolph of his own accord. He was sent to fetch me. This event is being carefully stage-managed, even more so than the last one."

"All for the greater glory of Lord Knaresfield?" I said.

"That and something else besides. The man has more than a financial stake in all of this. At the risk of sounding paranoid, I get the impression I am being singled out in some as yet indefinable way. Targeted, even."

"You mean he has a grudge against you? What for? What have you done to him?"

"I cannot for the life of me say. We have hitherto never met. It is something I shall have to look into. In the meantime, it would seem that Professor Quantock is ready. He has finished typing, and the Thinking Engine has started to grind its gears and gnash its cogs in earnest."

Shortly afterwards, tickertape was disgorged from the slot. Lord Knaresfield read out the message. Allowing for the fact that it originated from a machine, nothing on the tickertape came as any surprise to us. The Thinking Engine enumerated the facts of the case much as Holmes had, right down to the tell-tale Latin cipher revealing the identity of the sender of the three letters.

"The Engine states that Aubrey Bancroft was a dupe," said Knaresfield. "Somebody egged him on. Somebody incited him to get his own back on Dr Merriweather and confected for him the wherewithal to do it. This same person then turned on Bancroft and tried to kill him, evidently in order to protect their own identity."

"Does it say who?" Holmes asked.

"No. It does not. Why, Mr Holmes? Do *you* know?"

Holmes, with barely disguised chagrin, shook his head.

"Pity. That little nugget of information might have reaped you a pretty sum. As things stand, you and the Thinking Engine are again at level pegging. You have not demonstrated yourself its better yet, and at this rate, I don't reckon as you will."

The Thinking Engine let out a weird, hiccupping clatter that startled everyone in the room, not least Quantock, who leapt bolt upright in his seat with an elaborate flutter of the hands. Another few inches of tickertape scrolled out of the slot.

"What's this, then? An afterthought?" Chuckling at his own witticism, Lord Knaresfield tore the strip of paper free. "Hmm. Just a couple of words. 'Parson's Pleasure'. By heck, anyone know what that's supposed to mean? Sounds like a racehorse." He turned to Quantock. "Is your machine functioning properly? What's it up to, churning out a random phrase like that? Maybe it's in need of an overhaul. Cogs slipping or whatnot."

"W-well," said the mathematician, "I can't ex-explain why the Engine f-felt the need to attach an addendum to its analysis. That's certainly u-unusual and unprecedented. But the words themselves are a n-name well known to all Oxonians, especially academics. Parson's Pleasure. It's a p-place. In the P-Parks."

# CHAPTER SIXTEEN

## Parson's Pleasure

Holmes and I proceeded there forthwith, having obtained directions from Inspector Tomlinson. Tomlinson himself did not accompany us, on the grounds that he had spent enough of his weekend absent from home and Mrs Tomlinson would take it amiss if he stayed away a single hour longer. His wife understood that police work imposed heavy demands on his time and he must answer the call of duty even on a Saturday, but not for *all* of a Saturday.

"Sometimes I envy men like you," he said to us, "unencumbered by marital obligations." He corrected himself immediately. "Forgive me, doctor. I spoke out of turn. I forgot that you are lately a widower."

"Think nothing of it. I understand what you are saying."

"It's simply that a man who can devote all his time to his vocation is a man who succeeds greatly in that vocation – such as yourself, Mr Holmes."

"A man who can adequately discharge his professional responsibilities as well as keeping his spouse happy is no less successful," said Holmes in return. It was a rare, magnanimous gesture coming from someone who eschewed marriage and found the fairer sex, by his own admission, inscrutable. I think he had developed a fondness for Tomlinson that was akin to his toleration of our regular Scotland Yard sparring partner, Inspector Lestrade. Both were, to him, wayward whelps that might through patient training develop into useful working dogs.

Parson's Pleasure was situated in the University Parks, not far from a narrow island in the middle of the Cherwell nicknamed Mesopotamia. Reached by a gravel walk, it was a bathing area for men only and was frequented exclusively by dons who were in the habit of entering the water nude.

I did not anticipate that anybody would be indulging in that pastime today, given that it was early spring and the river was still freezing cold. However, there were half a dozen swimmers at the spot when we arrived. They splashed and sported in the weak afternoon sunlight, hurling themselves about with abandon, their pale bodies almost blue and their mouths giving vent to yelps that were equal parts delight and anguish. Nearby a weir gurgled, decanting the river from a higher level to a lower.

"Holmes, perhaps we should not be here."

"Nonsense, old chap. Don't be prudish. It is a perfectly harmless, healthful recreation. They are not ashamed, so why should we be? The naked human form is not *per se* offensive. Do you look at Michelangelo's *David* and recoil in disgust?"

"No, but then none of these fellows, with the best will in the world, is on an aesthetic par with that sculpture. I would not put any of them at younger than fifty, and their physiques bespeak decades of fine dining and good wines."

"If we cannot admire them as prime physical specimens, we can at least admire them for their courage in braving water whose temperature, as we know only too well, is capable of stopping the heart."

I thought of Nahum Grainger and did indeed feel a little more generously disposed towards these bathers, and at the same time less assured of their sanity.

"Gentlemen, good day to you," Holmes declared from a ramshackle wooden platform which protruded from the riverbank and served as a diving board. "I apologise for interrupting your recreation, but may I crave a moment or two of your time?"

The swimmers obligingly gathered below him, treading water. The murkiness of the river obscured their bodies from the chest down, somewhat to my relief. I am not a prude, as Holmes had asserted, nor am I squeamish about the human body – as a doctor, how could I be? – but I have never gone in for public nudity or this "naturism" business so beloved of continentals such as the Germans and the French, and have no truck with American writers like Whitman and Thoreau who have extolled the virtues of being outdoors unclothed in order to commune with the landscape. In the privacy of one's home one may do as one wishes, but elsewhere civilised society demands decorum and dress.

I can only speculate what these Oxford dons, amongst the wisest heads in the country, derived from their mutually disrobed state. Perhaps, cloistered in every sense, burdened by tradition, ritual and fustian, they relished the opportunity to cast off their constraints and revel in a wild, primitive liberty. At Parson's Pleasure, if only temporarily, they were emancipated from their lives of hidebound learnedness.

Holmes introduced himself to the men at his feet and enquired if they had seen or heard about anything untoward occurring at this location in recent days. Wet heads were shaken. Bare shoulders shrugged.

Then one of the swimmers piped up, "There was that theft, wasn't there?"

Holmes's ears pricked. "Pray tell."

"We presume it must have been a prank," said another of the swimmers. "Students. You know."

"I'm not convinced we should be confiding in you," said a third, addressing his colleagues as much as Holmes. "This is a place where privacy is valued and we prefer that word of anything that goes on here does not spread. It is an unspoken rule. Hence, we did not report the pilferage to anyone. We kept quiet about it then, and it is my view that we should keep quiet about it now. We are aware that you are a gentleman of repute, Mr Holmes, and you honour Oxford with your continued presence."

"You are too kind, sir."

"All the same, we would be doing ourselves a disservice if we did not adhere to the policy of discretion which enables us to behave in a free and uninhibited fashion here."

"That is the consensus amongst you?" Holmes said.

All heads nodded.

"How regrettable. This theft you speak of has piqued my curiosity and I would like to know more. What can I do to persuade you of my sincerity and trustworthiness? How might I convince you to supply me with further details? Ah. I have it."

So saying, Holmes doffed his overcoat and jacket and commenced unbuttoning his shirt.

Some of my readers, perhaps the majority, may find what Sherlock Holmes did next uncharacteristic of him, unbelievable, even shocking. I must say I had a hard time accepting it myself. In retrospect, however, I can see that it was the only logical way to ingratiate himself with the dons. To be accepted into their club, as it were, he had to fulfil the membership criterion.

I looked on agog, before averting my eyes, as my friend stripped off all his clothing until he had not a stitch on. He then retreated a few paces, took a running jump, and executed a graceful swan dive, plunging headlong into the frigid Cherwell.

He broke the surface spluttering and gasping. "Enlivening!" he exclaimed. "Quite bracing! I can see the attraction now. Sets the heart pumping, the blood racing. I haven't felt this invigorated in some while."

He breast-stroked over to join the assembled swimmers, who seemed pleased and a tad impressed. He had won their approval, and it wasn't long before they and he were in a bobbing huddle together, talking in low tones, while I in the meantime kept a polite distance, feeling out of place, somewhat as though I had turned up for an informal garden party clad in white tie and tails.

When they were done conferring, Holmes bade the dons adieu and clambered out of the river. He was shivering hard as he dressed, and I distinctly heard his teeth chattering. Still, he was bullish. "You should have a go, Watson," he said, plastering his hair down into some semblance of tonsorial order. "It isn't so bad. The sensation of all-over numbness fades after, oh, four or five minutes."

"And catch my death of pneumonia? No fear. You'll need to get yourself dry and in the warm as soon as possible, Holmes."

"All in good time. First, I need to check something."

He hastened over to a row of rough-hewn changing cubicles which faced the river. He inspected one of them inside and out thoroughly until, satisfied, he indicated that we could leave.

# CHAPTER SEVENTEEN

## A Kind of Agent Provocateur

As we headed at a brisk pace through the Parks, Holmes said, "Initially I expected this to be the proverbial wild goose chase. The Thinking Engine, I assumed, had blurted out the name of an Oxford location at random owing to some flaw in the mechanism. Now it seems that the damned thing is cleverer than I thought and the theft at Parson's Pleasure does have some relevance to the Merriweather affair."

"What was stolen?"

"Please understand that I have obtained special dispensation to share this information with you, Watson. I managed to coax my fellow bathers into accepting you into our 'bare brotherhood of the water', even though you did not commit yourself as wholeheartedly as I did."

"What you call commitment I call the act of a man who should be committed," I said, and receiving nothing in response from Holmes but stony-faced silence, added, "To a lunatic asylum, that is."

"Yes, I got the joke. You didn't need to spell it out. My lack of evident mirth should have clued you in to the fact that I did not find it amusing. To answer your question, what was stolen was an academic gown, a convocation robe belonging to a certain doctor of Divinity. The act of taking it would have been child's play. The walls of the changing cubicles do not extend all the way to the ground. There is an aperture of some six inches at the bottom, intended so that the water from the bathers' bodies may flow out rather than accumulate in the corners and rot the planking. The cubicles do not have hooks from which to hang clothes. Everything must be folded and placed on a low shelf. It would be the easiest thing on earth to reach in from underneath, through the aperture, and pluck whatever garment one wished."

"That was all that went missing, a gown?"

Holmes nodded. "The fact that the culprit was not spotted suggests one of two things. Either he is a don himself and was able to mingle freely amongst his colleagues at Parson's Pleasure, or he crept up to the changing cubicles from the rear and performed his act of larceny clandestinely, unnoticed. I err towards the latter explanation, simply because I cannot fathom why one don would purloin another's gown."

"It might just have been a prank carried out by students, as was suggested."

"Naturally. But consider this. The Bulldog, Stanway, stated that the moustachioed don who identified me as an intruder had a gown with a red hood. The gown of a doctor of Divinity has a long hood of scarlet silk which hangs down the back."

"Good grief!" I said. "You're suggesting the thief and the don at Magdalen are one and the same?"

"More than that. The don at Magdalen is the man who poisoned Aubrey Bancroft."

"Holmes, that is a leap of logic too far, surely."

"And," Holmes continued, undaunted by my objection, "he

is not a don at all but an impostor. Think about it, Watson. If you wished to go anywhere in Oxford, enter any college, pass unobtrusively amongst its quads and cloisters, what better disguise could you wear than that of an academic? No porter would think to challenge you, nor any Bulldog. You could come and go as you pleased. People would barely notice your face; all they would see was the gown. It would not even matter if you looked uncertain rather than purposeful or if you had to stop a passer-by to beg directions. Academics are such unworldly creatures; no one expects them to behave in a conventional manner. No great thespian talent would be required, just the confidence that your garb will shield you like some cloak of inconspicuousness, the perfect camouflage."

"Still, it would take some audacity to pull off the pretence."

"I believe we are dealing with an individual who is not deficient in boldness, or in ruthlessness."

"Why not simply buy a gown?" I said. "I've seen a shop selling them on the High Street. Why go to the effort of stealing one?"

"Because a shopkeeper might remember your face and be able to provide a description, and because the theft of an item of clothing from Parson's Pleasure is not only easy to execute but will not be reported to the authorities. Our malefactor knew that. He is, it seems, a wily one. Even his choice of disguise – a doctor of Divinity – was calculated to deflect suspicion. A theologian. One step short of the priesthood. The last person you would think capable of wrongdoing."

"So this man, the bogus academic, was Bancroft's co-conspirator?"

"The gown was stolen just over three weeks ago," said Holmes. "It wasn't long after that that Merriweather received the first poison pen letter. The dates line up. My theory is, our phoney theologian presented himself to Bancroft, befriended him, gained his confidence, then worked his wiles on the youngster, making him his cat's paw. Perhaps he claimed to share Bancroft's dislike of Merriweather, citing some long-running scholastic feud, a common-room rivalry. It wouldn't have taken much to spur Bancroft into action, with the added incentive of offering to help by drafting the letters for him to write out. Such larks, the gullible aristocrat must have thought, little realising that the instigator of the deed had a hidden agenda: the letters were not as anonymous as they appeared."

"But then to attempt to kill him…"

"As I said – ruthless. Aware of Bancroft's taste for champagne, the felon knew he would have no difficulty coaxing him into drinking a bottle of the stuff which he surreptitiously laced with strychnine while uncorking it. He himself refrained from taking even a sip, professing to be an abstainer."

"To think, we might have run into him, had we visited Bancroft just a few minutes earlier."

"My view is that we came nearer to encountering him than we realised. He must have spied us as we were entering Bancroft's staircase, put two and two together, and fled the scene, but not before taking the precaution of warning the Bulldogs about us so that we would be waylaid and unable to give chase. I would go further than that and say he had been monitoring the whole situation at Magdalen and was not ignorant of the fact that Merriweather had contacted me. This informed his decision to kill Bancroft."

"Holmes," I said after a pause for thought, "do you discern any connection between the Merriweather letters and the Jericho murders? It strikes me that there are correspondences there. In both cases a third party provided the impetus and the structure for an offence which someone else then committed."

"Watson, that is by far the most intelligent thing you have said all day. All year, even."

The warmth with which my friend uttered the remark did little to mitigate its condescending nature. As was often the way with Holmes's compliments, it carried more than a hint of disparagement.

"I have been coming to that conclusion myself," he went on. "What if the same individual who cajoled Bancroft into writing the letters also gave Grainger the idea for murdering his family and then building himself – almost literally – an unassailable alibi? It is fantastic, yet it is also only too possible. We are looking at a kind of agent provocateur, someone who derives an obscene satisfaction from driving others to acts of wickedness and then disposes of them afterwards at his convenience. He is at large in Oxford, a serpent in human form, a tempter and enabler, and we must find him and stop him before he strikes again, as he doubtless will."

We had by this time put the rolling landscaped greenswards of the Parks behind us and were wending west along streets lined with towering hornbeams that were just coming into leaf. I assumed we were returning to the Randolph, but Holmes, as was his wont, had other plans, and presently we were approaching the Radcliffe Infirmary, an imposing late-eighteenth-century edifice built in the style of a grand country house, with double gates, ivy-wreathed wings and a fountain in front featuring a statue of a muscular Triton.

"We need to talk to Aubrey Bancroft," Holmes said. "The more we learn about the doctor of not-such-great-Divinity, the better."

"What *you* need," I said, "is to change into dry clothing, or risk becoming an inmate of this hospital too. But it would be wasting my breath to tell you that."

The last comment fell on deaf ears, thus proving its acuity. Holmes entered the building, I trailing in his wake.

Soon locating a physician with responsibility for Bancroft's care, we learned that an interview with the young noble would not be possible.

"Are you friends of his?"

"Acquaintances," said Holmes. "Is he unavailable? Asleep, perchance?"

The look that came over the doctor's face was one I have had to adopt many times myself over the years. It was blandly neutral, with a tinge of compassion. It is the look we in our profession use when we are called upon to deliver the worst kind of news.

Holmes was sanguine as we exited the Radcliffe; I was angry.

"Dash it all, it's not fair!" I seethed. "What Bancroft did was mischievous, unpleasant, malicious even – but he did not deserve to die for it. That is far too severe a punishment. And him barely in his twenties…"

"Watson, you did all you could for him. He had ingested too much of the poison already. It was coursing through his bloodstream. His lungs had been affected irreparably and in the end gave out. You pursued extreme measures to revive him, you went above and beyond, and it is not your fault that it was insufficient. You must not berate yourself."

"I am not berating myself," I said, although I was, just a bit. "At the very least, Holmes, promise me we will find his murderer. Promise me we will catch the wretch and build an ironclad case against him so that a judge will have no choice but to reward him as he has rewarded his victims."

"Further evidence from Bancroft would have helped in that respect," Holmes said. "Without it, we do not have much to go on. Even so, I vow that the villain will not escape. If I have to remain in Oxford 'til kingdom come, no matter. So be it. He will not get away with this."

# CHAPTER EIGHTEEN

## Pressure from the Press

It was not long after these events that Holmes was engaged to solve the diverting case which I wrote up and published nine years later as "The Adventure of the Three Students". Readers of that tale will recall that it centred on the displacement of galley proofs of an examination paper in the rooms of a lecturer named Hilton Soames, the implication being that someone had moved the sheets in order to copy down their contents for the purpose of cheating.

In that narrative I went to some pains to disguise the name of the college where the incident took place, dubbing it St Luke's. Anyone reading *this* narrative may be able to intuit that the actual college was one that was named after another of the Four Evangelists, to wit St John's, which is amongst Oxford University's older and more prestigious constituents.

"Hilton Soames" was also a pseudonym, and I likewise rechristened each of the three undergraduates on whom suspicion for the misdeed fell, my principal aim being to spare the blushes of the one – "Giles Gilchrist" – whom Holmes was able to single out as the perpetrator. I am glad that I did so, for I have it on good authority that the young man, after a self-imposed exile in southern Africa and a stint in the Rhodesian Police, settled in the Transvaal, married a Boer woman, forged a career for himself in the diamond mining industry, and has gone on to lead a blameless and profitable life. His minor infraction was, in the long run, the making of him.

For Holmes, the affair was something of a palate cleanser, a break between courses of a meal. It bore no attachment to the larger mystery at hand; nor did it come to the attention of Professor Quantock and hence was not subjected to the ministrations of the Thinking Engine. An isolated occurrence, incidental, *co*incidental one might say, it offered respite from the somewhat oppressive chain of circumstances in whose toils we had become enmeshed.

I have a pair of letters which Holmes sent to me during this period, both of them on the Randolph's handsomely embossed notepaper and adorned with my friend's usual spidery penmanship. In the first, he described his efforts to track down the deadly agent provocateur, who was proving an elusive quarry. "Various avenues of investigation, which look promising, turn out to be cul-de-sacs," he wrote. "I seem to make inroads, only to find myself up a blind alley." His tone was sprightly, but reading between the lines one can sense a frustration. Holmes was not enjoying being repeatedly stymied.

In the second of the letters he related, in a most ironical fashion, how the Thinking Engine had begun to make headway even as he was wallowing in the doldrums.

> I have heard tell, mainly through the auspices of Inspector Tomlinson, that people have been travelling to the University Galleries to consult the Engine on personal matters – the loss of some valuable item, the whereabouts

> of an errant spouse on certain evenings, the mislaying of a wallet or purse, even a pet cat gone astray. They are like pilgrims visiting a shrine, hoping to have their prayers answered. And, Watson, the machine obliges. Each time, it spits out a tickertape response, and damn me if it isn't invariably right! Not least about the cat (which had got itself locked in a neighbour's tool shed by accident, in case you're wondering). I am astonished at the Engine's perspicacity, and beginning to ask myself if this isn't truly the miracle of science that Quantock and Knaresfield have been saying all along. It directed us to Parson's Pleasure, did it not? How did its mechanical brain know that there had been a theft there? How on earth did it winnow down all of the available probabilities to arrive at the conclusion that a man in a stolen academic gown was the *éminence grise* behind the letters to Dr Merriweather?

These rhetorical questions went unanswered, in that letter at least, and I descried in them a crumbling confidence, a deepening bewilderment. My friend was not one to give in to despair, not easily, but here he was, expressing an inability to decipher an enigma. That was anathema to a man in his line of work, with his track record and his keen skills of ratiocination.

For further evidence of the Thinking Engine's mounting public prestige, a sampling of Knaresfield-owned newspapers from that time is instructive. Holmes would not have been ignorant of their coverage of its doings, and this could not have alleviated the pressure that he was under.

A copy of the *Midlands Gazette* dated Monday 11th March 1895 devotes space to an article about the Duke of Marlborough, whose financial straits at the time were common knowledge and who was keen to find some way to repair both his failing family fortunes and his decaying ancestral home, Blenheim Palace, situated some ten miles north of Oxford.

The Thinking Engine steered him towards America and William Kissam Vanderbilt, the railroad millionaire whose wife had aspirations for their only daughter, Consuelo, to marry into the British nobility. The resultant betrothal rescued the duke from bankruptcy and his property from its remorseless slide into dilapidation, although it was not, by all accounts, a match made in heaven. Seldom can wedding vows have seemed more like the clauses of a business contract.

The *Coventry Gleaner* of Wednesday 13th March contains a story of almost tragicomic proportions about the Reverend Charles Lutwidge Dodgson, one of Oxford's most famous denizens, better known to his many, many readers around the world by his pen name Lewis Carroll. The venerable author of delightful nonsense, then nearing the final chapter of his life, paid a call on the Thinking Engine in his role as a semi-retired lecturer in mathematics at Christ Church College. He was in the throes of writing a new treatise on linear and algebraic equations, and sought the Engine's aid in constructing a method of evaluating determinants in square matrices, a theorem he was working on. This action he undertook in a light-hearted, jocular manner, little thinking it would yield a result.

What happened next is not exactly clear. The Engine, after nearly half an hour of calculation and computation, churned out several dozen yards of tickertape, which Dodgson spent a further half an hour poring over. He then left the Galleries in a state of some flusterment with the coils of tickertape bunched up under his arm.

The story was picked up by two further Knaresfield newspapers, the *Northampton Argus* and the *Birmingham Echo*, the following day. In both, Dodgson is said by eyewitnesses to have "blanched" when he read the Thinking Engine's answer and to have been "close to fainting". The *Echo* article concludes,

> Was this a Snark that Mr Dodgson discovered, or a Boojum? Did the Thinking Engine send him down a rabbit hole from which he may never return? Has it imparted some profound piece of wisdom to him with an enigmatic Cheshire Cat smile? What is certain is that Mr Dodgson departed from the University Galleries in high dudgeon, with anything but a "carol" in his heart.

I can imagine whoever wrote the piece was especially pleased with that closing sentence.

It has been said that his encounter with the Thinking Engine hastened Dodgson's demise. He had been sickly since childhood, suffering from a weak chest, persistent migraines and epilepsy, but some have argued that the rapidity and facility with which the Engine solved the mathematical problem he put to it broke his spirit and was a blow from which he never recovered. A mere metal machine had cracked a riddle that had been confounding him for months, perhaps even years. He was an Anglican deacon and a staunch Christian, too, so the Engine's triumph may have wounded him on a religious as well as an intellectual level: something unliving, not blessed by God with a soul, was able to outshine the supposed pinnacle of Creation, *Homo sapiens*. What is undeniable is that the Reverend Dodgson's already precarious health deteriorated sharply thereafter, until pneumonia took him in 1898 just a fortnight shy of his sixty-sixth birthday.

Finally, I shall quote from the *Nottingham Mercury* of Saturday 16th March, in which it was reported that a delegation of students from St Edmund Hall had quizzed the Engine about one of Oxford's queerest little oddities, namely a tombstone in the churchyard of St Peter-in-the-East on Queen's Lane, adjacent to their college. Marking the last resting place of one Sarah Hounslow, the tombstone proclaims that the lady shuffled off her mortal coil on "31.2.1835". This impossible date has been ascribed to a simple slip of the stonemason's chisel. There is nothing in the parish records giving the correct date of death.

The Thinking Engine proposed that the error occurred because the stonemason commenced his work on Ash Wednesday, the first day of Lent, which fell on 4th March that year. Sarah Hounslow must have died the day before, three days after the end of February. The stonemason, the machine suggested, may have overindulged himself on that same day, Shrove Tuesday. If he was of French or Eastern European origin, this would have meant drinking heavily in addition to gorging on pancakes and other rich foodstuffs. That, or he had been a guest of Brasenose College, where the consumption of a yard of spiced ale is traditional on the eve of Lent. In other words, the man was reeling from a titanic hangover as he hammered out the tombstone inscription and forgot that February customarily has only twenty-eight days, twenty-nine at most. "The Thinking Engine," the *Mercury* article said,

> prefixed its reply with the phrase "A polite speculation only", suggesting that there are some conundrums that are beyond even its dazzling computational capacity to unravel. Yet there is a playfulness about the offered solution which suggests hitherto unplumbed depths. Is it possible, is it even conceivable that Professor Quantock's machine possesses a latent humorous streak?

The perfidious Archie Slater of course made hay. The *Illustrated London News* of that same Saturday sees him describe the Engine's escalating popularity in Oxford: "People approach in a spirit of scepticism and leave with the beatific smiles of the converted." He is then provoked to muse, "What need have we of detectives when the Engine has all the answers? What becomes of Sherlock Holmes and his ilk now?"

The last was more than just a jeering taunt. It was something I was beginning to ask myself, and I asked it all the more intently on my next trip up to Oxford, as Holmes and I tackled "The Mystery of the Missing Stroke".

# CHAPTER NINETEEN

## The Mystery of the Missing Stroke

Mist. Mist hung over Oxford. Mist draped itself across the rooftops, masking the city's towers and spires and muffling the peals of its multiplicity of church bells. Mist slid along the cobbles and mud of the streets. Mist flowed around the dome of the Radcliffe Camera and shrouded the cupola of the Sheldonian Theatre, Sir Christopher Wren's masterpiece with its palisade of sagely stone heads. Mist rippled and writhed through the air, turning the sun to a pale silver disc.

"Makes one quite nostalgic for home," Holmes remarked as we headed along the towpath on the east bank of the Isis, past Christ Church Meadow.

"A London fog is yellower and more mephitic," I said. "It leaves a foul taste in the back of the throat."

"An Oxford mist runs it a close second. This is in many ways a dismal place, Watson, dank and damp. Built on marshland, which tells you a lot. Floodplains all around. Cambridge University is no better, perched amid the Fens. What is it that compelled the founders of our two supreme seats of learning to choose such low-lying, uncongenial sites for both?"

"No education worth having can be achieved without discomfort?" I suggested.

I was speaking in jest, of course, but Holmes took the comment at face value. "Perhaps so. The late Cardinal Newman, at any rate, was far from fond of Oxford. He said something along the lines of 'Its air does not suit me. I feel it directly I return to it.' This from a man all but synonymous with the city. No wonder he threw himself so enthusiastically into ecclesiastical reform, seeking refuge from unpleasant physical conditions in the embrace of doctrinal debate. Might the name the Oxford Movement have been a latent expression of the desire to be somewhere else? Then there's Thomas Hardy, who has described Oxford's air as 'extinct' and 'accentuated by the rottenness of the stone.'"

I too had read *Jude the Obscure* the previous year in serial form in *Harper's*, but could not quote from it as accurately as Holmes did, or indeed at all. His mind was an incredible repository of retained facts. I wonder if he forgot anything.

"I am experiencing that for myself," he went on, "now that I have been here nearly three weeks. There is something deadening and enervating in the local atmosphere. It creeps up on one like catarrh. I am not at ease. I am not at home."

His face took on a haunted, lugubrious cast. I had seen the look before, but normally it manifested when Holmes was bored, in a lull between cases, under-stimulated. I was surprised by its presence now. Weren't we in the middle of an investigation? Weren't we on our way to interview a group of people who had been present during an inexplicable abscondment? At a time when, in the normal course of events, he ought to have been at his most excitable and energetic, Holmes seemed to be lapsing into one of his episodic depressions. That worried me. I feared a resumption of the needle and the seven-per-cent solution of cocaine, whose effects were so detrimental to the health. The pupils of his eyes were not dilated, nor was he speaking with the agitated prolixity which use of the drug commonly engenders. He was not under its influence at that precise moment. But how long before he resorted to it once more?

On the river, a sleek clinker-built eight emerged from the mist, its crewmen pulling heavily through the iron-grey water. The cox exhorted them with shouts which matched the rhythmic splash of the blades and the grunts of the rowers. The boat passed us by in a flash and was swallowed by the mist again, the sounds of its progress swiftly dwindling into silence.

"If being here is getting you down," I said, "why not remove yourself back to Baker Street? A change of scene might do you the world of good. It might restore some perspective."

"Not while *he* is still out there." Holmes swept an arm around him vaguely. "Not while he continues to evade me."

"Is it the agent provocateur who is vexing you so, or is it the Thinking Engine?"

"Why would you say that? There is no comparison. One is an evil, the other merely an annoyance."

"It cannot help your mental equilibrium, though, to be waging a war on two fronts. Ahead of you is an opponent, entrenched, lurking out of sight, while behind is another opponent nipping at your heels. You are stretched thin, your resources divided."

"Watson, sometimes you really do talk utter rot," Holmes snapped. "I have operated under far greater strain than this previously. My powers are up to the task. Tut! I make a few passing remarks about the inclemency of the weather, and all at once you're inferring some sort of debility."

He snorted in irritation and picked up the pace. So long and rapid did his strides become that I had to all but run to keep up.

We crossed a footbridge over a spur of the Cherwell and

arrived at a row of boathouses. Our destination was the sixth one along. Outside, waiting for us in the mist, was a handful of hale and hearty young men of assorted shapes and sizes. They were dressed in boating caps, short-sleeved cotton shirts and neckerchiefs patterned with blue and white stripes. A couple of them wore blazers with navy blue piping and cuff rings and an emblem of three feathers embroidered on the breast pocket. All looked sheepish and a touch sullen. Their smiles, as they greeted us, were forced.

"These, Watson, unless I am very much mistaken, are the crew of the Oriel College 1st VIII," Holmes said. "Gentlemen, you are kind to have agreed to convene here. You need not have come in your rowing outfits, but it is appropriate to have you looking the part, I suppose."

"We have not got changed since this morning," the tallest of them said. "We have, as you can imagine, been in a state of perturbation. For Trenchard to do as he did…" He shook his head. "It beggars belief."

"You are…?"

"Stevens."

"Ah yes. You row at number five."

"How did you…?" Stevens turned to an older man present, who was clad not in rowing wear but in plain flannels. "Of course. You have told Mr Holmes about us, Mr Gill."

The man called Gill gave a curt nod. "I gave him all the information he asked for, Stevens. Your names, your positions in the boat, whatever details he deemed pertinent."

"You also insisted he try to discover what prompted Trenchard's strange behaviour. I suppose it was inevitable."

"If it helps us find Trenchard, where is the harm?" said Gill. "As your coach, your welfare is my responsibility. Trenchard is gone, God alone knows where. Torpids starts tomorrow, and if we cannot locate our stroke and captain of boats, then we are in trouble."

"Torpids?" I said.

"It is one of the university's two annual rowing races," Holmes explained, "and is held over four days of Hilary Term. Every college fields a crew, often more than one, and the boats set off from staggered starting positions. Each boat attempts to hit the boat immediately in front. When this happens, it is known as a 'bump', and the crew which does the bumping ascends one place in the rankings while the crew that is bumped descends one place. The outcome of each day's racing sets the starting positions for the next. At the end of the four days, whichever boat is at the top of the rankings is crowned Head of the River and holds that post until the following year."

"Sounds inordinately complicated. Why not race side by side and have elimination rounds, as at an ordinary regatta?"

"The Isis is too narrow and winding for that," said Gill. "We make do with what we've got."

"But isn't it hazardous, one boat trying to hit another? Surely there must be sinkings."

"On very rare occasions. It is considered a bump, however, if the chasing boat's bow merely overlaps the stern of the boat ahead. Actual contact need not be made."

"Brasenose College has been Head for the past nine years," said Holmes. "Oriel is favourite to catch them this year."

"But not without Trenchard," said Gill sourly. "He is a titan amongst oarsmen, a one-man engine room, and the best stroke I have ever coached. It's a wonder he isn't in the Blue Boat."

"They don't want him," said one of the crew members, the smallest in stature. "They know what he's like, how he rubs people up the wrong way. That's why *we're* stuck with him."

"You are the cox," said Holmes. "Preston, isn't it? A cox needs to be light and slender, and you fit the bill." He held out his hand,

and Preston shook it. Puzzlement registered on his face, since Holmes had not shaken Stevens's hand earlier in much the same circumstances; the act seemed gratuitous. The cox then shrugged, clearly thinking no more of it.

"You are not fond of Trenchard," Holmes said.

"If I'm honest, no," said Preston. "It's fair to say that no one in the boat is. We acknowledge that he is a fine oarsman, and as a stroke he keeps the rating like a metronome. As a human being, though..."

"Arrogant," said one of the crew.

"Overbearing," said another.

"A harsh taskmaster," said a third.

"He demands as much from himself as he does from any of you," Gill pointed out, but this argument carried little weight with Trenchard's crewmates, judging by the frosty glares it elicited.

"So his absence is a blow to your hopes of sporting glory," said Holmes, "but not to any of you personally."

"He can be replaced," said Stevens. "The stroke of the 2nd VIII, Hargreaves, is highly talented. He would be only too happy to be promoted, and we would be only too glad to have him."

"Why don't you tell Watson and myself exactly what happened this morning? I have had one version of events from Mr Gill, but he – no disrespect meant, sir – did not see everything. It would be useful to hear about it from the perspective of those who were actually in the boat."

"Why don't we tell the Thinking Engine instead?" said a brawny, swarthy lad who was only an inch or so taller than Preston the cox and whose face seemed to bear a permanent mischievous smirk. "That thing has all the answers."

A few of the oarsmen sniggered. Beside me Holmes bristled. I could see him doing his utmost to maintain his composure.

"I posed that very question myself to Mr Gill when he came to me at the Randolph," my friend replied. "Do you know what he said? 'I don't trust machines, Mr Holmes.'"

"Especially ones that purport to think like men," said Gill. "It isn't natural."

"There you have it," said Holmes to the swarthy lad. "It's Llewellyn, yes? The bow man?"

"What gave me away? My Welsh accent?"

"Mr Gill told me there was a joker in the pack, one who hailed from the Valleys. The deduction was beyond elementary."

"El-em-ent-ar-ee," said Llewellyn in his orotund tones, with a triumphant gloat. "Hear that, boyos? Mr Holmes used his magic word, his abracadabra. That's a shilling each you owe me."

There were more sniggers.

"You were right, Taff," said one of the rowers. "You said he would say it."

"I've read the stories. He always does."

"I do not," Holmes countered. "Watson may have me use the expression in several of his narratives, but I assure you, in life it seldom passes my lips."

I refrained from pointing out that he had last uttered the word only a fortnight ago, shortly after our visit to the Graingers' house in Jericho.

"Well then, this was a rare instance of life imitating art," said Llewellyn, "and that's me better off to the tune of more than one crown. Much obliged, sir. *Diolch yn fawr*."

Holmes drew himself up to deliver an even sharper rebuke to Llewellyn. I was afraid that the young Welshman might be scorched to a cinder by the full force of my companion's scorn, so I placed a hand on Holmes's arm, a gesture of restraint.

"Come, come," I said. "It doesn't matter. Perhaps I do attribute 'elementary' to you more often than you actually say it. Put it down to creative licence. Now, are we here to locate the missing Trenchard, or what?"

My words had the desired salutary effect. Holmes calmed and said, "Very well. It was a dawn training outing, was it not? As the sun rose, the ten of you gathered at this very spot – eight oarsmen, one cox, one coach. The mist was as thick as it is now, if not thicker. You carried your boat out from the boathouse and deposited it in the water. And then…?"

# CHAPTER TWENTY

## An Impromptu Self-jettisoning

The story came out in dribs and drabs, the crewmen taking it in turns to be narrator, sometimes interrupting one another to chip in with some extra detail or expand on a point the previous speaker had made.

The thread of it, when assembled, was as follows.

Once the boat was afloat in the water, Gill set off on his bicycle along the east bank towpath to the road bridge called Folly Bridge. Crossing this, he came back down the river along the west bank. The towpath on that side is unbroken all the way south to the Iffley Lock, beyond which Oxford crews do not row, whereas the towpath on the other side terminates at the university boathouses.

By the time Gill drew level with the Oriel boathouse, the crew had pulled out from the landing pontoon and were already some way downriver, going at a fair lick. He pedalled hard to catch up but lost sight of them at the first bend. He called out to them through his megaphone, telling them to slow down and wait for him, but the cox, Preston, stated that he did not hear the instruction. Neither did any of his crewmates. The mist was too dense.

Eventually coach and boat were reunited just past the bend, a zigzag turn known picturesquely as the Gut. The boat had come to a halt, oars at rest, and was drifting gently with the current. It was then that Gill observed that one of his oarsmen was gone. The stroke's seat was empty. Trenchard was nowhere to be seen.

Gill asked, with some astonishment, what had become of Trenchard. An answer was not immediately forthcoming. The remaining crewmen were in consternation, flummoxed by the unexpected turn of events.

Trenchard, it transpired, had leapt from his seat and dived into the water. He had swum the few yards to the bank, crawled out and begun running. Not a word of warning had he tendered, nor of explanation. He had waited until the cox had given the order to stop – "Easy all! Hold her hard!" – and the boat had been braked by the insertion of the oar blades perpendicular in the water. Next moment he had, in a manner of speaking, abandoned ship.

Gill raced off after him along the towpath, cycling as fast as he dared given the limited visibility. He failed to find him. Trenchard might well have cut to the right and headed across the fields between the river and the Abingdon Road. Equally, he might have continued southward to Donnington Bridge and joined the main road there. He was a fit athlete, a strong runner. Staying ahead of a much older man on a bicycle, especially after a decent head start, would not have been difficult for him.

Gill returned to the Gut, out of breath, unsuccessful, despondent. The crew then had no choice but to limp home minus its stroke, with Trenchard's oar shipped and Jenkins at seven filling in for him as pace-setter. Gill meanwhile went to Trenchard's rooms at college, hoping he was there, but no luck. He tried the common rooms, the dining hall, the library, stopping anyone he passed to enquire if they had seen him; no one had.

When asked if anything had occurred prior to the outing

which might have precipitated Trenchard's impromptu self-jettisoning, the remaining crew members confessed there had been a slight contretemps. Trenchard liked to give pre-training "pep talks", which consisted of him cataloguing his crewmates' flaws as rowers and inviting them to concentrate on improving their skills. Llewellyn had, on that morning, found this habit particularly irksome and had called Trenchard various choice names. Bad blood had been festering between bow man and stroke as the boat set forth. The rest of the crew had not been happy either. Perhaps Trenchard had been able to sense the discontent in the boat, the waves of resentment emanating towards him from behind, the stares piercing his back like daggers. That might account for his actions. Suddenly it all became too much for him and he snapped.

The crew were, by their own admission, labouring under a heavy burden of expectation. Hopes were riding on them. Oriel had never stood a better chance of dislodging Brasenose from the top spot and becoming Head of the River than it did this year. It was a college where sporting prowess was valued almost as highly as academic achievement. Winning the event and hoisting high the Torpids Challenge Cup would mean a lot.

"If you ask me, Trenchard couldn't take it any more," said the number four man, Allardyce. "The strain, I mean. He just cracked."

"As captain of boats as well as stroke, he would have been feeling it more than any of us," said Stevens. "He isn't what you'd call sensitive, but still waters run deep. He may just have had enough and wanted to be shot of the whole thing."

"Surprising of him to quit in so rash and dramatic a fashion," said Knight, who rowed at number two. "But then, prone as he is to fits of uncontrolled temper, perhaps not that surprising."

"Anyway," said Llewellyn, "now we can recruit Hargreaves. It shouldn't take long to integrate him into the boat. He stroked for us a couple of times earlier in the term, when Trenchard got injured. He'll slot right in, no trouble."

"Trenchard injured?" said Holmes. "How?"

"He 'caught a crab', Mr Holmes. Nasty it was, too. Oar handle flew up and whacked him in the mouth. Broke a tooth. He had to visit the dentist and have it seen to."

"How unfortunate for him."

"Very. And him such an expert rower. Mind you, it wasn't his fault. Turns out there was a problem with his rigger. Couple of the bolts had worked themselves loose. The whole thing nearly fell off mid-stroke."

Llewellyn looked spectacularly sly as he said this, and there was little doubt in my mind that the bolts had not just "worked themselves loose" of their own accord. Someone, most likely Llewellyn himself, had tampered with them with the aim of triggering some sort of mishap. The stunt had succeeded better than hoped, causing Trenchard not simply embarrassment but actual bodily harm.

"In sum, then," said Holmes, "you are a man short but you are none of you too bothered by the fact."

"*I* am," said Gill. "Hargreaves is good but he's no Trenchard. I want the best in my boat and only the best."

"So you would still like me to locate him for you?"

"If you would be so kind."

"Yet your crew wouldn't care if he remained lost."

The seven oarsmen and one cox shuffled their feet.

"They may think they can manage without him," said Gill, "but I am their coach and I'm saying they cannot. If they want to win their blades this year and give Brasenose a bloody nose, it will be with Trenchard stroking or not at all. I know he is a disagreeable so-and-so. I know he puts people's backs up. I'm not blind. But I know, too, that he is passionate about this sport. Lives for it. It's that passion that drives him to excel and makes him impatient with those who don't meet his high standards. And it's that passion that will lead us to victory this coming week."

It was a rousing speech, both a rallying cry and a plea for peace and unity. The Oriel 1st VIII were affected by it, I could tell, but not swayed. Their faces remained set in defiance. They didn't want Trenchard back. They had no wish for Holmes to find him.

"It seems to me," Holmes said, "that I would be none too popular were I to retrieve Mr Trenchard from whatever hiding place he has holed up in."

"You can say that again," Llewellyn muttered.

"How about if we were to come to some sort of compromise, then? I shall limit my investigation to an examination of the boat. If I cannot deduce the fellow's whereabouts from that, I shall refrain from any further efforts."

There were puzzled frowns all round, the deepest belonging to Gill.

"How would that help?" he said. "At best you'd be doing half the job. The boat itself can't reveal anything. It's just a boat."

"If that is all Mr Holmes wants," said Preston, "why not let him?"

The crew murmured assent.

"But Trenchard could be miles away by now," said Gill. "He could be in London, Manchester, anywhere. I've sent a wire to his parents in Lowestoft. If he returns home, they are to let me know as soon as possible."

"How far do you think he will have got in sodden rowing clothes?" said Holmes. "With no money in his pockets? No, if he is anywhere, it is somewhere nearby, and the boat may well reveal where."

# CHAPTER TWENTY-ONE

## A Kind of Mutiny

The boat was duly lugged out of the boathouse and laid onto a pair of trestles fitted with canvas straps which cradled the hull in the manner of a sling. Holmes then set to inspecting it from end to end, giving it his customary microscopic attention. Not a plank, not a bolt, not a screw went unstudied. He checked the gates on the riggers, the leather bindings which fastened the oarsmen's feet to the footrests, and the runners on which the seats slid. In particular he scrutinised the narrow niche at the stern where the cox sat. He tugged the cords which controlled the rudder and ran a finger along the inside of the saxboards, the top edges of the gunwales.

The crew were bemused by the amount of time he spent looking over the boat. To anyone unaccustomed to Holmes's methods it might have appeared that he was in the grip of an obsession, a mania even. No detail, no minutia of the vessel's construction seemed too small to be of notice.

Finally he pronounced himself done. "I am satisfied," said he, "that there is nothing further to be gleaned here. You may return the boat to its rack, gentlemen. Before you do, however…"

The crew, who had assembled on either side of the boat to pick it up, halted.

"Yes?" said Stevens.

"Perhaps you might explain why you have lied to me."

"I?"

"Not just you. All eight of you."

"That's preposterous. I've told you only the truth. We all have."

"No, you have not. You have lied consistently all day, first to Mr Gill, now to me. Trenchard did not jump out of the boat."

"He did," said Stevens, "and I defy you, sir, to prove otherwise."

"Oh, that will not be a problem," said Holmes. "The evidence is right in front of us. You, Stevens, and your cohorts have colluded in a rather cunning ruse, all to cover up the fact that Trenchard did not abscond in the colourful fashion you have collectively described. On the contrary, he is sequestered in a place of your choosing – trussed up and gagged, I'll wager."

"That's a blatant—"

"Were I to enter the boathouse," Holmes said, gesturing towards the entrance, "and look around, might I not find a storeroom of some sort?"

"There's one at the rear of the building," said Gill. "A cupboard, really. We keep cans of grease in it, and spare seats, tools, other paraphernalia. It is hardly used. My goodness, do you mean to say Trenchard has been there all along? I must go to him."

Gill moved towards the boathouse, but Holmes stopped him.

"I daresay another five minutes of captivity won't hurt. Before he is freed, I would like to hear what his crewmates have to say for themselves."

The members of the Oriel 1st VIII blustered and protested, but guilt was writ large across their faces. The game was up and they knew it.

"After all," Holmes continued, "if they come clean now, we can work on a strategy for dealing with Trenchard once he is released. He will doubtless be extremely irate and will regard their cavalier treatment of him as a kind of mutiny. I imagine he may wish to punch at least one of them, if not all. Appropriate contrition will mollify him, and perhaps he and his crewmates can be reconciled in time for the regatta tomorrow. I think the best tactic is to identify the ringleader, the person on whom the lion's share of the blame can be apportioned and onto whom Trenchard can vent his spleen. And that would be…"

Holmes raised a forefinger, running it back and forth along the ranks of the crewmen as though lining up a shot at tin ducks in a fairground shooting gallery. His aim came to rest on Llewellyn.

"You."

"What? No. Ringleader? Me? You're mistaken."

His crewmates took an unconscious step back, leaving him isolated, unsupported.

"We all agreed to it," Llewellyn insisted. "It was a shared plan. We're all equally responsible. Isn't that what we said? All in it together. That's what we said. Boyos?"

"You're the one who proposed it in the first place, Taff," said Allardyce. "You encouraged us. If it wasn't for you, we'd never have gone through with it."

"I will not be made a scapegoat!" Llewellyn said hotly. "That's not fair. Yes, it was my idea to nobble Trenchard, but you wanted it as much as I did. Isn't that so, Stevens? Preston? Jenkins? You swine, how dare you turn on me! We should be presenting a unified front. Instead, you're making it out to be all my fault. That's what Mr Holmes wants, don't you see? Divide and conquer. So we'll confess more easily."

"There's no need for a confession," said Holmes. "You've made one already, as good as. Nor is there any need to divulge how you managed to make it look as though Trenchard went overboard. I know."

"Oh yes, I'm sure you know," sneered Llewellyn. "Mr Holmes always knows. Mr Holmes is so terribly clever. Everything is elementary to Mr Holmes."

"You won't goad me into saying that word again, if that's what you're after. But I will happily explain the trick you pulled."

"Go on then. If it makes you feel better."

"Simply put," Holmes said, "Trenchard did not jump out of the boat this morning because Trenchard was never in the boat."

"I beg your pardon?" said Gill. "I saw them with my own eyes, rowing away from the pontoon. There were quite clearly eight oarsmen, plus Preston. It was misty, I admit. Visibility was poor, twenty yards at most. But I am adamant that Trenchard was in his seat."

"Someone was in his seat," said Holmes, "but it wasn't Trenchard. It was in fact you, Preston."

The cox lowered his gaze, abashed.

"You," Holmes went on, "rowed in Trenchard's place. From the opposite bank, through thick mist, the substitution would have been hard to tell. One silhouette of a rower would have been all but indistinguishable from another. You may not be the oarsman Trenchard is, but the boat only had to travel a short way, approximately a third of a mile, from here to the Gut. For that span of distance you could serve as an adequate replacement. How do I know this? Remember how I shook your hand earlier? I had observed that there was a blister on your right palm. You winced slightly at my grip, showing that it was a fresh one. Your hands are soft, and the blister would have been raised by using an oar for a few hundred yards. Your crewmates' palms and fingers are, by contrast, well callused. The blisters they have accrued during months of training have hardened over. I didn't have to discover that by shaking hands with any of them. One can tell just by looking. The calluses are quite prominent, and are typical of those who participate in this sport."

Preston inspected his palm. A blister the diameter of a sixpence obtruded from the ball of his thumb, inflamed and red.

"But if Preston was in the stroke's position," said Gill, "then who was coxing?"

"No one," said Holmes.

"But I distinctly saw someone."

"What you saw was an effigy. It had been prepared beforehand, dressed up in suitable clothing, and no doubt secreted in the same store cupboard where Trenchard currently resides."

"Effigy?"

"Made of this." Holmes reached into the cox's seat and produced a tiny strand of straw. "I found it lodged in the crevice between two planks."

"But Holmes," I said, "the cox steers the boat, surely. How then did they navigate?"

"Again, bear in mind it was only a short way. Minor course corrections may be achieved by the crewmen on one side pulling slightly harder than those on the other side. To veer left, the stroke-side men increase their effort. To veer right, the bow-side men. With careful co-ordination, the boat can wend its way without the application of the rudder."

This time it was Gill who raised the objection. "True enough, but the rudder must be held fixed, otherwise it will swing fully one way or the other and no amount of pulling on either side will prevent the boat turning in a circle."

"I noted small circular marks on the saxboards just where the toggles on the rudder cords would be positioned were a cox keeping the rudder dead straight." Holmes looked at the crew. "Clamps, am I right? You screwed them into place to hold the toggles steady. The ends of the clamp bolts left indentations in the wood."

One or two of the crewmen nodded.

"Then what became of this effigy?" asked Gill.

"It did what Trenchard didn't: went overboard. The straw would have become waterlogged in a trice and the effigy would have sunk quickly. Weighing it down with bricks or rocks would have helped."

He looked to the crew for confirmation. Again, there came a few sheepish nods.

"The clamps went to the riverbed with it," Holmes carried on. "All of this took place during the period while the boat was out of your sight, Mr Gill. Down went the cox effigy, and Preston resumed his rightful position, nipping across from the stroke's seat to his own, where he undid the clamps, tossed them out, and took command of the rudder. When you at last appeared on your bicycle, 'Trenchard' was no longer at his oar. The crew then fed you their cock-and-bull story about him spontaneously leaping into the Isis and swimming to shore, prompting you to give fruitless chase. You looked for him everywhere except the last place you would have thought to look for him, which is right here."

Gill was clearly having trouble absorbing the revelation that the crewmen he had coached so assiduously had deceived him. It was a profound betrayal of trust.

"So I presume they must have supplanted Trenchard with Preston just after they put the boat in the water," he said, "as I was cycling over Folly Bridge."

"You were out of earshot as well as out of sight," Holmes said. "You wouldn't have heard his cries of protest as his crewmates set upon him and bundled him into the boathouse. Eight against one – he wouldn't have stood a chance. The mist, you see, was crucial to their whole plan, in particular the way it occludes both sound and vision. I doubt they could have succeeded without it. Today was the first day this term that the climatic conditions were just right for their purposes."

"It's true," said Jenkins. "We've been waiting over a fortnight for a mist like this. We were beginning to think it wouldn't happen. Then, just in time, it did."

"Why?" said Gill plaintively to the Oriel 1st VIII. "Why would you do such a thing? Don't you see you're sabotaging your own chances of victory?"

"To teach the high-and-mighty Trenchard a lesson," said Preston. "Put him in his place. Show him he's not indispensable."

"This close to Torpids," said Knight, "we were hoping he might even take the hint and resign."

"Failing that," said Allardyce, "we'd have kept him in the store cupboard until tomorrow at least, and have Hargreaves stroke for the first race."

"We would have fed and watered him," said Stevens. "Made sure he's comfortable. We're not monsters."

"Llewellyn," said Holmes. "You've gone quiet. Before we fetch Trenchard out and you face the music, do you have anything to add?"

"Not that you'd want to hear, Mr Holmes."

"As the man who meddled with Trenchard's rigger earlier in the term so that he would catch a crab, you would be the best candidate for organising an even nastier offensive against him, such as this one."

"So?"

"Your ploy of picking a fight with him just before the outing – that was to provide a plausible motive for him quitting. It would be consistent with his character to respond petulantly to personal slights. He would see them as a challenge to his authority."

"Again, so?"

"Such keen psychological insight."

"Are you talking about me or you?"

"Such intricate forward planning, too."

"You're insinuating something, but I don't know what it is."

"I have to ask myself, did you manage it alone?"

I knew, as Llewellyn did not, what Holmes was driving at. He was probing to see if there was a connection between this incident and the Jericho murders and the poison pen letters. He suspected the hand of our Oxford agent provocateur behind the Oriel mutiny. Llewellyn was just another cat's paw.

"For the last time, it was all of us," said Llewellyn. "All eight of us. I'll not be made a pariah here. Bad enough that I'm Welsh. Not many of my countrymen get to Oxford. You should hear the things the other students call me, the jokes they make about me. 'Leek eater,' they say. 'Wash the coal dust off you.' And that's just the least of it. 'Taffy was a Welshman, Taffy was a thief,' they chant. Then there are the various sheep-related remarks, which I shan't go into. I put up with it, I play the clown, I grin and try to be accepted. But I will not put up with—"

A shot rang out.

The instant before we heard it, Llewellyn keeled over, clutching his chest.

# CHAPTER TWENTY-TWO

## "Gas Par"

With the *crack* of the gun report still echoing across the water, everyone stared in shock at the hapless Llewellyn, who was sprawled on his back, a patch of blood blossoming across the front of his shirt. Even Holmes was momentarily paralysed, although he was the first to recover his wits.

"Quick!" he cried. "All of you, take cover!"

I, who knew what it was to come under fire, sprang into action. The oarsmen, cox and coach were still frozen in alarm. I set about chivvying them away from open ground, shepherding them urgently towards the shelter of the boathouse. Holmes did the same. At any moment I expected further gunshots, more bullets whizzing our way.

With the rest of the Oriel men safely indoors, I darted back for Llewellyn. I had no idea where the sniper was, but judging by the sound of the gunshot he was positioned on the opposite bank, most likely in the lee of one of the tall trees there, concealed amongst a stand of shrubbery and thick undergrowth.

Crouching, making myself as small a target as possible, I edged alongside the boat, which sat perpendicular to the river. Llewellyn was alive, shuddering, one hand clawing the air spasmodically. There was a space of five yards between him and the vessel. To reach him I would have no choice but to cross it, leaving myself fully exposed to the sniper. I wished I had my service revolver on me; I could have used it to lay down return fire. I wouldn't have had a hope of hitting anyone at that range, but it would have given the gunman something to think about and deterred him long enough for me to retrieve Llewellyn.

Holmes appeared beside me.

"What are you doing?" I hissed. "Trying to get yourself killed?"

"No more than you are, Watson. We can't just leave Llewellyn. His would-be killer is lining up a second shot even now, to put his fate beyond question. The mist has thickened, but it is shifting. When it parts again…"

"If only there was some way of protecting ourselves so that we can get to him."

"Yes, but… Ah! I have it."

Holmes grasped the nearest rigger and spun the boat over in its trestle sling until it was at right angles, stroke-side pointing to the sky. Then he kicked one of the trestles flat, taking the weight of the boat on his shoulders as he did so. With a grunt he sank to a squatting position, supporting the boat in the meantime so that it did not crash violently to the ground. It came to rest tilted, still partly perched on the remaining trestle, its bow in the air.

"Now, Watson," Holmes said, "if you could see your way to doing the same…"

I emulated him, kicking out the other trestle. Together, teeth clenched, grimacing with effort, we lowered the boat until it was lying horizontal again, balanced on its bow-side riggers with us braced beside. We did this as carefully as we could, but it was difficult to be delicate about it. The two of us were performing a job which normally demanded the combined strength of eight men.

I heard a groan of dismay from the boathouse. This was Gill lamenting the abuse being meted out on his crew's precious craft. I personally thought Llewellyn's life more important than any boat, but then I was not a rowing coach. Besides, other than a couple of dented rigger gates, the thing was not faring too badly.

"Now," said Holmes, "we must slide it round." He reached either side of him to grasp a section of the boat's ribs. I followed suit. Both of us dug in our heels and heaved, and the boat began to rotate on its central axis. Its stern swung out towards the river, its bow round towards Llewellyn.

A break in the mist came, allowing the sniper to unleash his next shot. The delay cost him, however, for when he did fire, the bullet struck the boat and ricocheted away, raising a shower of splinters. I felt the impact reverberate through my neck and arms, and redoubled my efforts. The boat slithered and grated across the ground. It seemed to weigh a ton.

Then it was in position. Holmes and I had manoeuvred it through ninety degrees, and it now fully shielded Llewellyn's supine form. Holmes hooked a toe over one of the flattened trestles, dragged it towards him and stuck it up under the boat as a prop. This enabled the boat to continue resting at a shallow angle with my friend taking a lessened proportion of the weight. I was at liberty to crawl on all fours over to Llewellyn.

The Welshman was babbling incoherently, his lips smeared with a froth of blood. The bullet had pierced a lung. It was what is known as a sucking wound. Air was entering the pleural cavity during inhalation and was unable to escape during exhalation, as though trapped by a one-way valve. The pleural cavity was inflating, in turn squeezing the lung flat. Llewellyn was developing a tension pneumothorax. Pressure would continue to build inside his chest until his lung collapsed and, after that, his vena cava would be compressed, leading to catastrophic heart failure. He was mere moments from death, and every breath he drew pushed him that little bit closer.

I tore open his shirt, then took out my handkerchief and my penknife. I wadded the handkerchief up and clamped it over the wound. Then, holding the penknife in my free hand and opening it with my teeth, I attempted chest decompression by inserting the blade through the intercostal muscle between the second and third ribs, just below the clavicle. Blood sprayed out over the knife's handle. Escaping air hissed wetly. Llewellyn writhed.

I thought I had saved him. At the very least I had relieved the tension pneumothorax, giving him a fighting chance.

He looked at me with a flicker of gratitude in his terrified, pain-wracked eyes.

"Gas," he said.

"Gas?"

"Par."

"Par? Gas par? Did I get that right? What does it mean? Llewellyn? What are you trying to say?"

But no further words emerged. Llewellyn went into convulsions. He began choking. Blood welled in his throat and gurgled out of his mouth like crimson lava from some ghastly volcano. Under my hands, with my penknife still embedded hilt-deep in his chest, he perished.

# CHAPTER TWENTY-THREE

## The False Armour of Rage

I reared up from behind the boat.

"You!" I yelled across the river. "Villain! Murderer! Animal! Happy? Proud of yourself? He's dead!"

"Watson," Holmes said, "are you mad? Get your head down."

Mad? No, I wasn't. Furious was what I was. Incensed beyond reason. So irate, it did not even occur to me I was putting my life in danger.

"We're coming for you, whoever you are," I roared. "You won't get away with this."

I don't know if I was expecting an answer. None came, at any rate.

I could have sworn, however, that I heard a faint ripple of mocking laughter.

After which, silence.

My surge of anger abated and common sense reasserted itself. Panting, I slid down behind the boat.

"Never, ever, do anything so imbecilic again," Holmes admonished. "You're lucky you didn't get your brains blown out. Not that you have any, on current showing."

"I— I just…"

"He's an expert marksman. Can't you tell? To have made that first shot through this mist – that was no mean feat. Your great fat head would have presented an easy target. You damn fool."

My friend was quite right, of course, but he could perhaps have expressed his sentiments with a little more tact. I consoled myself that he would have been less insulting, had he not cared so much. His vituperation was a marker of his concern.

"So what do you propose? Should we rush him?"

"You are thinking like a former serviceman, Watson, which is tantamount to not thinking at all. Rush him how? By swimming across the river? Some kind of amphibious assault?"

"We run round to the bridge and—"

"—and get shot before we've gone a dozen yards."

"Not if the mist stays thick enough."

"Can you guarantee that? Do you have divine powers that I'm unaware of? Are you a weather god?"

"Damn it all, Holmes, are we just to huddle here and hope he gets bored and goes away?"

"It is about the only viable option," my friend said. "We are pinned down. We have no weapons. To attempt to move on him would be suicide. We must play the waiting game. Besides…"

"Yes?"

"If I am right, he has got what he came here for. He has achieved all he set out to do. You have handily announced to him that Llewellyn is dead. If he has any sense, he will now withdraw. He knows that our fear will keep us *in situ* for the next few minutes. Plenty of time for him to make a clean getaway."

"You're saying he might not even be there any more? We're ducking down here for nothing?"

"It is likely. But it is not a theory I am eager to put to the test just yet."

We remained doubled over behind the upturned boat for another quarter of an hour before Holmes, very tentatively, poked his head up over the hull to take a peek. He raised a hand and waved, in a spirit of experimentation. No gunshot came. He rose to a half-standing position, then straightened fully upright. Still no gunshot.

"I would venture," he said, "that the sniper has gone."

Not without reluctance, I stood too. Now that I was no longer clad in the false armour of rage, I felt exposed and vulnerable. I imagined gun sights aimed at me, a finger on the trigger, a bullet in the breech destined for my body.

It was a long time before my heartbeat settled into a stable, steady rhythm.

Holmes and I made our way to the boathouse, where the Oriel men bombarded us with anxious questions.

"Who was that?"

"Is someone trying to kill us?"

"Is he still out there?"

"Is Llewellyn really dead?"

"What on earth is going on?"

Holmes deflected their entreaties with a shake of the head. "There is little I can say at this juncture that will be of any benefit, other than to tell you that I believe you are all safe and have nothing to worry about. The assassin has fled the scene. His work here is done."

"Brasenose would stop at nothing to make sure we don't beat them," Knight said. "It can't be their doing, though. Can it? It can't be."

"No, your intercollegiate squabbles are not the issue here. It's about Llewellyn alone."

"Why him?" Stevens asked. "What did he do wrong?"

"Nothing, apart from fall in with a bad person who preyed

on his insecurities and deceived him. Did he ever mention that he had made a new friend this past month? Did he talk to any of you about a co-conspirator, someone who helped him devise his scheme for deposing Trenchard?"

Llewellyn's crewmates returned blank looks.

"We aren't in the habit of socialising with him that much," said Jenkins. "I mean weren't. Weren't in the habit. Bit of an outsider was Taff. A loner."

"He might join us for a pint at the Wheatsheaf now and then," said Allardyce, "but otherwise we wouldn't see him except at the river."

"I feel awful," said Preston. "Perhaps if we had—"

At that point Trenchard put in an appearance. Clearly Gill had gone to the storeroom and untied him. He was a hulking, barrel-chested figure, and he was quite understandably in a state of near apoplexy.

When he had finished bellowing at the other rowers and threatening them with all manner of dire ramifications, he grew somewhat more tractable. The sight of Llewellyn's corpse certainly sobered him.

"My God," he sighed. "This is a pretty mess, isn't it? How can this have happened?"

Holmes asked him the same questions he had put to the rest of the crew, and received much the same response. Trenchard, indeed, was the last person who would have known anything about the Welshman's private life, given the antagonism that existed between them. "We rowed at opposite ends of the boat," he said, "and that is about as close as we ever got."

Holmes despatched two of the crewmen to the police station with instructions to fetch Inspector Tomlinson. Then he and I went round to the opposite bank via Folly Bridge in order to pinpoint the spot where the sniper had lain. Along the way

Holmes interrogated me about Llewellyn's last words. He had seen the dying man speak to me but had been unable to discern what he said.

"'Gas par'? You're sure about that?"

"Quite sure."

"Not Casper, by any chance?"

"I don't think so."

"So it might have been?"

"Well, maybe, but it definitely sounded like a *g* at the beginning, not a *c*."

"Casper is a name. A first name and a surname. Perhaps it is the name of Llewellyn's secret associate, our agent provocateur. Mind you, Gaspar is a first name and surname too, one of Mediterranean origin. Either way, was Llewellyn trying to tell us who he had consorted with? Did he know who shot him?"

"It could be a Welsh word or phrase," I suggested. "*In extremis*, Llewellyn might have lapsed into his native tongue."

"Doesn't sound very Welsh, does it? 'Gas par'. But I take your point. My knowledge of the Cymric language is limited."

We traipsed up and down the section of the river's west bank opposite the boathouses until Holmes ascertained exactly where the sniper had hidden. As I had surmised at the time, he had secreted himself in a thicket of evergreen shrubbery. Holmes indicated broken twigs and a patch of flattened earth.

"He has left barely any trace, though, Watson. To the casual eye, it is as if no one was ever here. This is a man practised in the art of concealment. I would not be in the least surprised to learn that he has a military background. And see? No spent shell casings littering the ground. A professional killer knows to pocket those and take them with him, so that he cannot be identified by his choice of weapon. We may assume it was a high-powered bolt-action rifle of some sort, a Lee-Metford perhaps. No, more likely it's the gun that is superseding the Lee-Metford, the Lee-Enfield."

He sniffed the air.

"I smell cordite, rather than black powder. Cordite is smokeless and less pungent, leaves less telltale residue, and is becoming the common propellant in rifle cartridges. The Lee-Enfield takes smokeless rounds, and also has the appropriate effective firing range. Then again, our assassin might have used one of those brand new Mannlichers. They are becoming popular. Without the shell casings to determine calibre, one may only speculate."

"Not only is he a master manipulator and a cold-blooded murderer, then, but a crack shot to boot," I said. "What have we got ourselves into, Holmes? This business becomes murkier and more insidious by the minute."

Holmes nodded sombrely. "Death seems to be dogging us, and we are never quite quick enough to catch it before it strikes. It is as though we are being toyed with."

I too had that impression. Innocents were being slaughtered, right before our eyes, and us powerless to prevent it. Our enemy seemed to be deriving great satisfaction from our inability to catch him. He was a ghost, as opaque and evanescent as the mist around us.

As a footnote to this chapter, I must relate that Torpids did not go ahead as planned. The records of the Oxford University Rowing Clubs for 1895 state simply that there were "no races" that spring, citing poor weather conditions. In truth, a terrible frost set in the day after the mist, the Isis turned to ice, and although proposals were made to postpone the event by a week, it wound up being abandoned altogether.

Ice, however, was not the only reason or even the main reason for the cancellation. The killing of the Oriel 1st VIII's bow man, Hugh Llewellyn, was. The rower's death cast a pall over the proceedings.

Just as it cast a pall over my spirits.

Just as it cast an especially deep pall over Holmes's.

# CHAPTER TWENTY-FOUR

## Dr J. Collis Browne's Chlorodyne

I elected to remain in Oxford for the next few days. I can't say there was a rational basis for the decision. It was instinctual more than anything, a feeling in my vitals. Holmes needed me. Or rather, I sensed I might be needed. Not for any practical assistance I might provide, not even for my companionship and moral support, but for his own good. He was troubled and frustrated, the worst possible combination under the circumstances. To Sherlock Holmes, nothing counted so much as forward motion. If he was not making progress in a case, he was apt to brood and the consequences of that were rarely agreeable.

When I told him that I was staying, I expected him to be pleased. I also expected him to volunteer to put me up at the Randolph at his own expense. Neither outcome occurred. Holmes greeted my announcement with an air of indifference, almost of disdain. "As you wish," he said. I had hoped for at least a modicum of enthusiasm. That he exhibited none was a telling sign, not to mention hurtful.

Since I could not afford the Randolph's exorbitant room rates on the income of a general-practitioner-cum-freelance-scribe, I found myself more modest accommodation. Inspector Tomlinson recommended a guesthouse up in Summertown, which is a pleasant residential area in the north of the city, full of large villas, neat terraces and quiet, secluded avenues. The guesthouse, run by a Mrs Bruell, boasted decent amenities, although I was obliged to share a bathroom with four other lodgers and the hot water boiler frequently failed to keep up with demand. Mrs Bruell provided a good, solid cooked breakfast, however, and was not one of those termagant landladies who make unreasonable demands about tidiness, punctuality, outside visitors and the keeping of hours. Guests were free to come and go as they wished, with the stipulation that they make as little noise as possible when returning at night, her husband being a light sleeper.

The weather that week was miserable. The mist had been merely a harbinger of worse to come. A low pressure system moved in from the north and overnight the mercury plummeted. I can honestly say I have never been as cold as I was in Oxford in late March, 1895; not even the windswept foothills of the Hindu Kush in midwinter could compare. The damp chill seemed inescapable, and even beside a blazing hearth or tucked up in bed, one could not mitigate it. The only remedy was to get the blood flowing. Accordingly, wrapped up in several layers of clothing, I would head off on brisk walks, with frequent stops for hot toddies or pots of tea.

The Isis and the Cherwell became sluggish, capped with a layer of floating slush; likewise the canal. Parks, meadows and playing fields were white all day long with frost. Trees were ivory skeletons, their new buds glazed with ice. Everyone – students, dons, citizens, myself – moved with a hunched-over, shuffling gait, as though uniformly stiff and ancient. Faces were pinched, cheeks chapped.

And Holmes?

Holmes succumbed to torpor, like some hibernating animal. He refused to leave the cosy confines of the Randolph. Many a time I invited him to come for a stroll, only to be rebuffed. He was busy, he said. He was reflecting, he said. But it didn't look that way to me. All I could see was lassitude, enervation and an air of incipient hopelessness. Nothing I could say or do would shift his mood.

By the fourth day of this, I had become seriously concerned, not least when I espied a bottle of Dr J. Collis Browne's Chlorodyne on the dressing table in Holmes's room. It was half empty, and the pallor of my friend's cheeks and the pinkened glassiness of his eyes put it beyond question that he had partaken of a heavy dose of the patent medicine. A liquid suspension of laudanum, chloroform and tincture of cannabis, Chlorodyne was in my view dreadful stuff, dangerously addictive, and I regret to say I rather lost my temper.

"What is this?" I thundered. "Cocaine I can understand. Tobacco too. But an opiate? Holmes, you hate opiates. You refuse to have anything to do with them. The only time I have seen you even come close was in that den on Upper Swandam Lane, and that was only in order to entrap the Lascar who ran it!"

My friend barely raised his gaze to mine. "What can I say, Watson? I crave not stimulation now but release. This damnable business. This deadly agent provocateur who plays people like musical instruments and discards them mercilessly when his tune is finished. This city with its frigid air and mean beauty. What have I to show for my time here? Nothing. Nothing but disappointment and failure. If Dr Collis Browne's concoction can offer an antidote to that, why should I not take advantage of it?"

"Come now, you are not some housewife with the hysterics or some dreamy poet who finds the world altogether too sharp and cruel for his aesthete's soul. You are Sherlock Holmes, damn it. Sherlock Holmes!"

"For all the good *that* has done. Ask Aubrey Bancroft and Hugh Llewellyn how beneficial it has been to them to have known Sherlock Holmes."

"I will not have this!" I snatched up the Chlorodyne, threw open the window sash, and emptied the bottle into the street below.

Briefly Holmes's eyes flashed with indignation. Then either the opiate or his depression regained the upper hand, and he shrugged his shoulders contemptuously, saying, "So what? I can always buy more. The chemist on Broad Street is open 'til five."

"Holmes. Please. Don't do this to yourself. Shake off your brown study. Apply yourself anew to the problem at hand. Use that incomparable brain of yours."

Holmes turned away. "You know what, Watson? I am tired of detection. It yields so little bounty beyond the pecuniary. Perhaps I am finished with it, or it is finished with me. I have talked before of retiring to the country. Sussex beckons. The landscape down there is congenial, especially by the coast. I have accumulated a sizeable nest egg. I could live comfortably, if a little more frugally than I am accustomed."

"You cannot retire. You have only just returned from a three-year sabbatical, if I may call it that. There is still work to be done, work only you can do. You are barely forty. Who retires at that age?"

"The exhausted. The weary. The depleted."

I apprehended that my friend had reached a point of crisis. His threat of retirement was not an idle one. I could foresee him abandoning his investigation in Oxford as a lost cause, relinquishing all his detecting duties, and slipping away into obscurity somewhere in the wilds of the Home Counties. Perhaps his three years of supposed death, the period Tomlinson had described as a "hiatus", had given him a taste for solitude. Although he had wandered the world and mingled with the masses, he had done it under various aliases such as a Norwegian explorer named Sigerson, and not as Sherlock Holmes. He had been free of the onus of his renown and had had to meet no one's expectations or play any role other than that of roving traveller and tourist. He had been able to indulge himself in scientific researches and obtain audiences with grandees – lamas in Tibet, sultans in Khartoum and the like. He had been a peregrine falcon, beholden only to his own whims and the vagaries of the winds. It must, I realised, have been a time of pure bliss.

When I thought of this and of how self-assured he had been at the start of the month, and now saw how low his sojourn at Oxford had brought him, it fair broke my heart.

I moved squarely into his line of vision. I bent before him, head bowed, hands out, almost in supplication.

"Old friend, I beg of you, snap out of this… this despondency. It is simply a trough. Troughs are followed by peaks. Such is the way of it. You must ride out the swells like a ship at sea. You must rise again."

"What an adorable turn of phrase you have, Watson. Ever thought of becoming a writer?"

"For pity's sake, I am trying to help you. I am your friend, possibly your only friend. Don't spurn me. Without me, you'll have nobody else to turn to."

"Mycroft."

"Your brother? Pah! Mycroft only sees you when it suits him, when he has a use for you. He calls, you come running. That is not brotherhood. It is certainly not friendship."

"Watson, I am—"

"Holmes." I put my face right up to his, so close that I could smell the peppermint-oil flavouring of the Chlorodyne on his breath. "I am telling you to accept help. You will not find answers in a surfeit of some spurious cure for neuralgia. You will find at best a temporary respite from your woes. Let me do something for you. Let me get you out into the daylight, away from that unmade bed and these meal trays which the chambermaid hasn't been allowed to clear for days, I'll be bound. Let us go eat at a riverside inn, or amble amongst the bookcases of the Bodleian, or maybe – here's a thought – revisit some crime scenes and see if we cannot turn up any fresh clues. How about that? Does that strike you as a good idea?"

I seemed to be getting through to him. His gaze regained some of its focus and potency. His mouth lost its slackness, becoming tighter. A phantom smile flitted across his lips.

He rose, slowly, falteringly, like a man recovering his balance after a dizzy spell. I experienced a burst of relief. I had succeeded. I had galvanised him back into action.

"You are right, Watson," said he.

"Of course I am," I chuckled.

"I should accept help."

"And who better to provide it than me?"

He collected his hat, his coat, his gloves, his scarf. "And there is one source of help which I have, through pride alone, been unwilling to exploit. You have persuaded me to think otherwise."

"I'm sorry, what?" I was thoroughly confused.

"I should not have been so pusillanimous. I am, as you said, better than that. It feels as though I am stooping, but I am not. When in a trough, one has no alternative but to reach up to those above. It is an invidious position to be in, but one must acknowledge it as one's lot."

"Holmes, I don't follow."

"I am going," Holmes said, "to consult an intellect which I must perforce recognise as surpassing mine."

"You don't mean Mycroft? Granted, you have claimed that he specialises in omniscience and that he is your superior in observation and deduction. All the same..."

"No, not Mycroft. Honestly, Watson. Why would I consult him? I am referring, obviously, to the Thinking Engine. What else?"

# CHAPTER TWENTY-FIVE

## The Voice Cabinet

It crossed my mind, as Holmes and I once more traversed Beaumont Street to the University Galleries, that my friend had taken complete leave of his senses. The Thinking Engine? *He* was seeking aid from *it*? He must be at an extraordinarily low ebb if he reckoned that Quantock's machine could unearth a solution where he could not. Evidently the Chlorodyne was impairing his judgement. His brain had become fogged, so that what seemed logical to him was, by any objective estimate, the opposite.

Then I wondered whether this was all just some artful ploy. The Chlorodyne, his intoxication, his impulsive decision to consult the Engine – it was one of Holmes's subterfuges, an illusion he had concocted, like a conjuring trick, in order to generate some outcome that I could not as yet guess. He was only purporting to have imbibed such a large quantity of the medicine, just as he had only purported to be an opium addict in order to infiltrate the Lascar's lair (in the adventure I have recorded as "The Man With The Twisted Lip"). It was all a performance, a bluff, and at some stage he would turn to me and the old familiar Holmes would reassert himself, glint in his eye, mind on fire, and I would know that I had been hoodwinked and so had the intended victim or victims of his scheme, and all would be well.

I clung to this hope, flimsy though it was, as we entered the underground chamber where the Thinking Engine was ensconced. Holmes was implementing some ingenious stratagem that would crack the case. He had to be. The alternative was too distressing to contemplate: the case had cracked him.

Professor Quantock was on site. It appeared he seldom left his Engine's side. He was engaged in some complicated piece of repair or modification, in his hands a wax phonographic cylinder which he was delicately installing into the interstices of a teak cabinet stationed in the front of the Engine. The cabinet had not been present the last time we visited. It was large, the size of a double wardrobe, and I spied dozens of similar cylinders arrayed on racks within, connected to one another by wires.

So absorbed was Quantock in what he was doing that our arrival startled him and he nearly dropped the fragile cylinder.

"Oh! You're early. N-no, wait. You are not who I was exp-expecting. Mr H-Holmes. Dr Watson. I did not know y-you would be joining us too. I was not t-told. I d-did not know you were even in Oxford st-still."

"Still here. Still soldiering on," said Holmes. "What are you up to?"

"Th-this?" Quantock glanced down at the cylinder. "An improvement to the Engine. The next step. You c-could say I'm enhancing its per-performance."

"In what way?"

"Tickertape is not the m-most efficient form of communication. Slow and time-consuming. I have construed a faster and more d-direct method. I am just p-putting the finishing touches to it, and am due to d-demonstrate it shortly. To, as it happens, a roster of v-very important personages."

"Really? I thought Lord Knaresfield had returned up north."

"Not h-him. Others."

"Ah. And this improvement to the Engine – it involves phonographic recordings somehow?"

"On each cylinder is etched a s-selection of syllables, carefully chosen and arranged according to frequency of use, the commoner ones more readily accessible than the less common. I d-dictated these myself – some three thousand of them in all, the building blocks of our mother tongue – via speaking tube assembly and cutting st-stylus. No mean feat, in light of my sp-speech imp-impediment, but I rose to the occ-occasion. The cylinders sit on their r-respective mandrels, and the Engine has been programmed to know the precise l-location of every syllable on every one of them. Instead of im-imprinting its answers onto t-tickertape, it sorts through these syllabaries algorithmically to find and play the individual sounds it needs. Putting them together one after another, it thus cr-creates words and ultimately sentences, somewhat in the manner of syllable-based languages such as Chinese and Japanese. The sounds c-come out here."

He patted an amplification horn mounted on the side of the cabinet.

"In sh-short," he concluded, "I have given the Th-Thinking Engine a voice."

I could not suppress a low whistle. "You mean it talks now?"

"It will do, once the f-final few cylinders are in pl-place. If you'll excuse me…"

He completed installation of the cylinder, holding it by the ends so as not to besmirch the playing surface with his fingerprints. Three further cylinders were removed from their tins and slotted onto the remaining vacant mandrels. I noted a small brass plate beside each mandrel with a numeral on it. There were corresponding numerals on the tins. Quantock then lowered a series of playing needles mounted on notched armatures, one for each cylinder.

Holmes watched the operation with a bleary concentration, as though he was interested but it took an effort to be so. I noticed that he was swaying slightly where he stood, and once or twice he had to stifle a yawn. If he was acting the part of an opiate-addled wastrel, he was doing it very well indeed. By which I mean – though it pains me to relate this – he was not acting at all.

Quantock fussed with a web of cables at the back of the unit which linked it to the Engine proper, made some meticulous calibrations to its interior, then pronounced himself satisfied and closed the glass doors that fronted it.

"The voice cabinet is r-ready," he said. "Perhaps a dr-dry run before our g-guests arrive would be in order."

The motor was started up, and the Engine embarked on its preliminary cycle of clicks, whirrs and chirrups, like a field of crickets responding to the first warming touch of sunrise.

"This is rather fortuitous," Holmes remarked, "since we have come to solicit your machine's advice."

The mathematician's hands expressed his surprise by flapping in opposite directions like a pair of birds parting company. "You…? My m-machine…? Well, that's a turn-up for the b-books, I'll say. From being its ant-antagonist, all at once you n-now wish to become its petitioner?"

"Such antagonism as there was, was largely Lord Knaresfield's doing. He was the one who put the Engine and me on a collision course with his extravagant wager. Circumstances have since changed, and in the quandary in which I find myself, it would be foolish not to exhaust every possibility before finally conceding defeat."

"I see," said Quantock. "Then the Engine is a l-last resort. All else has failed, so you come cr-crawling to my door." For the first time I saw a flash of spite in the little man's eyes.

"That is not what Holmes meant," I said, interceding. "What he meant is he has come to the realisation that there is more to be gained through co-operation than competition. Isn't that right, Holmes?"

"If you say so, Watson."

"To which end, if your invention can shed any light on the mystery that is currently plaguing us, professor, we would welcome it."

It seemed to me wiser to help Holmes than hinder him. The sooner his consultation with the Thinking Engine was over with, the sooner we could move on. I was taking the path of least resistance, with the view that once this particular caprice of Holmes's had been sated, I could get on with the more important process of pulling him out of the vortex of despair into which he had fallen.

"When you p-put it l-like that," said Quantock, "I suppose it would be churlish of m-me not to accommodate you. I built my Engine to help others, after all." He settled down at his typewriter station. "What do you req-require to know?"

"Anything it can tell us about the Oriel 1st VIII incident earlier in the week," said Holmes.

"The killing at the river, yes? A very b-bad business."

"Also, the meaning of the phrase 'gas par' or 'cas par'. It may be Welsh, it may not. I have referred to the latest edition of the Anwyl brothers' revised version of Spurrell's Welsh-English dictionary. I browsed through a copy at Blackwell's. However, the results I have drawn are inconclusive. There is a Cymric word '*cas*', meaning 'hatred'. There is no 'par' but there is a verb, '*peri*', which is a close analogue and translates as 'produce' or 'cause'. So '*cas peri*' might simply be an expression of intense dislike, which, given the event that precipitated its utterance, would not be inapt whatsoever. I am not sure the grammatical or syntactical construction is authentic, but one has to make allowances both for the speaker's compromised condition and the possibility that the listener did not hear with absolute clarity."

Quantock typed energetically for several minutes, nibbling his lip in concentration.

"You didn't tell me you had looked up 'gas par,'" I said aside to Holmes.

"It was just something I did," he replied airily, "for something to do."

"So you have not been entirely idle since the shooting."

"Not that it availed me much." He heaved a sigh of deep futility. "It was a vain attempt to breathe life into a moribund investigation. The game no longer seems in any meaningful way afoot."

"We shall see, shall we not?" I said with a jollity I did not feel.

Quantock ended his typing with a flourish, and the Thinking Engine commenced the loud, protracted chattering and clattering that attended its calculations. The noise went on for quite some while, reaching a pitch of intensity such as I had not heard from it before. I was obliged, indeed, to stop my ears with my fingers, so boomingly raucous did it become, and even then I found it painful. The mighty cotton mills of Lancashire in full flight could not have been as deafening. The entire chamber around us vibrated until the high fan-light windows were rattling in their frames.

Then, all at once, a stunning silence fell. Echoes of the Engine's activity faded away.

And the machine spoke.

# CHAPTER TWENTY-SIX

## A Chip off the Old Block

Its voice – such was the label Professor Quantock had assigned to it, so voice it must be –issued from the amplification horn in fits and starts, sometimes pausing part way through a word, other times cramming syllables so close together that they overlapped, and every so often giving a monosyllable a peculiar double-stress as it conjoined two phonemes. It was staccato and monotone, lacking the cadences and variations in intonation which humans habitually use. It lacked, too, many of the niceties of the English language, such as pronouns and definite and indefinite articles. On first hearing, it little resembled speech.

Yet speech it was, indisputably. The Thinking Engine was talking to us, sounding crackly and etiolated but still eerily like its progenitor, Quantock. I could not help but think of a son who grows up to emulate the vocabulary and phrasing of his father, the proverbial chip off the old block. Quantock had not merely created a lifelike machine; he had fashioned it in his own image. The Engine now possessed not just intelligence but the ability to express itself audibly. It was to all intents and purposes a sentient being. I found this notion both thrilling and repellent. What next? A face? A working mouth? An automaton-like body? Where might it all end?

"Oarsmen rebelled against disliked captain," the Engine said. "Replaced cox with straw figure. Cox rowed for captain."

I watched the needles slide along their armatures in the voice cabinet, propelled by small pistons. Reaching the appropriate notch, they pecked down onto the wax cylinders, which rotated obligingly and played whatever syllables the machine required.

"Substitution veiled by mist," the Engine continued. "Captain was held in captivity."

"All of which is common knowledge," Holmes muttered.

"Bow man Llewellyn was shot dead." The machine stumbled over the Welshman's name, teasing it out like a child encountering a difficult word for the first time in a storybook. Perhaps the double *l*'s confused it. "Assassin lay in wait on opposite side of river. Assassin was bow man's collaborator. Assassin was getting rid of witness who might incriminate."

"Again, nothing new." Holmes rubbed his face languidly.

"Llewellyn's dying words: 'gas par.'"

The Thinking Engine seemed to hesitate. Cogs reeled. Rods pulsed up and down. The needles in the voice cabinet were poised on their armatures. We all three of us looked expectantly at the amplification horn.

"Maybe it has drawn a blank too," Holmes said.

"Surname," said the Engine. "Not in full. Unfinished. The first section. Italian. Gasparini."

I turned to Holmes to see what effect the machine's declaration had on him. He, in his state of narcosis, did not reveal much. I observed a narrowing of the eyelids, an almost imperceptible flaring of the nostrils, but these tiny fluctuations in expression gave scant clue as to his inner processes.

"Does that signify anything to you?" I prompted him. "Ring any bells?"

He pursed his lips. "Is that all you have for me?"

"Are you add-addressing me," said Professor Quantock, "or the Engine?"

"Whichever. It makes no difference. An Italian surname, Gasparini. I am being given no more to go on than that?"

The Thinking Engine ceased its computations, which implied it had said its piece and had nothing further to add.

"It is, perhaps, just a s-suggestion," said the mathematician. "The Engine, like any of us, ex-extrapolates from existing data. It c-could not resolve the con-conundrum of the St Peter-in-the-East tombstone inscription, after all, only submit likely scenarios to account for the impossible d-death date. I have n-never pretended the thing is infallible. Gas par, Gasparini – an ed-educated guess, maybe that is all. B-but at least it has offered you a p-potential direction for your investigation that you did n-not have before. You m-must give it credit for th-that."

My friend let out an abrupt, derisive laugh. "Shall I hunt through Oxford, then, for a Signor Gasparini who may or may not be our unseen gunman?"

"In the past, you have chased down considerably slimmer leads," I said, "with great success. The murder by Boscombe Pool, for instance. From just the words 'a rat' gasped out by the victim, you deduced that the killer hailed from Ballarat in Australia."

"There was ancillary evidence which aided me in reaching that conclusion. The words alone would not have been enough. Likewise a name alone."

"Mr H-Holmes," said Quantock, "far be it for me to c-criticise, but is it not at the l-least unwise, if not downright foolhardy, to ignore the Engine's conclusion? If you l-look for this Gasparini but find that no such person exists, what h-have you lost? Whereas, by not looking for h-him at all, you c-could be letting a mur-murderer slip through your grasp."

"What he's saying, old chap," I said, "is don't cut off your nose to spite your face."

"P-precisely."

Holmes regarded us both with lofty disdain, much as if we were traitors ganging up against him, Brutus and Cassius to his Julius Caesar. "You know better than me, eh?"

"Far from it," I said. "But I do think you should give the Engine the benefit of the doubt. It was right about Parson's Pleasure. What if it is right about this Gasparini too?"

"If the machine is so deucedly clever, why doesn't it provide a Christian name for the man? An address? Why doesn't it tell us exactly where he is at this very moment?" Holmes brandished a hand for emphasis, as though rapping an invisible door with his knuckles. "That would be preferable to it spewing out a name and leaving me to do the legwork. You have clearly taken the Engine's side, Watson. You should go the whole hog, switch allegiance fully and make *it* the hero of your future stories rather than me. I can see it now. The front cover of *The Strand*. A strapline above the masthead. 'Inside: Sensational New Thinking Engine Adventure – Complete This Issue.' I'm sure your readers will be captivated by your descriptions of a machine delivering vague, sibylline hints which someone else then has to interpret. They'll be on tenterhooks as you fill your narratives with repeated depictions of the Engine talking like someone with a stutter reading out a telegram. No offence, professor."

"Some t-taken."

"Put simply," Holmes went on, as oblivious as a steamroller, "if there is a Gasparini, which I sincerely doubt, let the police find him. It is a task better suited to their resources than mine. Let him be their responsibility. I'm quite happy for Inspector Tomlinson to take up the burden on his donkey-like shoulders."

"Holmes..." I said.

"In fact, Watson, there's the secondary protagonist of your new series of stories. 'The Thinking Engine and its sidekick Inspector Eden Tomlinson.' What a team. The soulless machine and the mindless bobby."

"Holmes..." I said more insistently.

"I'll enjoy seeing you try to make capital out of such unpromising material as that. The pair of them could not be more undynamic. The one permanently stationary, the other moving at a snail's pace, thinking he understands my methods and can put them into practice but really—"

"Holmes!" I barked, frantically gesturing for him to turn around.

"What?" he sighed testily, and swivelled.

A half-dozen individuals had entered the chamber while he had been ranting. Amongst them were some very eminent figures indeed. I recognised Sir William Thomson, the President of the Royal Society, and Colonel Sir Edward Bradford, the London Commissioner of Police. I had met neither man in person but their faces were familiar from the newspapers, as was that of the Home Secretary, no less, H.H. Asquith.

Accompanying them were a pair of thickset, round-shouldered men whose deportment marked them out as plainclothes police – Special Branch officers, there to provide protection and security. I recognised one of them, a glowering gorilla called Grimsdyke whom Holmes and I had had a run-in with five years earlier during the Baron Cauchemar case. He had gained a cauliflower ear in the intervening period and, as his unkind grin revealed, lost a couple of teeth.

It was not the judgements of these men or any of the others that I was concerned about, however. They looked bemused to have walked in on Holmes lambasting me, but with them the worst he would have done was embarrass himself.

It was the man escorting the whole party whom I felt sorry for. Inspector Tomlinson had arrived in time to hear every excoriating adjective Holmes had used about him, from "donkey-like" to "mindless" to "undynamic".

The official's face was a picture of hurt, disappointment and dismay. He struggled manfully to hide it but could not. In front of some of the most important men in the land, at least two of them knights of the realm, he had just been openly and patronisingly traduced by Sherlock Holmes – by the person he idolised and thought of as a friend. More complete a humiliation could not be conceived.

Reddening, in choked tones, Tomlinson said, "Forgive the intrusion. I'm minded to return at a more opportune moment – when, say, Mr Holmes has calmed down or, better yet, absented himself from the room."

On any other occasion Holmes would have shown remorse. But on that day, whatever he might have been feeling deep down, he exhibited none. He shot a blank, unrepentant look at Tomlinson and said, "I can see I am not wanted. Surplus to requirements. Very well. Good day to you all, gentlemen."

With a tip of an imaginary hat – his real one was under his arm – Holmes swanned past Tomlinson and the august entourage he had brought with him. At the door my friend paused.

"Are you coming, Watson?"

"No," I said. "Frankly I think not." Holmes had behaved so abominably, I had no desire to remain in his company just then.

"You're sure?"

I dug my heels in. "Adamant."

"So be it."

And with that, he was gone.

# CHAPTER TWENTY-SEVEN

## The Soul of a Napoleon

After Holmes's departure an awkward silence hung in the air, which I felt honour-bound to break.

"I must apologise," I said. "My friend Holmes... Well, he is extremely busy. He is not himself. The stress..."

Asquith, consummate politician that he was, smoothed things over with a few well-chosen words. "That was Sherlock Holmes, eh? On the face of it, hardly the cool, cerebral superman we have been led to believe. But I imagine once one gets to know him, his decent side emerges. I am acquainted with his brother, of course. Few in Westminster are not. He too makes a poor first impression."

"You are most gracious," I said.

"Besides, Mr Holmes is not why we have come all the way up from London," the Home Secretary continued. "Our objective, unless I am much mistaken, lies yonder." He nodded towards the Thinking Engine. "The eighth wonder of the world, if the rumours are even halfway true. I shall be fascinated to see it at work."

The dignitaries gathered around Professor Quantock, who began delivering a lecture on his Engine – its origins, its construction, its purpose. It was clear from their demeanours that Grimsdyke and his colleague longed to evict me from the premises, but since no one instructed them to do so, they did not. They lingered nearby, however, Grimsdyke aiming the occasional reproving scowl my way. He obviously had not forgotten how Holmes and I had given him and Inspector Lestrade the slip in the cells beneath Scotland Yard, dashing off on an urgent errand before he could stop us. He seemed the type to hold a grudge, and to enjoy doing so.

I took the opportunity to draw Tomlinson aside and apologise again to him, this time man to man.

"I just don't know what's got into Holmes," I concluded somewhat lamely, even though I knew perfectly well what had got into him: a gnawing worm of self-doubt and the several fluid ounces of Chlorodyne with which he had tried to drown it.

"I can't say his comments did not cut me to the quick," Tomlinson said. "But I'm prepared to chalk it up to the pressure he's under. We are seldom at our best when the Devil is on our back."

"The Devil? Holmes, as an arch-rationalist, would have little truck with *that* notion."

"Then that is where he and I differ the most, for I am a Christian man, Dr Watson. A Quaker, to be precise."

"Then you are in an unusual line of work for somebody of that persuasion. Indeed, I think you are the first Quaker policeman I have met."

"I'll admit I am a rarity, but the two traditions are not so incompatible. I belong to one of the liberal branches of the Religious Society of Friends, less strict and evangelical in its practices than most. I am a pacifist, but then what is one of the roles of a policeman if not to keep the peace? Otherwise my ethics are broadly in line with the law of the land. I may personally oppose capital punishment, but in general I am in favour of tolerance, equality and fairness, and the law exists to promote those, at least in theory. I see my religious convictions as underpinning my job, not at odds with it."

"So that's how you can find it in yourself to be so forgiving towards Holmes – your faith inclines you towards charity."

"It goes hard sometimes, but yes."

"I wish I could follow your example."

The Thinking Engine began to clatter and grind once more, limbering up.

"Why," I asked, "have these worthies chosen to call on Quantock and his machine? Is it just curiosity?"

"More than that," replied Tomlinson. "The Commissioner of the Met? The Home Secretary? Why do you think *they* might have taken an interest in the Engine?"

I thought it through. "Because of its potential as an aid to police work."

"Nail on the head, doctor."

"A Thinking Engine at Scotland Yard, serving as an oracle for the London force. I can imagine what old Lestrade might have to say about that."

"You are thinking on altogether too modest a scale," said Tomlinson. "From what I can gather, Quantock has aspirations that are significantly bolder and further reaching. Hark at him."

Quantock, voice raised above the ruckus from his machine, was expatiating on the possibility of a Thinking Engine in each and every police headquarters in the land. Regional departments would compile information about criminals and criminal activity in their areas. Each Engine would become a treasure trove of data about robberies, murders, dens of iniquity and other manifestations of illegality.

But there was more. Quantock was proposing that these Engines be linked to one another telegraphically, so that the information could be shared across the country by wire. Thus the constabulary in Liverpool might trade intelligence swiftly and automatically with the constabulary in Newcastle, and a Liverpudlian felon would find himself as known to the Geordie police as he was in his hometown, and vice versa. Provincial forces would have access to the records of every miscreant at large, so there would be no lying low in the countryside for a suspect on the run, no rural bolthole for an escaped convict. What Quantock had in mind was nothing less than a revolution in national policing, based around his remarkable device.

As he expounded his vision, he became eloquent and oratorical, his stammer all but vanishing. He foresaw dozens, nay hundreds of Thinking Engines yoked together, constellations of them dotting the kingdom, their united computational power making a career in crime that much harder to pursue and successful prosecutions that much easier to achieve.

"I am not prophesying an end to the bobby on the b-beat. Far from it. There will always be a call for constables patrolling their patches, watching out for signs of wrongdoing, physically collaring villains. But they will also serve as the eyes and ears of their station's Engine. Their reports will supply it with the hard facts it n-needs to function and thrive."

This was intended to allay any fears that ordinary coppers might be made redundant by a network of law-enforcement Thinking Engines, but on Inspector Tomlinson it had almost the reverse effect.

"So we are to become glorified worker bees, is that it?" he grumbled softly so that only I could hear. "Drones, slaving in support of a mechanical queen. Fattening her up with juicy titbits of knowledge, fulfilling her needs, but allowed no initiative of our own?"

Quantock's immediate audience, by contrast, seemed quite

taken with the notion. Colonel Sir Edward Bradford was nodding along sagaciously, while H.H. Asquith – who would subsequently rise to become Britain's longest-serving but least-celebrated prime minister – opined out loud, with typical Liberal Party optimism, that anything which removed subjectivity from the application of the law and replaced it with cold, dispassionate reasoning could only be considered an advance. He added that he had been a Balliol man himself, a scholar at that college and subsequently a Fellow, which inclined him to look with approval on the handiwork of a Balliol professor.

Sir William Thomson of the Royal Society, as befitted a man in his position, adopted a more cautious, sceptical stance. "The proof of the pudding, Professor Quantock," he said. "Put this invention of yours through its paces, if you would."

"The Engine is all yours, good sirs. Ask it any question you like, issues of local interest a speciality. The acc-accuracy of its answers will astound."

Questions there came; at first of a tentative, even facetious nature, but gradually turning more serious and personal, as Asquith stepped forward.

"What is my political future?" the Home Secretary asked.

I was rather interested in what the Thinking Engine would say, but just as Quantock was inputting the enquiry into the machine, I felt a hand on my shoulder.

"Time to go, gents," Grimsdyke said, and he and his colleague ushered Tomlinson and me out of the chamber and shut the door firmly behind us. Clearly it was felt that we of the lowly rank-and-file should not be privy to serious affairs of state.

As we strode away we heard the Engine's reply to Asquith's query, a clamour of laughter, and some comments in response, every word muffled and unintelligible.

"Quantock is more ambitious than I gave him credit for," I

said. "That meek and mild exterior hides the soul of a Napoleon. I wonder what Lord Knaresfield would make of these shenanigans."

"How do you mean?"

"His lordship has a proprietary interest in the Thinking Engine. He wants to use it as a tool to bolster the efficiency of his newspaper empire. Now Quantock is offering its services as a policing tool as well, seemingly without Knaresfield's knowledge."

"Why can't it be both? An asset in both fields?"

"I suppose there is no reason why not. We appear, inspector, to be in at the birth of something that could well change the world. The creation and dissemination of the Thinking Engine look set to transform society as we know it. The future is taking shape before our very eyes."

"Am I wrong in regarding that with trepidation?" said Tomlinson. "Change often brings upheaval. Could it be a mistake to place too much faith in our inventions? The Industrial Revolution has given us much but it has also taken away part of our humanity, turning people into little more than machines. Might a computational revolution not push us one step further away from our natural selves? There are devices to do the work of our bodies for us. Now there are devices to do the work of our minds?"

He shook his head darkly.

"I don't know, doctor," he said. "If this is God's plan, I can't make sense of it, and I'm not certain that I want to."

# CHAPTER TWENTY-EIGHT

## STRANGER IN THE TURF

I avoided Sherlock Holmes for the next few days and he made no attempt to get in touch with me at Mrs Bruell's. I had never thought I would have cause to feel ashamed of my friend. There had been times when his brusqueness had given offence, both to me and to others, and I had longed for him to develop a little sensitivity, a little politesse. Yet I had come to accept that an occasional lack of manners was part and parcel of his soaring brilliance, the corollary of being a genius, and made the necessary allowances.

This time, however, Holmes had gone too far. His behaviour in the Thinking Engine chamber had been beyond the pale.

By rights, I ought to have returned to London. There was nothing tangible keeping me in Oxford, no real obligation to remain.

My loyalty to Holmes, however, prevented me going. We had been bosom companions for fifteen years – twelve if one doesn't count his *Wanderjahre* – and I considered him not only the best and wisest man I knew but the very dearest of friends. Certainly I could not desert him in his hour of need. There would come a moment, I was sure, when sense would return to him and he would reach out to me. He would find me waiting patiently, good Watson, faithful Watson, steadfast as a Shire horse.

The weather brightened and spring proper set in. As the last days of March played out, the students embarked on their termly exodus home. For a couple of days the streets were thronged with cabs and carriages of every description, their roofs and luggage racks piled high with trunks, suitcases and stacks of books tied with string. In front of every college there were scenes of parting, cheery farewells, and promises to meet up during the holidays if feasible, as though it were an eon and not just five short weeks before Trinity Term began. For a brief period the city was as busy and vibrant as it is possible to imagine.

And then it all went quiet. The undergraduates were gone, and with them the source of much of Oxford's vitality. University buildings stood unfrequented and forlorn. Pubs were notably emptier. The peals of the chapel bells sounded louder and somehow more plangent. No longer was there a burst of raucous laughter around every corner, knots of rosy-cheeked young men scampering to lecture or tutorial, hearty souls in sportswear racing to match or practice, lines of choristers filing to evensong, musicians and music lovers chattering on their way to a recital, a plethora of bicycles clattering to and fro. Many of the dons left too, taking the opportunity to visit friends or relatives elsewhere in the country, while others buried themselves in the libraries to concentrate on their dissertations and doctoral theses, rarely emerging into the light of day.

The Gown part of the Town-and-Gown equation dwindled to a negligible sum. Oxford's citizens were for the time being free of the conquering army of academe. They had some breathing space before the scholarly occupying force returned.

At Mrs Bruell's, I made the most of my free time by catching up on correspondence and making sure my journal was fully up to date. It was important to keep a thorough record of my adventures with Sherlock Holmes, setting everything down on paper while it was still fresh in my memory and annotating previous entries with afterthought marginalia.

The other lodgers at the guesthouse presented an ever-changing roster of overseas visitors, itinerant workers, and wayward eccentrics. On the whole they were a convivial lot, and I spent the evenings amiably with them in the parlour, passing around tobacco and brandy and swapping anecdotes. Naturally, since it was no secret who I was, they demanded I tell them stories about Holmes. Having no wish to disappoint, I regaled them with various cases that had already appeared in *The Strand*, and one or two I had not yet published and might never. I flatter myself that I made for an engaging raconteur, and I held the room spellbound for a good hour each night. Even so, I found it an increasingly wearisome practice and something of an imposition. My feelings were mixed as I recounted Holmes's exploits, aware of the contrast between the man he used to be and the man he was now. Our present estrangement coloured my affection for him and hence my storytelling. Now and then, unconsciously or not, I would exaggerate his more abrasive traits, to such an extent that one member of my audience, a travelling brush salesman in town on business for a fortnight, was moved to comment that my friend seemed less attractive and heroic "in person" than on the page. I assured him this was not so, but it felt like a lie.

Come Saturday, I chanced upon the latest edition of the *Illustrated London News* at breakfast. Mrs Bruell, like Mrs Hudson, subscribed to the paper. Perhaps it should have been subtitled "The Landlady's Favourite".

As I flicked idly through the pages, my eye was caught by a short piece headlined "Great Detective Stricken?" Its author, needless to say, was Archie Slater, and it suggested that Holmes had come down with some mystery ailment, influenza perhaps, while hinting there was more to this illness than met the eye.

"Has Sherlock Holmes fallen prey to a foe that even he cannot out-think?" Slater wrote.

> The famous sleuth has taken to his room at the Randolph Hotel, one can only assume because he has succumbed to the notoriously uncongenial Oxford climate and been afflicted with an infection of the lungs. This while the poisoner of Magdalen College student the Honourable Aubrey Bancroft has yet to be found and the murderer of Oriel College oarsman Hugh Llewellyn roams free. Mr Holmes has allegedly been investigating both deaths, yet of late he has been anything but active. It must be a serious malady, to have laid him so low. One can think of no other reason why he has been making so many trips to the chemists, save that it is to seek some form of analgesic or cough suppressant, in copious quantities.

Slater knew exactly what he was doing. The words "analgesic or cough suppressant" would conjure up only one thing in most people's minds: laudanum. He had, whether by intuition or observation, hit upon the truth of Holmes's condition.

The mention of "so many trips to the chemists" ought to have come as a surprise to me but somehow did not. Slater must have been keeping a weather eye on Holmes's comings and goings, or else bribed hotel staff to keep him apprised of my friend's movements. By this reconnaissance he had divined that Holmes was becoming an habitual opiate user. I did not doubt that this was so. Holmes, with his personality and propensities, was unlikely to stop at just the one bottle of Chlorodyne.

I was incensed by the article, more for its sly, wink-and-nudge tone than for its content, which after all could not be gainsaid. I was tempted to tear it out of the paper, but knew this would alter nothing so left it there.

I am not the sort to document dreams. I consider them of little material significance and the recital of them tedious and irrelevant. They interest the dreamer himself and none other. However, I will break my rule and mention here that that night I was visited in my sleep by Aubrey Bancroft and Hugh Llewellyn. The former had streams of greenish-yellow bile leaking from the corners of his mouth, while the latter emitted a pulsing jet of blood from a hole in his chest. Their faces pallid, they berated me for my inability to pull them back from death's door. Call myself a doctor? I was an insult to the medical profession. I should be struck off.

I protested that I was not the one who had fatally harmed them and I could not have worked harder to save either man, but my objections fell on deaf ears. The two corpses shambled towards me, arms menacingly outstretched, while behind them I glimpsed the hazy, featureless outlines of a woman and two girls whom I could only assume were Tabitha, Elsie and Flora Grainger. In moaning, high-pitched voices these three urged Bancroft and Llewellyn on. It seemed the deceased students wished to seize me and tear me limb from limb in hideous recompense for their suffering, and the female Graingers approved.

I tried to turn and run, but found myself incapable of moving. Cold fingers clawed at me. The stench of blood and putrefaction filled my nostrils. I remember pleading for clemency, and my assailants laughing coldly in response, saying that here, in Oxford, only the dead held the power over life. The dead held sway. It was a city of the dead.

I awoke in such a state of agitation and panic, my heart racing so hard, that I did not sleep again for the rest of the night. I found it hard to shake off the impression of terror the dream left upon me. Even in the cold light of morning, when I was able to reason to myself that the dream was simply my subconscious mind working through the residual guilt I was feeling about Bancroft and Llewellyn, still the recollection of those ghastly ambulatory corpses would not leave me. Their censure was somehow, I felt, merited.

Two days later, when the sun was out and there was a delightful breath of crisp vernal warmth in the air, I went for a walk. My mood had lightened, the corpse dream all but forgotten. Oxford wore a mellow glow and for once I was able to see it for itself, not as a place where a spate of foul deceptions and murders was in train but rather as a venerable and eternal institution, ancient but lent a kind of perpetual youth by the tides of students who came and went, year in, year out, washing through its archways and portals, leaving traces of their copious, invigorating energy on its well-worn stones. I lingered beside Merton College's playing fields, watching groundsmen lower the rugby goalposts and mow the grass in readiness for the cricket season. I whiled away some time in the Botanic Garden, wandering the paths between the beds and stooping to inhale the scents of a lemon verbena plant and an ornamental hyacinth just coming into bloom. I loitered in the mazy interstices of Blackwell's, where I was pleased to see that the quartet of books I had published so far – *A Study in Scarlet*, *The Sign of the Four*, *The Adventures of Sherlock Holmes* and *The Memoirs of Sherlock Holmes* – were all prominently displayed. I toyed with the idea of introducing myself to the proprietor and offering to inscribe every copy with my autograph, but I am innately reticent about such things anyway, and was further hampered by my current difficulties with Holmes, which had the effect of making me somewhat less proud of my opuses than usual.

My footsteps took me along Catte Street and beneath the covered outdoor walkway which links the two parts of Hertford

College and is known as the "Bridge of Sighs" for its resemblance to the Venetian bridge of the same name. Thence I ventured down a winding, shoulder-width alleyway in the shadow of New College. Halfway along this I came upon a tiny, dim-lit, low-ceilinged public house, the Turf Tavern, which judging by its higgledy-piggledy half-timbered construction dated back to the thirteenth century. It seemed like a pleasant enough place to halt and whet my whistle, and shortly I was seated inside with a tankard of foaming ale before me. There were no other patrons. I was alone with my thoughts.

Not for long, though. A man entered the pub barely three minutes after I did, ordered a stout from the landlord, and took it to the dingiest corner of the snug. Sitting with his back to me, he supped his beer. His coat lapels were drawn up, so that I saw nothing of his face other than one edge of a set of dark whiskers. His hair was glossily black. His hands were gloved.

I paid him no more heed than that, giving him the cursory glance that one does any stranger in a public place, then resuming my drinking.

A moment later, the man spoke.

"Dr Watson," he said.

I glanced up. "Yes? Do I know you, sir?"

"Know *of* me, perhaps. You are Dr John Watson, that is correct?"

"I am he. And you are…?"

The man gave a gruff chuckle. "I go by many a name, many a different alias. At the present time I believe you would be most familiar with my identity as a gentleman of Italian extraction, surname of Gasparini."

My jaw dropped and I felt the electrifying sensation of the hair across my entire scalp prickling and going erect.

"Gasparini?" I echoed. "My God…"

I made to stand, but the other, without looking round, raised an admonitory finger.

"I would not do that if I were you, doctor. I would stay put, compose yourself, and listen. I have a proposition for you."

# CHAPTER TWENTY-NINE

## The Proposition

I did as he recommended, if only because he gave the order with a certain chilling authority. The landlord had gone to the back room. There was nobody else around. I might as well hear what this Gasparini, or whatever his real name was, had to say. I was in the presence of a multiple murderer, our elusive agent provocateur. What did he want with me? What might this "proposition" of his be?

"Your mind is racing," he said. "Your thoughts are in disarray. 'Should I call for the police?' you are thinking. 'Should I launch myself at him? Should I at least alert the landlord?' I advise you against any of those courses of action, especially the last. Breathe one word to mine host when he returns, give him the slightest hint that all is not well, and I will be forced to act. And I think you know what I mean by 'act'. You have twice dealt with the consequences – with a signal lack of success."

"You fiend," I said. "You unmitigated scoundrel."

"I might be that. I might be worse. But I am, I assure you, not one to make idle threats."

"Turn around. At least show me your face."

"And why would I do that, my dear doctor? So that you may describe my features to your friend Sherlock Holmes later? I think not."

I was oddly heartened by his use of the word "later". It implied he did not mean to kill me. Not just this moment, at any rate.

"You don't sound Italian," I said. I was stalling, playing for time so that I could come up with a plan.

"Because I am not. I can be, of course." He affected a lilting Italian accent. "How about-a now, signor *dottore*? Does thees sound Italiano enough for-a you?"

"Not terribly."

"Well, it did to young Mr Llewellyn. He didn't doubt the nationality of his newfound chum Gasparini, not for one instant. Very engaging company, he found me, in fact. Both of us outsiders in this city, foreigners, ill at ease amongst the English. It helped forge a bond between us."

"And Aubrey Bancroft? You were able to forge a similar bond with him?"

"He liked me as a don. I was affable and approachable, unlike many of them." His voice went up an octave to an effeminate, fluting register. "'I am a Doctor of Divinity, ever so pious, on the side of the angels… but with a devilish streak.'" It dropped again to the low guttural rasp which might have been his normal speaking voice but might equally have been as artificial as either of the others. I had no way of telling.

"I do not rate myself a great actor," he continued. "I would not give Sir Henry Irving a run for his money. But I am good enough for my purposes. I can do what needs to be done when bagging my game. Stalking, camouflage, staying downwind of my quarry, making sure it doesn't suspect a thing – those are my skills. I can be your best friend, I can sneak up right beside you, I can smile and mesmerise like a snake charmer, and you won't even see the blade in my hand, not until it's too late."

"How very… picturesque."

"I'm telling you how it is, that's all."

"You are confessing, then, to the murders of Bancroft and Llewellyn. Nahum Grainger too."

"I am confessing nothing," said Gasparini. "Nor am I denying anything. I will say that it is a joy to see the mighty Mr Sherlock Holmes so flummoxed. He seems to have no idea which way to turn. He flops and flounders like a landed trout. How is his health, incidentally? I hear from backstairs staff at the Randolph that he seldom orders food to be sent up from the kitchen any more, and the trays almost invariably sit outside his room untouched. He goes out only to visit the chemists. Sometimes he pays the hotel's boots to run that errand for him. He must be in a bad way. I don't believe what I've read in the paper, about a lung infection. Not for one moment. I'd say it's the cards not falling as he'd like, that's what ails him."

"How Holmes is faring is none of your business." I nearly added that it had become none of mine either.

"Oh, but it *is* my business, doctor. While it is a pleasure to see him brought low, I do not wish him crushed utterly. Not yet. The privilege of destroying him belongs to another. My job is to soften him up first."

"Then this has all been about Holmes?" I said. "The intent behind your entire design has been to cause his ruination?"

"Is that so hard to credit? Sherlock Holmes has made many enemies in his life and put many a man behind bars. Should it surprise you to learn that some of them might seek recompense?"

Before I could respond, the landlord came back, drying his hands on his apron. He had heard our voices, and for a while he indulged in inconsequential chitchat about the weather and England winning the Ashes in Australia despite the absence of

W.G. Grace from the team. Gasparini and I both joined in the conversation, he with gusto, I in more desultory fashion. Moments earlier Gasparini had been softly crowing about his sinister achievements, and now he was debating the merits of the respective team captains, our Stoddart and their Giffen, for all the world as though he was just an ordinary man in an ordinary pub on an ordinary afternoon. The landlord was addressing him across the bar as he might any customer, blissfully oblivious to the fact that his life was in jeopardy, while I sat pretending hard that everything was normal. It was a disconcerting exercise, to say the least.

"Can I get you gents anything?" the landlord asked. "Refills?"

"Not for me, thank you," I said.

"Nor me," said Gasparini.

"Fair do's. Give me a shout if you change your minds."

The landlord disappeared into the back room again, leaving me alone with the killer once more. Gasparini had not shifted position at all during our exchange with the publican. He had contrived not to turn his head any more than a few degrees, so that I still had no clear, unimpeded view of his face.

Nonetheless I had become convinced there was something familiar about him. I was sure that we had met before. The set of his shoulders, the timbre of his voice – these were features I recognised but could not put in context. Sometime in recent history our paths had crossed. Holmes would have identified him in a trice, had he been here, but I was not Holmes, I did not have Holmes's incisive powers of observation and encyclopaedic memory, and Gasparini knew it. Hence he felt he could present himself before me, more or less openly, with impunity.

"You mentioned a proposition," I said. "Of what sort?"

"I wish you to do me a service."

"Is this one of your wicked pacts? I perform some self-interested deed, something seemingly for my own benefit, upon completion of which you kill me?"

The other laughed low and long. "No. I am not so rash as to think you would fall for that. I am asking you to save Sherlock Holmes. That is my proposition."

"Save him?"

"Before he can sink any further. I have, it transpires, pushed him harder than I intended. It is possible that he is made of less stern stuff than I thought. I do not relish seeing him collapse entirely before my plans come to a head. He needs to be around to witness my triumph and that of my associate. Otherwise where is the fun in it? What would be the point?"

"Let me get this straight," I said. "You are his foe, you harbour a deep grievance against him… and you are concerned for his wellbeing?"

"Only in as much as I would not wish him to perish too soon. His end should not be of his own choosing. Its time and manner should be for others to decree."

Gasparini stood, shunting his chair back.

"I have said my piece, Dr Watson," he said. "You would be advised to act upon it. Now, do not attempt to follow me as I leave. Stay for at least another quarter of an hour. In fact, here." He tossed some coins onto his table. "Have another pint. It's on me. My treat. I shall know if you come after me. I shall be watching out for you, and believe me, I have the eyes of a hawk. You are a brave man and might not fear for your own life, but remember – you are not the landlord of the Turf Tavern, and it would be a great shame if some harm were to come to that fine upstanding citizen."

He left by the nearest door, in such a way that I still did not get a good look at his face.

I was tempted to disregard his parting shot and give chase. I knew, though, that the life of yet another innocent would be forfeit if I did, so there was no alternative but to sit and stew while the minute hand of the pub's clock crept through a quarter turn. The landlord came and cleared Gasparini's table, pocketing the change that lay on it. He expressed delight at having been left such a generous tip and opined that the Turf could do with more patrons like the gentleman just gone and fewer students, who were often rowdy and for whom the notion of giving gratuities was an alien concept.

I enquired in a roundabout way whether he had seen the fellow's face at all.

"Not directly, no," he said. "Something of a nose on him, he had, and a piercing blue eye, but that's the extent of it."

The landlord had had a better angle than I, but still Gasparini had managed to evade his eyeline. It was agonising how adept our agent provocateur was at masking his identity. Rarely had I had such a sense of being manipulated and outmanoeuvred as I did that sunny Oxford afternoon. I felt as helpless as a mouse in a cat's clutches or a rabbit in a fox's maw, forced to lie limp in the vain hope that the predator might lose interest and drop me. Even when the allotted fifteen minutes was up, I waited a further ten. Just to be on the safe side.

# CHAPTER THIRTY

## A Living Scarecrow

"Holmes!"

I knocked on the door to his room.

"Holmes!"

I knocked again.

"Holmes, open up! I know you're in there. There's no point pretending you're not."

I heard a slither of shifting bedclothes, a heavy thump as of a human form tumbling to the floor, then a soft groan.

"Holmes, open the door this instant, or so help me God I'll break it down. You see if I don't!"

Further indistinct sounds came from the room. I gave it another minute, then took myself to the opposite side of the corridor. This afforded me a run-up of some ten or eleven feet. It might be enough. I tensed, lowering my shoulder and lining it up with the point where the edge of the door met the jamb. I imagined hurling myself into the thick of a maul on the rugby pitch, bent on getting the ball but also on biffing a couple of the opposing team's forwards into the bargain. Never let it be said that rugger is a gentleman's game. In my experience it is only a shade less brutal than war.

I charged across the corridor.

The door swung open a split second before I reached it.

I went stumbling through, headlong. My shins struck a coffee table some three yards beyond. I plunged prostrate onto the carpet, fetching up at the foot of an armchair. I lay stunned and dazed, feeling not a little foolish. I looked up to find Holmes, in pyjamas and dressing gown, staring down at me with mild bafflement, as though I were an exhibit in a cabinet of curiosities.

"Well," he said, "you certainly know how to make an entrance, Watson."

I scrambled to my feet. "Damn it, man. Couldn't you have told me you were going to do that?"

"Open the door? But isn't that what you were demanding of me? Why should it have come as a surprise, then?"

I dusted myself down and rubbed my barked shins, glancing around as I did so. The room was dingy and unkempt. The curtains were partially drawn, the grate brimmed with cold ashes, and the bed was a landslide of sheets and blankets. The air was stale and malodorous, musty with the smell of unwashed body, and as for Holmes, he was a caricature of himself, a living scarecrow: gaunt almost to the point of cadaverousness, hollow-eyed, his hair lank and tangled, his skin sporting a greyish pallor, his cheeks and chin unshaven.

"Good grief!" I ejaculated. "The state of you. Have you looked in a mirror lately? You're a fright."

"And how nice it is to see you too, Watson." Yawning, Holmes closed the door. "To what do I owe the pleasure? Or have you come purely to bandy insults about?"

"I have come," I said, "because I could not bear the thought of you debasing yourself any further. Look at this."

I indicated the various empty bottles of Chlorodyne which lay haphazardly around the room. Holmes had clearly quaffed prodigious amounts of the stuff, so much that it was a wonder he could function at all.

"You have been contributing far too freely to the coffers of that quack Collis Browne," I said.

"And, in one instance, to his rival's coffers," Holmes said, pointing to a bottle of Freeman's Chlorodyne, one of the many imitative products that had sprung up after Collis Browne's concoction became a roaring success. "The boots bought the wrong brand, in spite of the very specific instructions I gave him. A much bitterer taste, and in my view a less efficacious recipe."

"Holmes, Chlorodyne is poison. Deaths have been attributed to it. There have been articles in *The Lancet* calling for it to be banned. People are apt to become so infatuated with it that they lose all sense of themselves and waste away. A child in New Zealand died last year after his mother inadvertently gave him an overdose."

"I am not a child."

"You are acting like one!" I shot back. "It is childish to be this irresponsible with your body, this wilfully neglectful of your health. If that is not obvious to you, then you are not the man I have known all these years; you are, to put it bluntly, a blithering idiot."

"Please, Watson, do not shout." Holmes winced, clutching his forehead. "It makes my ears ring and my head thump."

"I *will* shout if it is the only way to get through to you. What you are doing to yourself is neither sane nor profitable. Is this some act of self-martyrdom? Is that it? Are you doing it out of a perverse sense of nobility? You would rather die than concede defeat? The word for that is *cowardice*."

"You know I am merely finding consolation in numbness. I have told you so already. Haranguing me will solve nothing, and if that is the sole reason you are here, then I would be grateful if you would do me the kindness of leaving." He held an arm out towards the door. "The exit is that way."

I was sorely tempted to grab him by the lapels and give him a good shake. "Holmes," I said, straining not to lose my cool entirely, "the reason I am here is that I have new information about the case. I was intending to share it with you, but the condition in which I find you makes me ask myself why I should bother. You seem unreceptive to any form of assistance or succour. I've half a mind to accept your invitation to leave, and to make that leaving a permanent state of affairs."

Something – a faint intimation of the old spark – glinted in Holmes's eyes.

"New information?" he said.

"I have had an encounter. A most unnerving one."

"With whom?"

"No less than our killer, Gasparini. He accosted me in a pub, of all places."

Holmes's reaction to the news surprised me. I had anticipated concern about my welfare, a demand for further detail, an expression of amazement at the agent provocateur's boldness.

I had not anticipated that he would collapse into the nearest armchair as though in a swoon and would lie there for a minute with his hand over his eyes, intoning, "Oh, thank God. Thank God. Thank God."

"Holmes?"

He removed his hand and peered at me through half-closed lids, much like someone squinting into bright sunlight.

"Finally," he said. "Finally the wretch makes his move. I had begun to think he might never. What has it been, a week? I wasn't sure if I could last much longer. I was starting to lose my grip. The Chlorodyne… Glorious, insidious substance."

"Holmes, I don't understand." I said this, but I had a glimmering of what he was getting at.

"Watson, you must help. I have gone as close to the edge of the precipice as I dare. Perhaps too close. I am teetering on the brink. It's up to you. You must pull me back. Only you can do it. Only you have the skill. Save me, my friend. I beg of you. Save me."

# CHAPTER THIRTY-ONE

## Saving Sherlock Holmes

It was just what the agent provocateur had said, the very proposition he had put forward in the Turf Tavern. "Save him." Now I was hearing it from Holmes's own lips. "Save me." How could I possibly refuse?

For the next three days I occupied myself with nothing other than extricating Holmes from the toils of the Chlorodyne. According to the medical literature, there were two ways of doing this: the tough and the slightly less tough. One entailed simply denying him any more of the so-called medicine. The other entailed weaning him off it by giving him progressively smaller doses or else substituting a milder equivalent such as paregoric. I put it to him that the latter option would be the less painful of the two but the more protracted. He plumped for the former. The sooner he was restored to normal, he said, the sooner he could get back to work. I expressed the hope that his constitution was up to the challenge of going from heavy dependency to none at all. He said that he hoped so too and that we were about to find out.

The bulk of my task lay in keeping vigil over Holmes,

monitoring him round the clock and nursing him through the withdrawal symptoms. It was an ordeal for me but more so for him. He was afflicted with all the classic side-effects that come with ridding one's body of the craving for opiates. His muscles ached. He trembled. Sometimes he was feverishly hot, other times shivering with cold. He sweated profusely and complained of nausea. His digestive system was in uproar, and he was often agitated to the point of frenzy.

I made sure he drank plenty of fluids – camomile tea and plain water, for the most part – to keep him hydrated. I ordered up simple soups and broths from the hotel's kitchen, and spoon-fed these to him when his hands were shaking too much to hold an eating utensil.

I synchronised my sleep patterns with his periodic catnaps, allowing myself to close my eyes and nod off only once he had. I needed to be awake whenever he was, else I could not regulate his behaviour or offer palliative care. On one occasion I was so tired that I failed to register that he had roused himself. I woke up to find the door wide open and Holmes almost at the head of the staircase. He would have gone further but his legs had given out under him and he now lay in a twitching heap, somewhat to the consternation of other guests, who were having to step over him to get past. I bundled him back into the room, but a few hours later much the same thing happened again. This time I had taken the precaution of locking the door and pocketing the key, but that did not deter him. A blast of outdoor air stirred me from my slumber, and there was Holmes, halfway out of the window, three storeys above street level, bent on shinning down the drainpipe. I coaxed him back inside and resettled him. His goal both times had been to get to the chemist and purchase more Chlorodyne. "Just a drop or two," he said. "It will ease my suffering." I doubt any self-respecting shopkeeper would have served someone in such a dishevelled state, clad in nightwear and slippers, plainly unwell, but you never know. It was a chance I could not take. There are unscrupulous types in every profession.

To forestall further escapes I fastened Holmes, with his consent, to the bedpost, using the cord of his dressing gown. It was a token gesture. He could have slipped his bonds with little difficulty, and we both knew it. I just needed to reinforce psychologically the knowledge that he should not stray.

"Were I Harry Houdini," he said, testing how securely I had tied his wrists, "you would require something more substantial than this." His voice was hoarse and thin, barely a wisp of sound.

"But you are not Harry Houdini, Holmes, and this is not some carnival entertainment. This is serious."

"Houdini spoke of death and rebirth as touchstones in his act – what could be more serious than that?"

"Your recovery," I replied, only partly in jest.

As the hours wore on, Holmes revealed piecemeal how he had surrendered himself to Chlorodyne on purpose, with a view to luring the agent provocateur into precipitate action.

"I could have feigned addiction," he said, "but our adversary – Gasparini, for want of a better name – is cunning and observant, and there was a danger of being caught out. The crucial thing was not that I appeared to have given in but that you, Watson, were in no doubt that I had. Your despair was more important than mine. You are not, with the utmost respect, an expert in dissimulation. I mean that as a compliment. You are the model of sincerity, your every emotion abundant on your face. I could not give Gasparini the least cause to suspect that I was trying to goad him out of hiding, thus my capitulation had to be real, and you had to see it was real and react accordingly, with resentment and disapproval."

"I was your stooge, in other words." I remembered the long years thinking my friend dead. He had used the same excuse then for keeping me in the dark.

"Come now, don't be so hard on yourself."

"If I am being hard on anyone, it is you," I said. "You could not count on me to play along convincingly with any kind of pretence, so you went ahead and did it for real, despite the danger. You used my gullibility as a tool."

"On the contrary. How is it gullible to be angered when a friend does something you disapprove of?"

"I have been a pawn nonetheless, just as Grainger, Bancroft and Llewellyn were the agent provocateur's pawns."

"No, because he uses deceit. I have not deceived you. My adoption of Chlorodyne was genuine."

"It is a fine distinction."

"It is a valid one."

I sighed. "How did you come to think of this deception?"

"I took my inspiration from Tabitha Grainger."

"I don't follow."

"Cast your mind back, Watson."

I did so, thinking of that cursed house in Jericho, the bed with its blood-stained sheets. "Dalby's Carminative!" I cried.

"Just so, Watson. The bottle on the woman's bedside table. How easy it is to seek refuge in drugs, and how commonplace. People do it all the time."

"So says the cocaine user."

"The former cocaine user, Watson. You have seen to that. And soon I shall be a former opiate user too, again thanks to you."

By the morning of the fourth day Holmes had rallied and was almost back to his old self. There was some colour in his cheeks and he had visibly gained weight. The tremors and sweats had subsided, although he was still prey to stomach cramps and bouts of anxiety. During one especially anguished spell he begged me to forgive him for enticing Gasparini to get so close to me.

"Followed you into a pub!" he wailed. "He might have murdered you on the spot."

"He wished to send you a message. I was the courier."

"A stronger message would have been your death. That would certainly have got my attention."

"And for all he knew, driven you right over that precipice you spoke of. It is not part of his plan that you die yet. He wants you alive."

"Still, I left you out there, alone, unprotected, just so that he would see you at a loss and it would tempt him to tip his hand. I should not have done that. I should not have been so casual with your life."

After weeks of thinking my friend had abandoned all care for me, his words were greatly appreciated, and I could afford to be magnanimous. "I'm still breathing, aren't I? Like all your risks, it was a calculated one."

Later, when he was calmer, Holmes said, "I need you to tell me everything you can about Gasparini."

"We should wait until you are stronger."

"I am strong enough." My friend, with some struggle, propped himself up on his pillows. I had removed the dressing gown cord restraints not an hour earlier, deeming them no longer necessary. "He presumably appeared to you in heavy disguise."

"I wouldn't know about any disguise, but he managed not to reveal his face to me. My impression of him was—"

"I am not interested in impressions, Watson! You know that full well. Pure facts, that's what I am after."

I had never thought I would be glad to hear Holmes chide me with his customary severity, but I was. It signified once and for all that he was on the mend.

I related my exchange with Gasparini at the Turf as best I could remember it. Holmes pressed me about certain turns of phrase my interlocutor had used.

"'Bagging my game'? Those were his exact words?"

"I believe so."

"Believe so or know so?"

"He used an extended metaphor about hunting, that's for sure. One about fishing too. Cards as well, if memory serves."

"And you say he referred to a snake charmer."

"He had the ability to mesmerise like one, he told me. He was not a little boastful."

"The pub landlord spoke of… 'piercing blue eyes', was it?"

"Along with a large nose. The queer thing is, Holmes, I'm convinced I've met Gasparini. Before the other day, I mean."

"You say that on what basis?"

"I'm loath to call it a hunch – yet a hunch is all it is."

"Nothing specific led you to that conclusion? His hair perhaps?"

"It was nothing out of the ordinary. Dark, collar-length. Very dark, in fact."

"So dark it might have been dyed?"

"Now that you mention it, yes. Lord Knaresfield dyes his hair, does he not? But it wasn't him, I don't think."

"No, his eyes aren't blue. They're brown. He was wearing a wig, then."

"Possibly. I'm sorry, Holmes. I'm trying my best. Your analytical methods seem so straightforward until we mere mortals attempt to apply them."

"You are doing adequately, Watson. What else can you tell me? He spoke of an 'associate', yes?"

"He is in league with someone, definitely. Reading between the lines, I think he is the subordinate in the partnership. The other gives the orders, he executes them."

"And their mutual goal is my downfall," Holmes mused. "I suppose I should be flattered."

"He implied he is an old opponent of yours."

"I've no doubt that is true, from what you've been saying. In point of fact, I have a notion that this man is one of the deadliest opponents I ever faced."

I asked him to expound on that remark, and after a moment, he did.

"If Gasparini is who I think he is, Watson, then we are both still alive only by his good graces. He could have slain us a dozen times over. He has had the chance to. Instead, he has led us a dance, calling the tune and watching us caper. He and his partner in crime have been keeping us preoccupied while some other subtler plot unfurls."

"Good grief," I said. "Well, out with it. Who is he?"

Holmes counted off attributes on his fingers. "A hunter. One who has spent time in India, judging by the snake charmer reference. Enjoys cards. Blue eyes. Prominent nose. It's all there, my friend, plain as day. But the principal clue is the name Gasparini itself. I would have spotted the significance of it sooner, had I been… clearer-headed than I was. It is by way of a joke."

"Some kind of pun? Wordplay, as in the poison pen letters?"

"Not as such. Call it a taunt. There is a relatively well-known Gasparini, a Swiss pastry chef who lived during the first half of the last century and whose main claim to fame is the invention of the meringue. Most cookery books, at any rate, ascribe its creation to him."

"The meringue?" I said, bemused.

"Bear with me. Gasparini was a resident of the village of Meiringen, from which the confection derives its name. Meiringen lies in the canton of Bern, in the Hasli region of Switzerland, on the banks of the River Aare."

"As I know full well. It was where we stayed when we were on the trail of Professor Mori…"

My voice tapered off. My blood ran cold.

"Oh no," I breathed. "Oh, this is too much, Holmes. You're telling me..."

"It is my firm opinion," Holmes said, "that Signor Gasparini, the unnamed Doctor of Divinity, and the friend of Nahum Grainger who provoked him into slaughtering his family, are guises adopted by a certain rogue shikari of our acquaintance, formerly an infantryman in the 1st Bangalore Pioneers, veteran of the Jowaki Expedition and the battles of Charasiab, Sherpur and Kabul, author of *Heavy Game of the Western Himalayas*... Need I go on?"

"You need not, and I would prefer that you *did* not."

I looked down at my hands, which had developed a slight tremor.

"All along," said Holmes grimly, "we have been contending with none other than Colonel Sebastian Moran."

# CHAPTER THIRTY-TWO

## Moran the Ronin

I tried to deny it but I could not. The evidence fit. All too well did it fit.

Moran was a callous, cold-hearted killer. We knew that from experience. He had twice made an attempt on Holmes's life, first at the Reichenbach Falls as Holmes was returning from his gruelling and deadly hand-to-hand tussle with Professor Moriarty, then three years later in London. He had hurled boulders at Holmes in the first instance, shot at him with an air-gun in the second, both times only narrowly failing to achieve his lethal objective, thwarted by my friend's quick wits and resourcefulness.

To Moran, life was not precious. Far from it. Not only had he bagged a larger tally of tigers than any other man, but he was wont to kill humans with as little compunction as he did big cats, and often for the slenderest of reasons. His murder of the Honourable Ronald Adair, to take one example, was motivated by nothing more than the fear that Adair was about to expose him as a card cheat and thus cause him to be barred from the Bagatelle and every other London card club worth being a member of.

As Moriarty's confederate and enforcer, Moran had been responsible for keeping the criminal mastermind's underlings in line and disposing of anyone who might compromise Moriarty's plans or rise in opposition to him. I recalled how we had come face to face with him in Blandford Street after he had shot at a wax bust of Holmes positioned as a decoy in a window of our rooms in adjacent Baker Street. Even under police arrest Moran had been like a wild animal – a raging tiger, one might say – and I had got the sense that here was someone with the soul of a barbarian, someone who wore only a thin veneer of sophistication and truly belonged in a bygone, more brutal age. I could see how he was able to play various roles, such as Signor Gasparini, because, for him, being any kind of human at all was a role. Holmes had been right when he had told Inspector Tomlinson that the jungles of the subcontinent were Moran's spiritual home. Moran was a bestial throwback, a savage who had learned to pass for civilised.

Who else but hawk-eyed Moran could have gunned down Hugh Llewellyn through the mist? He had carved himself out a hide on the riverbank opposite and lain in wait, utilising all the skills he had honed in the Eastern Empire as a soldier and a hunter. Likewise he had shadowed me through Oxford to the Turf Tavern, not once giving me cause to suspect I was being followed.

"An Oxford man himself," said Holmes. "This city is familiar terrain for Moran. He knows it as well as he knows anywhere, and he has used that to his advantage. Its lore, its byways, its quirks, its idioms – nothing will have changed much since his graduation back in the sixties."

"To think that I was within a few feet of him," I said. "Moran. I see now why he was wearing gloves and did not take them off in the pub. His swarthy skin might have been a giveaway."

"The question remains, who is he working with? Or rather,

for. It must be someone whose antipathy for me dovetails with his own."

"Could it be that that was just a bluff? That Moran is trying to muddy the waters? Why throw his lot in with another when he has the incentive and the wherewithal to topple you all by himself?"

"Colonel Moran is a follower, not a leader, Watson," said Holmes. "He lives to take orders. There is a Japanese concept I learned about on my travels in the Orient – the *ronin*. It refers to a samurai warrior who has lost his *daimyo*, his master. In feudal-era Japan, this was a shameful status. If the daimyo died or committed ritual suicide to atone for some disgrace, his samurai guard were obliged by their *bushido* code to join him in death, which they would administer to themselves with their own swords. Anyone who refused to do so became a ronin, and thereafter was considered to lack honour and had to find some illegal means of earning a living, usually as a mercenary or a bandit. Moran is, I would argue, a ronin. In the absence of Professor Moriarty, he has lacked direction and guidance. That is why I was confident he would not trouble us, even after he escaped from custody. He sought to silence me over the Adair affair and failed. He would not risk trying again now, not unless given an incentive by another."

"So some new master has stepped in to fill the breach, and Moran is active once more?"

"Very much so. And furthermore, I am quite convinced there is a direct connection between Moran and the Thinking Engine."

"What makes you say that?"

I was almost glad to hear the irritation in Holmes's voice. "Think, man, think. When he accosted you in the Turf, what did he say? 'You know me best as a gentleman of Italian extraction, surname of Gasparini', or words to that effect."

"Yes. So?"

"Watson, how could he know that we knew about a Signor

Gasparini in the first place? It was the Thinking Engine that furnished us with the name. All we had before then was Llewellyn's 'gas par.'"

"I see," I said slowly. "Damn it, yes. You're right."

"Of course I am. Even if he had heard Llewellyn's dying words from across the river, which I doubt, Moran wouldn't necessarily have been aware that we had made anything of them. The only way he could have been confident that you would recognise the name Gasparini is if he was present when the Engine supplied it, or else is in regular contact with someone who was."

"Was he eavesdropping on our last visit to the Engine somehow?"

"Conceivably. There isn't anywhere in the Thinking Engine chamber itself where a man could easily hide, though. What space the Engine does not occupy is open, without niches or recesses. It is more likely that his associate is someone closely linked to the Engine, someone willing and able to relay to him whatever information the machine yields up."

"You mean Quantock? That mouse of a man? Surely not."

"We cannot rule him out. But it may be that the associate is another person, one to whom Quantock is beholden, a more senior and authoritative figure."

"That would be Lord Knaresfield."

"Quite so. I imagine if Knaresfield insisted Quantock share with him everything the Engine says, Quantock would do so without demur. There is also the charming Archie Slater. It wouldn't be hard for him, like Knaresfield, to browbeat Quantock. And Slater, as we know, despises me."

"So Quantock, Knaresfield, Slater – they're all three of them candidates for the role of Moran's new overlord."

"There is one other you haven't listed."

"Who?"

"Inspector Tomlinson."

"No!"

"My recollection of the event is a tad hazy," Holmes said, "but I do seem to remember that when he arrived in the chamber with the party of dignitaries from London, I was in the midst of a diatribe against the Engine. I'm sure I used the word Gasparini in his presence."

"But Tomlinson has been our ally. He is a self-professed admirer of your work and mine. He has been nothing but accommodating since we came to Oxford. He is a Quaker, what's more. Frankly, if he is our enemy, I'm a Dutchman."

"So great a fan, Watson, that he mistook a reference to the Silver Blaze kidnapping for one to the Speckled Band case?"

"A pardonable error. Even I have been known to make mistakes in my own oeuvre."

"Such as the location of your war wound. Shoulder is it, or leg?"

"Yes, there is that."

"And your own Christian name. Are you John or James?"

"Ahem, that too. I blame Newnes. What is an editor for if not catching an author's occasional inconsistencies?"

"One man's inconsistency is another man's blunder," said Holmes. "But we digress. A single slip-up does not *per se* incriminate Tomlinson. We should, however, not ignore the anomaly of a helpful policeman, one who has gone out of his way to accommodate us."

"How dashed cynical of you."

"I point it out merely because, if I were wishing to keep tabs on an adversary, a good method would be to pose as a friend and manipulate his activities under the guise of supervising them. It would put me in a position of control, with my opponent unwittingly, heedlessly heading in whichever direction I chose to send him and making as much or as little progress as I permitted."

"But what is his motive?" I said. "What does Tomlinson stand to gain from seeing you brought low?"

"Could it be that I have embarrassed the police once too often for his liking? That he does not appreciate me showing them up on such a regular basis? That I make detectives like himself and Lestrade look bumbling?"

"It seems tenuous. His initiating a correspondence with you, his greeting you with open arms as a guest in his city – all a feint so that you will lower your guard and be easier to undermine? I don't find that consistent with the character of the man."

"You don't know him well enough to say that."

"I think I have the measure of him."

"Might he not have been playing the long game?" said Holmes. "Might he not have been biding his time, cultivating my friendship, carefully laying his snares? The bait luring me to Oxford was hard to resist: a juicy murder and the challenge of the Thinking Engine. Remember, too, that it was Tomlinson who brought up the subject of Moriarty when we were taking tea after Bancroft's poisoning. From Moriarty it is but a short leap to Moran."

"That, surely, is another score in Tomlinson's favour, rather than a black mark against him," I said. "Why mention Moriarty at all, if he knew we would be likely to discuss Moran also? His reaction to the name might have given away that he was in league with him."

"Or," said Holmes, "he was sounding us out, probing to see if we had any suspicions in that area."

"Hmmm..." I refused to be persuaded that Tomlinson was Moran's ally or any kind of evildoer for that matter. "By the same token, why would Lord Knaresfield wish you ill? You and he have never crossed swords, or even paths, until just recently."

"I am forming a theory about that. What I need to do now

is carry out some research. I need to look into his lordship's background, and Tomlinson's and Quantock's."

Holmes began to clamber out of bed.

I laid a hand on his shoulder, gently pushing him back.

"You are going nowhere," I told him. "You are still weak. As physician as well as friend, I am prescribing complete bed-rest for the next twenty-four hours."

Holmes plucked away my hand and resumed laboriously rising.

"With all due respect, Watson," he said, "I am going to ignore doctor's orders. I do not have the leisure to wallow around any more. Time is of the essence. Urgent action is called for. Moran has become overconfident and made a misstep, as I hoped he would. He has given us a break in the case. We now know more than we are meant to, and we must press home that advantage while we can."

"But, Holmes…"

My companion tottered as he stood upright. He looked as though he might faint.

Then, bracing himself on the bedstead, he took a deep breath and sallied forth, flinging open the wardrobe and inspecting his clothes with the air of a man unfamiliar with any attire beyond the humble dressing gown. Luckily I had taken the liberty of having his suit cleaned and pressed during his convalescence.

"Enquiries must be made," he said, "data gathered. All this time, the shikari has been employed keeping us distracted, drawing our attention away from some wider, more sinister scheme. I mean to find out what it is, the reason behind the misdirection. Our opponents' aim isn't just to humble me. There is a deeper current running beneath, I'm sure of it. Moran spoke of a 'triumph' that I am supposed to witness. We must determine what that is and, more importantly, how to prevent it."

# CHAPTER THIRTY-THREE

## A Brace of Errands

Holmes and I toured Oxford all that day, calling in at various destinations. As we traipsed back and forth across the city, I could not help but feel uneasy. Everywhere we went, I was constantly looking over my shoulder and sensing eyes on me – a beady, predatory gaze. Somewhere, anywhere, Sebastian Moran might be lurking. He might be tracking us on foot or, worse, observing us along the sights of a rifle from some window or rooftop.

If Holmes shared my apprehension, he did not show it. Although he was far from being at full strength, he had regained much of the vigour he had sacrificed to the Chlorodyne. I was still angry at him for the extraordinary risk he had taken by deliberately acquiring an addiction to the substance. I could now, however, dredge up a certain admiration too. So dedicated was he to justice that he would push himself to extremes, endanger his health and even his life, in its name.

Our first port of call was the offices of local weekly broadsheet *The Oxford Times*, where Holmes prevailed upon the editor to allow him access to its "morgue". He busied himself amongst the back issues and clippings for a good hour or so, and when he was done, he pronounced the archives of surprisingly high quality for a provincial newspaper.

We next dropped by the Bodleian. Holmes asked one of the librarians to steer him in the direction of the mathematics section. There, after some searching, he discovered a certain volume and perused it for several minutes, making notes. It was a treatise by none other than Professor Malcolm Quantock, and its subject was Vandermonde's Convolution, whatever that might be. Of as much interest to Holmes as the contents of the book, if not more, were the publisher's indicia page, the dedication, and the endmatter featuring the author's biographical details.

Last but not least, we went to Balliol College, where Holmes begged an audience with the Master, Professor Edward Caird. This was granted, and Holmes and Caird fell to discussing Quantock. Caird became cagey when asked about Quantock's aberrant behaviour earlier in the academic year and was unwilling to be drawn too deeply on the subject. The college's reputation was his foremost concern, he said, and besides, Quantock had since made up for any "misunderstanding" that may have occurred by bringing new lustre to Balliol, thanks to his Engine. The excitement about the machine, fanned by the press coverage, reflected well on Balliol, so much so that any difficulties there had been during its inception could be dismissed as "birth pangs".

"It was my predecessor, Jowett, who appointed Quantock to a professorship here," Caird told us, his Renfrewshire burr only a little flattened by years of living in southern England. "He admitted to me he had had some misgivings about it, although he never went into specifics. I gather Quantock left his previous post under something of a cloud. His academic credentials and qualifications are second to none, but there was talk of deficiencies of character. I would not have believed it myself had I not been on the receiving end of that temperamental outburst of his. It could simply be that Quantock is the type of person who has difficulty interacting with others and is apt to, as the expression goes, rub people up the wrong way. His stammer may also account for his social awkwardness. Life cannot be easy for one with such a defect. Owing to that and the exceptional brilliance of his work, I feel he deserves some latitude. I often speak in my lay sermons about the imperative of forgiveness, and I do try to – ha ha – practise what I preach."

"Can you tell me what it was the two of you argued about in the Garden Quadrangle?" said Holmes. "Was it by any chance the theological implications of the Engine?"

"Dear me, no. Wherever did you get that idea?"

"A source who now seems unreliable. It was inference on his part. Erroneous, clearly. Coloured by his own prejudices." Holmes was referring to Inspector Tomlinson.

"No, I am a progressive, Mr Holmes," said Caird. "Enlightened, in my way. Unlike some of my dourer Presbyterian countrymen, I do not look askance on the modern world and its appurtenances. Anything the Creator's creations create is fine with me, as long as it is used wisely and well. My clash with Quantock – the first cross words he and I have ever had, and I hope the last – was simply over the amount of time he was devoting to his machine, at the expense of his educative duties. He had missed a couple of tutorials, and when he failed to deliver a scheduled lecture as well, that was it as far as I was concerned. Enough was enough. I set out to remind him not to neglect his students. A stroll, a gentle chat, arm round the shoulder, that sort of thing. I must have hit a nerve, given how he flew into a rage. I like to think we have since made up. He has been nothing but civil to me in the Common Room and at table, and I have responded in kind. I have had no further complaints from his students, either. By all accounts Quantock has resumed being dutiful and punctilious as a tutor. Now, I have said more than I intended, and I have a pressing engagement elsewhere, so if you will excuse me, gentlemen…"

"Of course," said Holmes. "I shall trouble you no more, Master. I appreciate the time you have spared and such candour as you have been prepared to display."

Later, as we restored ourselves with Irish coffees at the Mitre Inn on the High Street, Holmes said, "Watson, I owe you a debt of gratitude – one I'm not sure I can ever repay."

"Oh pish! Think nothing of it."

"No." Those grey eyes of his regarded me levelly across the table. "You stood by me stalwartly when you had every justification for washing your hands of me. I shall not forget that. I don't know that I can ask anything more of you."

"I would be insulted if you did not."

"That's the spirit. Then listen. I have a few preparations to make. I am laying the foundations from which to launch a decisive counterattack against our enemies. You can assist me by running a brace of errands back in London."

"Name them."

He did.

"And afterwards," he added, "there will be one further imposition I will lay on you. Again, it will be asking a lot."

"What is it?"

"I cannot reveal any more until my plans are finalised. Please, continue to have faith in me. Is that acceptable?"

"Anything to halt Moran and his superior in their tracks, and end this nightmare."

"Then go. We shall reconvene at the Randolph tomorrow."

On the train to Paddington I mulled over the "brace of errands" I had agreed to discharge. The first was to fetch my service revolver from Baker Street. This I did eagerly and not without a sense of relief, for I had been feeling vulnerable without a weapon to hand, all the more so since learning that Sebastian Moran was on the prowl in Oxford. I took the pistol from its case, cleaned it thoroughly with wire brush and oilcloth, checked that the action was working smoothly, and slotted Eley's No.2 cartridges into the chambers of the cylinder. There is something about the heft of a loaded gun in one's grasp when one is in danger. It reassures. I sighted along the barrel, closing one eye. I pictured Moran standing before me. In my mind, he was cowed and cringing. "Put your hands up," I murmured, hoping my imaginary target would not obey, hoping he would give me an excuse to pull the trigger.

The revolver sat snug in my pocket as I pursued my second errand, and I was glad to have it there.

On Temple Lane, just off Fleet Street, Archie Slater met me punctually at six in the saloon of a public house, a watering hole favoured by newspapermen. They were all around me, editors, reporters and print compositors alike, hunched in packs, exchanging "war stories" and industry tittle-tattle.

"I can't say I wasn't surprised to receive a telegram from you, Dr Watson," Slater said, "given the history your friend and I share. How is Mr Holmes, by the way? Recovered from his bout of influenza?"

"It was no influenza and you know it. Your last article hinted as much, quite brazenly. For your information, he is much better now."

"I am so pleased to hear it. Still, I'm curious, and curiosity alone is why I am here. What can I do for you? Or is it something you can do for me?"

I regarded him as warily as I might a rabid dog. Holmes had identified Slater as a candidate for being Moran's new master. The man struck me as too weasel-like for that, an insinuator rather than a doer. He was the sort to take sly verbal potshots from the safety of a newspaper column, but was he the sort to machinate against someone directly? I thought not. But then what did I know? Was I a better judge of such things than Sherlock Holmes?

"I'll get straight down to business," I said.

"You'll buy me a pint first," said Slater. "A journalist is like a motor. He does not work well unless lubricated."

I ordered a beer for him grudgingly and watched him swig it down.

"That's the ticket," he said, wiping froth from his top lip with his shirtsleeve. "Well then?"

"Holmes has tasked me with making you an offer. He is willing to give you a journalistic exclusive. A 'scoop', I believe you people call it."

"Go on."

"Holmes wishes to resolve his competition with the Thinking Engine once and for all."

"Intriguing. How?"

"He is going to present the Engine with a puzzle it is incapable of elucidating fully."

Slater's eyebrows rose a fraction. He took out his notebook. "You don't mind if I scribble?"

"By all means. You may quote him verbatim: 'a puzzle it is incapable of elucidating fully'. He proposes to do this two days hence, on Sunday."

"And what's in it for me?"

"Spoken like a true pressman. By way of an incentive, once Holmes has accomplished his goal, he will grant you an hour-long, one-to-one interview during which you may ask him any questions you like. However personal or impertinent their nature, he will answer them with absolute frankness."

Slater's tongue darted out to lick his lips. He jotted further shorthand notes. "How obliging of him. I daresay our paper's readership would lap that up. Forgive the scepticism, but where's the catch?"

"The catch?"

"Come off it, doctor. I wasn't born yesterday. He's up to something, isn't he? He wouldn't all of a sudden be getting cosy with me if he didn't stand to profit by it."

"Your choice, Slater," I said, gathering up my coat. "Take it or leave it. Plenty of other journalists I could approach. This pub is full of them. I could throw a stone and hit someone who'll snap up the opportunity I'm handing you."

"But Mr Holmes doesn't do interviews. He's shy of publicity. Doesn't even take credit for half the cases he solves."

"All that means is that your piece on him will have an even greater impact."

"Why me, though? Why, of all people, the man who regularly criticises him?"

"To show he's unafraid. To meet your hostility head-on." I turned as if to leave. "You'd better hurry, Slater, if you're going to take me up on this. Holmes wishes his challenge to the Engine be announced as soon as possible. Your deadline for copy is tonight, isn't it?"

"Ten p.m."

"Then there's still time for you to cobble something together. Do that, get your article in this Saturday's edition, and the interview is yours."

As I headed for the exit, I heard rapid footfalls behind me. My hand stole to my pocket, ready to draw my pistol.

I did not need it. Slater shouldered past me with a perfunctory, mumbled apology and barged through the door. By the time I got outside, he was halfway down the street, hastening in the direction of the Strand.

"Hook, line and sinker," I said to myself.

I prayed that Holmes had gauged his move correctly and we hadn't just handed the initiative back to the opposition. We needed Moran and his master rattled but not to the point where they resorted to drastic measures. They were to know that we were gunning for them, but must not know how.

Slater was running to reach the *Illustrated London News* offices, but I also hoped that, if he was Moran's master and our true adversary, he was running scared.

# CHAPTER THIRTY-FOUR

## MIDNIGHT AT THE MUSEUM

Holmes crouched beside one of the fanlight windows that provided the Thinking Engine chamber with illumination during the hours of daylight. In his hands was a jemmy, the tip of which he inserted between the window frame and its setting.

"Hold that light steady, if you will, Watson."

I focused the beam from his pocket lantern onto the spot where he was working. The window itself was a solid artefact of metal, lead and glass, but it was embedded none too securely in the mortar surrounding it. By dint of levering the jemmy around its rim, Holmes soon began to pry it loose.

I glanced about, eyes peeled and ears pricked. We were in a courtyard on the St Giles' side of the University Galleries, to reach which we had climbed onto a low wall and vaulted the railings surmounting it. I tried to shield the lantern's glow with my body, lest it catch the eye – and arouse the suspicions – of a passing pedestrian. At this time of night, there was every chance that such a pedestrian would be a policeman out on patrol. Had it been term-time we would have had Proctors and Bulldogs to worry about as well, so at least the odds of being apprehended by the authorities were partially reduced.

Bells chimed in the dark, heralding midnight. The peals came from Oxford's score of chapels and churches, all seemingly vying with one another to announce the time, in prolonged concatenation, near and far. Loudest and lengthiest was the monotonous song of Great Tom, the bell in the gate tower at Christ Church which every day at that hour tolled 101 times in commemoration of the number of scholars who enrolled at the college when it was founded. This lasted twenty minutes and helped cover the noise Holmes was making as his efforts with the jemmy became more strenuous. Not for nothing had he chosen precisely this time of night to effect our break-in.

The jemmy kept grinding, mortar crumbled, and then at last, with a screech, the fanlight window came free. Holmes caught it with a deft hand.

"We have ingress," he said. "Come, Watson."

He slithered through the semi-circular aperture, down into the Thinking Engine chamber. I picked up the knapsack he had brought and lowered it in after him. He took it from me, then bade me follow.

During some of our investigations in the past, Holmes and I had engaged in practices which might not strictly be considered illicit but which certainly nudged at the boundaries of legality. My friend was not above bending the law when it suited his purposes.

What we were doing now, however, was a flagrantly criminal act: breaking and entering, with intent to steal. If discovered, we would have little hope of justifying or excusing ourselves. No court in the land would exculpate us on the grounds that it was all for the greater good; no jury would take pity on us. A hefty jail sentence would be warranted.

Thus I hesitated, feeling that by passing through the window

I would be irrevocably crossing a line. Here was a moral Rubicon.

"What are you waiting for?" Holmes said from below. "We haven't got all night."

"I'm not sure—"

Holmes cut me off abruptly. "This is no time for cold feet, man. I said I'd be asking a lot of you. I explained what was in store. You consented. Back out now, by all means, but don't expect ever to be held in my full esteem again."

"Oh I say, that's rather harsh," I declared, but Holmes had touched on a truth. How could I look him in the eye hereafter, having failed him at a crucial moment?

I thought I heard the shade of Mary Watson, née Morstan, tutting heavily as I slid feet first, backwards, through the window.

"A... tight fit..." I gasped.

Holmes grabbed my legs and pulled, making some disparaging comment about my girth which I affected not to hear. With him manhandling and me wriggling, we managed to insinuate me into the room, on whose floor I landed with something less than balletic grace.

The Thinking Engine hulked at the far end of the chamber, a bristling geometrical silhouette in the gloom. The odours of grease and metal were strong as ever, and strong, too, was the sheer presence of the thing. Though silent, the machine seemed pregnant with potential noise, the thrumming racket which lay latent in those myriad moving parts. As I stared at it, I was overcome by the impression that it might spontaneously spring into life. Worse, it might speak, addressing Holmes and me in those uncanny, halting quasi-sentences. I felt as one might in a room full of marionettes or clockwork automata, well aware that they were inanimate but nonetheless afraid that at any moment they would start to move of their own accord, impelled by some hideous otherworldly force. It was not a rational fear, but that did not make it any less potent.

"Watson? Are you planning to stand there forever, gawping? We've work to do."

I started at the sound of Holmes's voice, then shook off the creeping apprehension. I nodded. "Yes. Work to do."

Holmes shouldered the knapsack, which clanked with larceny-related paraphernalia, and made his way out of the chamber and up into the main body of the museum. I of course went with him, not displeased to be leaving the proximity of the Engine.

As we tiptoed up the staircase, I reflected on the fact that this was the second time in as many months that Holmes and I had been nocturnal visitors in a museum. At least during our previous escapade – unravelling the mystery of the revenant Pharaoh Djedhor – we had been granted permission to be there. This time we were intruders, little better than common thieves.

Holmes had ascertained beforehand that the University Galleries boasted but a single nightwatchman, one who, it had been established, was far from being the most conscientious exponent of his trade. Holmes, while spying on him as he settled in for his duties at closing time the previous-but-one evening, had observed a bulge in his jacket pocket corresponding in size and shape to a hip flask. In addition, he had followed him home from the museum the next morning and noted that he appeared well rested, much as someone would who had slept the night through rather than diligently staying awake and making his rounds. Indeed, the lackadaisical watchman did not go to bed when he reached his house on Osney Island but instead set about energetically weeding his front garden, then took himself to the pub for lunch.

"I don't think we have much to worry about where he is concerned," Holmes had said, but just to be sure we peeked into the entrance hall, where the watchman's booth was situated. As anticipated, the booth's occupant was fast asleep in his chair, feet up, arms folded, snoring softly. His hip flask sat on the desk in front of him, uncapped, beside an unlit oil lamp.

Skirting the hall, we negotiated a path through the building, through room after room housing Elias Ashmole's extensive collection of Raphael drawings, pre-Dynastic Egyptian artefacts, Minoan sculpture, Anglo-Saxon treasures and majolica pottery. To this had been added Old Masters, bas-reliefs, tablets, swords, coins, statuary and papyri bequeathed by other benefactors such as John Tradescant, along with unique oddities such as the death mask of Oliver Cromwell and the lantern used by Guy Fawkes during the Gunpowder Plot.

Amongst this gallimaufry of treasures, our goal was a golden chain, kept under glass before a portrait of its erstwhile owner, none other than Ashmole himself. The portrait, painted in 1681 by John Riley and set in an ornate gilt frame carved by Grinling Gibbons, showed its subject resplendent in full-bottomed wig and rust-red velvet coat, posing beside a leather-bound book on the Order of the Garter, which stood on end with the selfsame golden chain snaking about its base. Antiquary, astronomer, astrologer and alchemist, Ashmole had been a highly influential man in his day, qualities captured in the haughty stare with which he transfixed the viewer and the emblems of eminence surrounding his likeness.

Holmes paused briefly before the portrait, as though in reverence, one accomplished polymath paying his respects to another. Then he turned his attention to the lock which secured the display case. Producing a set of picks and torsion wrenches, he made short work of it, while I again held the lantern to shed light on his labours and tried not to think how, with every passing second, I was sinking deeper into a swamp of transgression as sucking and relentless as Dartmoor's Great Grimpen Mire. Yes, we were not planning to hold on to Ashmole's golden chain indefinitely. Yes, we would return it as soon as was convenient. This was not so much a robbery as a necessitous borrowing. We did not stand to profit financially from the deed in any way. All the same, we were committing a felony. There was no denying it.

The case door opened, and Holmes fished out the chain from within and passed it to me for safekeeping. I installed it in the left-hand pocket of my overcoat, where it sat in almost perfect counterweight to the revolver in the right-hand pocket.

From the knapsack Holmes then produced a replacement chain which he had commissioned from Oxford's premier forger of valuables, paying over the odds in order to guarantee timely delivery of the item. The forger had used a print of the portrait as his guide in creating the replica, which matched the original exactly, link for intricate link.

Holmes arranged the counterfeit chain in the same position the real one had sat in, then closed and refastened the door. He surveyed the substitution and gave a satisfied grunt. The fake chain was made of copper with a minimal amount of gold blended in to give it the requisite aureate lustre. An expert would spot the difference in a trice, but to the untrained eye it looked the part.

The worst was over. All we had to do now was make our exit from the museum the same way we had come in. I allowed myself to think that we were going to pull off the theft successfully, without coming to grief.

Beside me, Holmes stiffened.

"Watson," he hissed. "Did you hear that?"

I had heard nothing except the throbbing of my pulse in my ears. "No. What was it? The watchman?"

"I don't know. No. He would be using his lamp. Quick! Douse the light."

I closed the pocket lantern's cover and turned down the wick until the flame was extinguished. In the ensuing darkness – made all the darker by the sudden absence of artificial illumination – I strained my eyes, looking for movement. All I could see were the shapes of the exhibits, their edges limned by the faint streetlamp glow coming in around the window shutters.

"Holmes," I whispered, after standing stock still and barely daring to breathe for at least a minute, "are you sure you weren't mistaken?"

There was no reply.

"Holmes? Holmes? Holmes!"

I scanned to the left and right, then behind me. Of my companion there was no sign. He must have stolen off while I was preoccupied staring into the dark. If a foe was present – if, God forbid, Sebastian Moran was in that very room with us – Holmes evidently was trying to outflank him. I only wished he could have warned me that he was going to leave my side. I supposed that he feared any sound at all, even a few murmured words, might have given away his intentions.

I slipped the revolver out of my pocket and cocked it as noiselessly as I could. Gun held to the fore, I began to move, going slowly not just for reasons of stealth but also to avoid accidentally bumping into any of the exhibits.

In this fashion, painstakingly, half blind, I travelled from room to room, encountering no one until I reached the entrance hall. The watchman was still there, pursuing his endeavours as assiduously as ever. If anything, his sleep was deeper, his snores more stentorian, than before.

I padded past his booth, debating whether or not I should wake him. Assuming there was an intruder on the premises – another, that is, besides myself and Holmes – ought I not to alert the museum's official guardian and enlist his aid? It would be good to have an ally, someone to share my burden of anxiety.

I told myself not to be absurd. How would I account for my own presence there? What if the watchman tried to apprehend me and found Elias Ashmole's chain on my person? Moreover, I was carrying a gun. With such *prima facie* evidence stacked against me, they might as well not bother with a trial. I would be as good as convicted.

I moved onward until I reached the stairs. The cold stone steps whispered underfoot as I descended. I had no idea where Holmes had got to, but my principal aim was to quit the building as fast as I dared. Holmes had left me to fend for myself. The least I could do was return the courtesy.

As I re-entered the Thinking Engine chamber I spied a tall, lean figure stooping in front of the machine. My forefinger was curled round the trigger of my gun, and my nerves were so on edge that I very nearly fired. Some instinct prevented me, and I am more than glad that it did, for the figure straightened up and I perceived the angular posture and unmistakable aquiline profile of Sherlock Holmes.

"Holmes!" I declared. "Good God, it's you!"

"Who else would it be?"

"Well, Moran for one. Or some other undesirable, perhaps Moran's master. Did you not say you heard a sound when we were upstairs? Isn't that why you crept off, to investigate?"

"Oh, that," said Holmes airily. "Yes, it seems my ears were playing tricks on me. There was no one."

"Really?"

"Really. I apologise for alarming you without cause."

"Never mind alarming me. I just came within an inch of shooting you."

"I am grateful for your restraint," said Holmes.

Sometimes his unflappability could be maddening. I uncocked the hammer and stowed my revolver.

"You still have the chain on you, I trust," he said.

"Of course."

"Good. I was concerned you might have jettisoned it, for fear of being caught red-handed."

"You do me an injustice," I said, although the thought of ditching the purloined artefact had occurred to me and I had been tempted to act on it.

Holmes proffered the knapsack with the flap open, and I dropped the chain within.

"Shall we take steps to remove ourselves now?" I said. "We have done what we set out to do. Ashmole's chain is ours, the forgery installed in its place. I, for one, would like to put the whole episode, and the University Galleries, behind us."

"You're right. Best not push our luck and outstay our welcome. Give me a boost, would you? There's a good fellow."

I helped Holmes up into the fanlight aperture, he in turn hauled me through, and presently we were reinstalling the window, using glazier's putty to secure it in place. The putty would not hold indefinitely but would suffice for the time being, affixing the window frame so that nobody would notice it had been jemmied out, not unless they examined it closely.

I wasn't at all sad to be climbing back out of the courtyard, feeling nothing but relief to be on the street once more. At a stroke, Holmes and I were no longer burglars; we were a pair of friends out for a late-night stroll. At least that was what anyone might think, to look at us. In the event, there was no one else around. St Giles' was empty, flickeringly gas-lit.

"A good night's work," Holmes said.

Having exchanged a few further words, we parted company, he heading round the corner to the Randolph, I northward along St Giles' towards Mrs Bruell's.

Tomorrow would see the fruition of Holmes's plan and, I

hoped, make the trauma of tonight's exploits worthwhile. If all went well, then, at last, we would be finished with Oxford, and we could return to Baker Street. I looked forward to that outcome with no little eagerness.

# CHAPTER THIRTY-FIVE

## The Nuances of Language

The following day, at 11a.m. sharp, we gathered in the Thinking Engine chamber. Aside from myself and Holmes, present were Professor Quantock, Archie Slater, Inspector Tomlinson and Lord Knaresfield. The last had journeyed south from his Yorkshire home especially for the occasion and made no bones about the fact that he regarded this as an intolerable imposition.

"I have better things to do than be summoned – summoned, I say, as though I'm some manservant – down to Oxford for no apparent reason."

"My letter, your lordship, was more in the way of a request," Holmes said. "If you interpreted it as anything other, I crave your forgiveness."

"Up to Oxford," said Quantock quietly. "One al-always goes up to Oxford, n-never down."

"Up, down, what ruddy difference does it make?" snapped Knaresfield. "I had to be here, or so Mr Holmes told me, and here I am, but I don't have to be chuffed about it."

"Again, I can only crave forgiveness," said Holmes. "As for

there being 'no apparent reason' for your attendance, I assure you it is otherwise. You will want very much to know the truth about the Thinking Engine and the part it has played in recent events in this city."

"Aye, well, you hinted as much, didn't you? Your letter implied dark dealings, and if you're accusing me of being in any way involved in those – me! – I should like you to say it to my face. I may have a title, I may be all gentrified, but that won't stop me from giving you a right good pasting, sir, if I perceive a personal slight."

"Oh, you are involved," said Holmes, "and you know it. There has been villainy afoot here, villainy of various stripes."

"What's this?" Slater piped up. "Villainy? You had me write about an impossible puzzle, Dr Watson, and I duly did so. You'll have seen yesterday's edition of the *News*. There was my piece, on page ten. Just a couple of column inches, but we had to reset the whole page to fit it in. 'Sherlock Holmes vows to turn the tables on the Thinking Engine...' You never said there was anything more to it than that."

"Watson told you as much as I told him to, Mr Slater," said Holmes, "and not one word of it was a lie. He just didn't give you the whole picture. We desired your presence, like Lord Knaresfield, and we knew you would come if only to follow up on the article. You sensed there would be some sort of denouement today, the capstone to your series of features about the Engine. How could you stay away?"

"A rotten trick," Slater huffed.

"I imagine you have used underhand tactics more than once in your career in order to obtain a story. You cannot really complain if someone does the same to you. The biter bit, et cetera."

"Do I still get my exclusive interview?"

"I am not one to renege on a promise."

"Well, that's something, I suppose."

"I should be at the Friends Meeting House right now," said Tomlinson. "I'm not happy about giving up my Sunday morning worship for a work-related matter. The wife is even less happy about it. Mind you, the message you left for me at the station made it seem as though I didn't have a choice, Mr Holmes. Catching a 'Machiavellian multiple-murderer', isn't that how you put it?"

"That is my goal today, no less," said Holmes, "and even Mrs Tomlinson must appreciate that there can be few things more important than that."

The policeman grumbled discontentedly but said nothing further.

"For my p-part," said Quantock, "I'm keen to know how my Engine can f-fail to solve this puzzle of yours. Why w-would you wish to keep t-testing it anyway? Has it n-not proved its worth several t-times over?"

"Perhaps you should start it up, professor," said Holmes, "and then we'll see."

While Quantock got the motor going, my friend paced the room. He had not vouchsafed to me the full extent of his plan, and I was somewhat concerned that the Thinking Engine would unequivocally identify the two of us as thieves. What's more, it would do so in the presence of a police inspector and a journalist. Only by some nimble footwork would we be able to extricate ourselves from *that* predicament.

Once the Engine was up and running, Holmes said, "Gentlemen, you are all aware that there has been a rash of murders in Oxford. They began more or less when Professor Quantock's device first came to public attention. One might be inclined to regard this as a coincidence. Certainly the city was not immune to the blight of murder before the Thinking Engine was built, and the tawdry business of the Grainger killings in Jericho seemed the kind of violent domestic crime which is, alas, all too commonplace amongst the lower echelons of society. The only thing that was unusual about it was the level of guile shown by the culprit in deflecting suspicion away from himself. I myself would have thought little further of it, had I not been drawn ineluctably towards the conclusion that Nahum Grainger had an accomplice."

"Accomplice?" said Tomlinson. "This is news to me."

"Is it? Next, we had the matter of the poison pen letters to Professor Merriweather of Magdalen College, which culminated in the death-by-strychnine of Aubrey Bancroft. Bancroft, like Grainger, had an accomplice who, it seemed, turned on him. The pattern was repeated with Hugh Llewellyn, shot to death outside the Oriel boathouse."

"Yes," said Tomlinson, "and try though we might, Oxford police still haven't got to the bottom of that one. They're all three of them linked, these cases? Is that it?"

"Very much so. They are all shoots from the same plant, and it is a highly toxic specimen of flora which has its roots right here, in this very room."

"You're saying the Thinking Engine is involved?" said Knaresfield.

"M-my Engine?" said Quantock. He gave a brittle laugh. "That's ab-absurd. I know it's ingenious, but to accuse it of b-being at the heart of a c-criminal operation…"

"That is exactly what I am accusing it of," said Holmes. "At every turn the Engine has swiftly and readily provided solutions to the conundrums placed before it."

"Just as it was d-designed to."

"And how convenient that I have been present in the city all along to be outsmarted by it."

"If you are res-resentful of the Engine's prowess, th-that is your lookout. It reflects p-poorly on you, not on my m-machine."

"My point is," said Holmes, "what better way to solve puzzles than if one knows the answers already, and what better way to know the answers than if one sets the puzzles oneself?"

Knaresfield barked a laugh. "Now I've heard it all. Somehow the Thinking Engine has gone rogue and organised a series of elaborate crimes? Mr Holmes, it is an assemblage of cogs and dials and wires and other metal whatnots. It can no more do what you're suggesting than a locomotive can stand up and walk."

Holmes shot me a wry, surreptitious wink. Some five years earlier, he and I had seen something almost exactly matching Lord Knaresfield's metaphorical comparison. Warned by Holmes's wink, I refrained from commenting to that effect. Not that I would have. Mycroft Holmes had sworn us to secrecy on the topic, and moreover it would in no way enhance our credibility to bring it into the argument now. To this day, the memory of the ambulatory locomotive seems phantasmagorical, akin to one of H.G. Wells's wilder imaginings; yet I know it to have been real, not fiction.

"Perhaps the Engine is just a machine," Holmes said. "Perhaps it is more. I should like to establish that by asking it one simple question. Professor? If you'd care to start typing?"

"I'm not sure I want to," said Quantock. "This is n-nothing but a cheap attempt to invalidate all my hard w-work. You have d-dreamed up some impossible problem, purely in order to d-discredit me and my invention."

"Have you and your Engine not striven to discredit me? Can two not play at that game? Besides, I have never said that the problem is impossible, just that the Engine will be incapable of elucidating it fully. The two are not the same."

"They sound the same," said Slater.

"I would have thought a writer such as yourself would be attuned to the nuances of language, Mr Slater," said Holmes.

"Watson here would have no trouble fathoming the distinction."

I nodded, even though I couldn't myself see a significant difference between the two syntactical constructions.

"I still feel under no ob-obligation to g-go along with this farce," said Quantock, folding his arms. "My Engine is n-not some plaything, built to assuage childish whims."

"This is no whim, professor," Holmes said. There was steel in his voice and a flinty spark in his eyes. "I should not like to force you to co-operate, but neither would it be wholly against my nature to do so."

"F-force me?" The mathematician all at once looked very fierce, like a cornered rat.

"Or," said Holmes, "I could simply thrust you aside and carry out the typing myself. Which would you rather?"

Quantock dipped his head and glowered. His nostrils were flaring, and I could sense the deep reservoir of anger beneath the meek exterior, the same temper that Edward Caird, the Master of Balliol, had unwittingly aroused.

Inspector Tomlinson stepped between him and Holmes, like a referee at a boxing match.

"Let there be no threats, please," he said. "Let us behave like the cultured, civilised people we are. Professor, I'm not taking sides, but I am of the opinion that Mr Holmes has made a reasonable request. This all started with your Engine being set up in direct opposition to him, on the back of a wager. Is it not fair that he is given the opportunity to counter that challenge with one of his own? Natural justice demands it, even if there is no legal compunction for you to do as he asks."

Further support came from an unexpected quarter. "Yes, professor," said Slater. "Why the reluctance? Let Holmes have his head. The Engine will run rings around him. It has before."

Lord Knaresfield added his voice to the chorus. "Go on,

Quantock. Give us a show. Otherwise I'll have come all this way for nowt!"

Quantock gave Knaresfield a hurt look, as though betrayed. Sullenly, he moved to the typing station.

"Very w-well," he said. "If you in-insist. What's the puzzle?"

Holmes bowed graciously. "It's quite straightforward. What did Watson and I steal from the University Galleries last night?"

"Eh?"

Quantock's surprise was echoed by Knaresfield and Slater, and most of all by Tomlinson.

"Steal?" the inspector said. "I hope, for your sake, that you're joking, Mr Holmes."

I, too, was taken aback. Holmes was deliberately incriminating us? With Tomlinson right there to witness it, and Slater on hand to write about it in a national newspaper?

My friend maintained an air of placid composure. "Just input the question, professor, would you?"

Quantock tapped at the keys, looking marginally less surly than before, as if buoyed by the prospect of seeing Holmes and me exposed as lawbreakers.

"That's all?" he said. "No m-more?"

"It should suffice," said Holmes.

The Thinking Engine rattled heavily, calculations manifesting in audible form.

"It talks now, by the way," Holmes told Knaresfield, Slater and Tomlinson. "Don't be startled when you hear it. Professor Quantock has given his Pinocchio a voice."

We waited on tenterhooks, until at last the Engine arrived at a conclusion.

"Elias Ashmole's golden chain," it said in its weird, arrhythmic approximation of speech.

"By gum!" Lord Knaresfield exclaimed, although I couldn't tell whether it was the answer that shocked him or the phenomenon of words issuing from the voice cabinet's amplification horn. It could have been both.

"There," said a smug Quantock. "Puzzle solved. Not so imp-impossible after all. Even with only the b-barest of information to go on, the Engine comes up tr-trumps. Impressed, your l-lordship?"

"More than ever, professor," said Knaresfield.

"That was the easy part," said Holmes. "Making an assertion is one thing. Can the Engine prove it? That's altogether another thing."

"It had better prove it," said Tomlinson, "although for my peace of mind as much as anyone's, I hope that it cannot."

Quantock typed. He looked confident now, utterly assured of his creation's brilliance.

"Done," he said.

Once again the Engine thought, and once again it spoke.

"Chain replaced with replica. Replica copied from portrait. Substitution may be confirmed by counting links."

"Counting links?" said Slater.

As if in reply – though it was merely continuing its explanation – the Engine said, "Chain in portrait longer than chain on display. Several links removed from original in 1776."

"Why?" said Holmes. "Ask the Engine why the links were removed?"

Quantock complied, saying, "You sh-should not try to catch the Engine out on l-local knowledge, Mr Holmes. There is little about Oxford that it is ig-ignorant of."

"That is what I'm relying on."

"Links stolen," the Engine said. "Used as payment to landlord for board and lodging."

"By whom?" Holmes pressed. "It was someone famous. Notorious, one might say."

Quantock typed.

"By French revolutionary," said the machine.

"His name?" Holmes demanded.

A pause, then the Engine said, "Moriarty."

# CHAPTER THIRTY-SIX

## Moriarty and the Turk

Tomlinson and I both gasped, I the more sharply.

"Th-that's not r-right," said Quantock. "A French revolutionary called Moriarty? Surely, if anyone, the Engine means Marat."

"Why not ask it again?" said Holmes.

"I w-will."

But the Engine offered the same name as before: "Moriarty."

"There's s-something awry," said Quantock, flustered. "The voice cab-cabinet must be m-malfunctioning."

"I would concur," said Holmes. "'Marat' and 'Moriarty' begin with syllables that are not dissimilar sounding. It may be that the needle on the relevant cylinder is slipping, mispronouncing the second part of the name."

"But that c-can't happen. The syllabary system doesn't operate that way. A single syllable cannot b-be rep-replaced by three."

Quantock opened the voice cabinet's glass front and began checking the phonographic cylinders.

Holmes, meanwhile, turned to the rest of us and said, "Now do you see? I never said that the puzzle could not be solved by the

Engine. The machine has amply shown itself to be equal to that task. However, it has not been capable of elucidating the puzzle fully, as I predicted. It cannot supply the final telling detail, the surname of the infamous and ill-fated Jean-Paul Marat, one of the fathers of the French Revolution, who while practising medicine in England as a young man stole links from Ashmole's chain to pay off a debt. The Engine has instead stumbled and named another."

"But 'Moriarty'?" said Tomlinson. "Why that name, of all names?"

I was asking myself the same thing. First, Colonel Sebastian Moran. Now the Engine had blurted out the surname of Moran's deceased master. Could that be an accident? I sincerely doubted it.

Then I recalled coming across Holmes in this chamber after we had become separated the previous night. With hindsight, it occurred to me that he had not simply been standing static beside the Engine. He had been carrying out some sort of furtive activity, which he had completed just as I entered.

He had been tampering with the voice cabinet.

Professor Quantock arrived at the same conclusion. He rounded on Holmes, eyes flashing. A wax cylinder was in his hand.

"This is n-not one of my cylinders!" he said hotly. "Someone has interfered with my Engine. *You* have, sir. It must be you."

I thought Holmes might at least try to deny the accusation, but he actually seemed pleased to own up to it.

"Guilty as charged," he said. "I availed myself of the services of a phonographic supplies shop on Cornmarket Street. I hired a recording machine for an hour and etched a cylinder of my own, repeating the same collection of sounds – 'iarty' – over and over until there was no space left. That was my voice you heard. When Watson and I were treated to the first public demonstration of the Engine's voice, I noted which cylinder was called into use when the syllable 'at' was required. Number seventeen. That was the one

I replaced last night with my own cylinder."

"But… wh-what for?"

"All to produce this effect, the utterance of the name Moriarty."

I had to marvel at Holmes's ingenuity, even while wondering why he had not taken me into his confidence about this particular aspect of his plan. No doubt he had wanted me to be as awestruck by his little *coup de théâtre* as everyone else in the room. How he loved to pull the wool over people's eyes, strangers and bosom friends alike.

"But why Moriarty?" said Tomlinson. "I presume it's a reference to your erstwhile nemesis, who now lies dead and has, I am sure, been judged in the hereafter according to his deeds on earth."

"To show that I know the truth of what has been going on," said Holmes. "You see, I have for some time harboured the suspicion that there is more to the Thinking Engine than meets the eye. I am minded to compare it to the Turk."

"The Turk?" said Lord Knaresfield. "What in blazes are you jabbering on about now? What Turk? Is there some Turkish person hereabouts?"

"Don't you remember? It wasn't so long ago. Built in 1770, the Turk was a miracle of mechanical engineering, an automaton that could play chess against grandmasters and win. It could also perform the knight's tour, a vexing puzzle which requires the player to execute a sequence of moves with the knight so that the piece visits every square on the board once and once only – more a mathematical problem than anything. In short, the Turk was every bit as clever as the Thinking Engine."

"I dis-dispute that," said Quantock.

"As well you might, professor. The Turk could even be regarded as the Engine's forerunner, more so than any of Babbage's creations."

"I think I know what you're talking about," said Slater. "It was a model of a turbaned Levantine seated at a boxed-in table, yes? And it shunted the chessmen about with its hand. But wasn't it revealed as a—?"

"The Turk," said Holmes, butting in, "convinced many people that its Hungarian creator, Wolfgang von Kempelen, was some kind of engineering genius. It was shown all around the world and defeated several notable chess aficionados, including Frederick the Great of Prussia, Benjamin Franklin and Napoleon Bonaparte. The front of the table could be opened up to show off the complex workings inside, yet some who saw the Turk in operation were convinced it was not a machine at all but possessed by some supernatural entity. So lifelike did it appear that ladies in the audience were known to faint as it moved. I imagine one would find it eerie, watching this mysterious metal figure nod twice when its opponent's queen was in danger and three times when its opponent's king was in check. Emperors and nobles were very taken with it. Just as a member of our own nobility, none other than Lord Knaresfield, has been taken with the Thinking Engine."

"What of it?" said his lordship. "The Engine is an amazing thing."

"But that wasn't all that attracted you, was it? That isn't why you agreed to put your considerable clout behind it."

"I distinctly recall telling you that I regard the Engine as potentially a powerful tool for the advancement of journalism. It could be the way forward for my industry in the twentieth century. Hence my advocacy of it."

"I don't doubt that. But you also wished to exploit it as a weapon against me."

"Against you, Mr Holmes?" Knaresfield gave vent to a chuckle which, to my ears at least, sounded hollow and sly. "Why ever would that be? I have no beef with you – not until now, at any rate, when you've started to level wild accusations."

"You yourself hold no grudge against me," said Holmes. "The same cannot be said for a transatlantic counterpart of yours, Mr Wallace Rubenstein, one of America's foremost newspaper proprietors."

It took me a moment to place the name. Rubenstein, of course, was the owner of the collection of antiquities to which Pharaoh Djedhor's mummy had belonged.

"Mr Rubenstein and you," Holmes continued, "are acquaintances. I might go so far as to call you friends. I unearthed a record of your relationship in the archives of *The Oxford Times*. You have made several trips overseas to be a guest of him and his wife at their summer residence in New Haven, Connecticut. He, in turn, has stayed with you in Yorkshire. You boasted to me the other day about the advanced printing presses you intend to buy and the new typesetting and photogravure techniques you wish to introduce for your stable of publications. You said they are American in origin, and it takes no great stretch of the imagination to deduce that you came upon them courtesy of Rubenstein. It may even be that he is the one from whom you will be purchasing them."

"Those are facts," Knaresfield admitted. "They cannot be gainsaid. But so what? What bearing do they have on the present situation?"

"You know full well the answer to that. Earlier in the year, Watson and I caused Rubenstein some embarrassment – mostly of the financial kind. We obliged him to pay out compensation to certain individuals whom he had incommoded. I imagine Rubenstein was keen to enact retribution and ensure that I got my comeuppance. He recruited you as an intermediary, asking you to act as his proxy in Britain, his right hand. You agreed to it, not wishing to jeopardise your future business ventures with him. Opportunity arrived in the shape of the Thinking Engine, a machine that might outwit me. You put money behind it, in the form of a handsome wager which brought the Engine to my notice and that of the wider world. You have since been using your newspapers to promote the device and trumpet its successes at my expense."

Knaresfield seemed set to refute this, but his pride would not let him.

"All right," he said. "Well done. I can't deny it. You've rumbled me. It's nothing personal, of course. You do know that? Just business."

"Which is why I feel no great animosity towards you, your lordship. You are a businessman to the core. Love of profit runs through your veins. To you, helping an attempt to engineer my downfall has been a transaction, nothing more. A deal. The same goes for Mr Slater."

"What? Me?" said the journalist.

"I would say that your days at the *Illustrated London News* are numbered. Your tenure there is coming to an end. You are barely clinging to your position as it is, given your insalubrious habits and the use of blackmail against your editor. How much longer can you hold on? Your mother's consignment to an insane asylum is a drain on your purse, which is already depleted thanks to your gambling. Your actress mistress must be costing you a pretty penny as well. Lord Knaresfield has money. You need money. You are, I would suggest, already covertly on his payroll. That or he has offered you a well-remunerated post at one of his many papers, yours to take up once your role in this Thinking Engine business is discharged."

"I don't think that's—"

"I don't care tuppence what you think, Slater," Holmes said. "You and his lordship have done well, acting as though you are strangers to each other. All the while, at his lordship's behest, you have been penning articles that add to the weight of opinion against me. You have never been an admirer of mine. Lord

Knaresfield gave you the incentive to develop that into a full-blown *ad hominem* mania."

Slater continued to protest, but Knaresfield silenced him with a mid-air slash of the hand. "Slater, the game's up. Holmes has us bang to rights. The manly thing to do is accept it. Don't you understand the implications here, you daft beggar? We thought all we were doing was ruining a reputation. It seems, though, that we have been a party to something far more heinous. There have been deaths. The Engine wasn't solving them. It has been instrumental in *causing* them. We, whether we like it or not, are complicit in that. We bear some small part of the guilt."

Slater acknowledged this with a tight-lipped shrug. "I regret nothing."

"No, because regret implies a conscience, and that is an attribute you signally lack," said Holmes. "But I feel no great animosity towards you, either. Like his lordship, you are a victim of your personality. You are not evil, just pragmatic, a creature comprised entirely of self-interest and necessity. Whatever suits you best, you do, and the consequences be blowed."

"Now hold on a minute, Mr Holmes," said Inspector Tomlinson. "I think I've followed this so far. His lordship has waged a campaign of sabotage against you, with the connivance of Professor Quantock and the assistance of Mr Slater. You are being admirably sanguine about that, for which I commend you."

"Thank you, inspector. I have tried to behave rationally and not let resentment get the better of me."

"What I don't see is how Professor Moriarty ties in. And what the relevance of the Turk?"

"For the answer to that," said Holmes, "we must look to the person here who would seem to be the most innocent of wrongdoing but is not. He knows perfectly well how Moriarty and the Turk fit in. Don't you, Professor Quantock?"

# CHAPTER THIRTY-SEVEN

## Unholy Trinity

"I b-beg your pardon?" Quantock blinked rapidly, his hands darting like spiders. He appeared flabbergasted.

"Let us consider your background," said Holmes. "You came to Oxford from another, lesser university. I discovered its name from your book on Vandermonde's Convolution. It so happens to be the same university where Professor Moriarty was a Fellow. You and he were contemporaries there. Edward Caird told me you had left the place 'under a cloud'. So had Moriarty, and at roughly the same time. I wonder if the rumours of misconduct which became attached to you are similar to the ones attaching to him. I would not be surprised if they are."

"Good Lord," I said. "You mean he and Moriarty were friends?"

"Both mathematicians, at a relatively small provincial university. It would be highly unlikely they did not know one other, and that is confirmed by the dedication at the front of Quantock's book. 'To J.M., *magister arithmeticae et animi mei*.' Who else could J.M. be but James Moriarty? 'Master of arithmetic and of my soul.'

The two of them may have forged a bond of mutual admiration, or else – and this is the scenario I lean towards – Moriarty made Quantock his willing thrall, as he did so many others. A strong, charismatic personality such as Moriarty's would have easily overpowered that of a meeker, more hesitant man, to make him a fellow traveller in whatever shady habits he indulged in."

"Then," said Tomlinson, "Professor Quantock has been enacting a sort of revenge against you for Professor Moriarty's death?"

"I believe that to be the case."

"With Moran as his accomplice," I said.

"And not the only one. Isn't that so, professor?"

Quantock looked petulantly around at the rest of us. He had the air of someone under siege, harried, but far from defeated.

"Your silence is as good as a yes," said Holmes. "Not only have you allied yourself with Sebastian Moran, Moriarty's thuggish second-in-command, but with another Moriarty too. A former soldier and colonel, like Moran himself."

"The brother," I said.

"That is my belief," said Holmes. "Here is where the Turk comes in. That automaton, it transpired, was no such thing. The Turk is one of the greatest hoaxes of all time. It fooled princes, statesmen and chess grandmasters alike. The model of a human figure was merely a puppet. The so-called workings built into the table were in fact elements of the mechanism by which the chess pieces were controlled. This consisted principally of a set of levers that opened and closed the model's hand and moved it to the desired location on the board, matching a second board set within the machine, in the manner of a pantograph. Clockwork sounds were manufactured so as to give the impression that the Turk was being driven by some intricate inner apparatus."

"Whereas in fact it was not," I said, the light dawning. "It was driven by a man."

"A chess expert, hidden inside the table," said Holmes. "There were at least five of them all told, at various different times. Wherever the Turk was exhibited, one of them would be operating it secretly from within, fostering the illusion of a machine with the mind of a human."

"And the Thinking Engine – it is the same? There's someone in there?"

From Knaresfield, Slater and Tomlinson there were expressions of astonishment, none of them feigned; from Quantock, just a shifty glance to the side and a hand flap that could be interpreted to mean many things or nothing at all.

"I can allege that with confidence," said Holmes, "because there is no earthly way the Engine could have known of the theft of Ashmole's chain *unless* there was someone inside it. This someone has been inhabiting it all along, like a hermit crab in its borrowed shell, and was here last night when Watson and I were discussing what we had just done. He overheard everything – exactly as he was meant to. He then, just moments ago, made the tactical error of revealing what he knew. He simply couldn't help himself. The Thinking Engine could not betray ignorance, could it? It could not be wrong. Especially when, by being right, it could land Sherlock Holmes and John Watson in hot water."

"Last night we were laying a trap for it?" I said. I thought back to our time in the British Museum all those months ago, and suddenly light dawned. "My God, Holmes," I cried. "Are you saying that Houdini has performed the same trick and is living within the Thinking Engine, as he did the mummy? That Rubenstein sent him to aid Knaresfield in bringing you low?"

My companion shook his head, a familiar look of condescension on his face. "No, no, Watson. We have already ascertained that while Knaresfield and Rubenstein took advantage of the Engine's existence, they are not the prime movers in this case, merely the enablers." He waved a dismissive hand in Knaresfield's direction. "And consider, our friend Mr Houdini is skilled in physical feats and showmanship but this endeavour required a great mind, one the equal of the late unlamented Professor Moriarty."

He drew himself up to his full height. "We were indeed laying a trap for the man inside the Thinking Engine. A man who shares the blood – and the mind – of the Napoleon of crime. His brother, Colonel Moriarty himself. The man who took it very hard when I exposed his older sibling as the head of the vilest and most extensive criminal organisation this country has ever known. He and Quantock have been collaborators in a monstrous fraud, while a third member of their unholy trinity, Moran, does their dirty work."

A loud *crack* made me jump. The cylinder which Quantock was holding, fragile like all of its kind, had shattered into a dozen pieces in his grasp. He had gripped it too tightly. Now it lay in fragments on the floor.

Quantock looked down at his hands. A couple of his fingers, lacerated by the shards of cylinder, were bleeding. Seemingly untroubled by the pain, he looked up again, and his lips pulled back from his teeth in a terrible, leering grin.

"Not bad, Mr Holmes," he said. "Not b-bad at all. There's only one problem."

"Oh? And what is that?"

"Right surname," said Quantock. "Wrong Moriarty."

# CHAPTER THIRTY-EIGHT

## A Great Brass-and-Steel Sham

There were times when it was hard to gauge Sherlock Holmes's reaction to an unexpected development or a reversal of fortune. Usually he would respond as anyone might, with a flinch of surprise and perhaps an oath. Occasionally, however, he would go blank, his face taking on a flat affect, as though a part of him had shut down, screening itself off from the world. A stage curtain would descend, as it were, obscuring the theatre of his mind.

This was one of those occasions. Quantock's words seemed to freeze him, rendering him immobile and mute. They stunned him just as effectively as a blow from a cosh might have.

On me they weren't much less incapacitating, although I did manage to splutter out a sentence or two. "There's another Moriarty. A third one. Some cousin, some nephew we've not heard about before."

I said it more in hope than expectation, and Quantock's slow head-shake told me I was destined for disappointment.

"There is only one," the mathematician said. "Only one M-Moriarty that matters. The original. The inimitable."

"But he is dead!" Tomlinson objected. "We've been assured of that. He perished at the Reichenbach Falls, by Mr Holmes's hand, with his criminal organisation in smithereens."

"You b-believed Holmes himself to be dead," said Quantock. "Yet he stands before you t-today, large as l-life. If he survived their encounter, why could the same not be tr-true of his archenemy? Professor Moriarty, after all, is ev-every bit his equal."

"Am I missing something here?" said Lord Knaresfield. "There's a man inside that machine, and he's some professor friend of Quantock's who is supposed to be dead but isn't. Is that about the long and the short of it?"

"It's a little more complicated than that, your lordship," said Tomlinson. "Professor Moriarty is no ordinary man. He's a legend amongst criminals – their god-king, their Alexander. Surely you've heard of him?"

"The name rings a bell, but I'm not always up to date on current events. I print the news, but that doesn't make me an expert on it."

"In the East End, people still talk about him in hushed tones," said Slater. "I've a couple of underworld contacts I use for tip-offs and information. Even to this day, four years after Moriarty was last seen or heard from, my snitches are wary of mentioning him. They'll take the Devil's name in vain but not his. That's the kind of awe he held people in."

"Oh well then, that's the explanation," said Knaresfield. "It's London stuff and I'm a northerner. No wonder I don't know so much about it."

"And now, allegedly, he's here," I said. "But it's preposterous. I don't credit it for one moment. Professor Moriarty is inside the Thinking Engine? Come now, Quantock. You're bluffing. It's wishful thinking on your part, that's all. Holmes may have come back from the dead but he never actually fell into the Reichenbach

Falls, whereas Moriarty assuredly did. No man could survive that! Your old friend is gone but you're desperately trying to resurrect him somehow, keep his memory alive. It's a nice try. We're all shocked, just as you hoped. But it's *Colonel* Moriarty in there, not Professor. Don't you agree, Holmes?"

My friend was still inert, although I sensed calculation in his eyes, his brain rapidly running through permutations. His gaze was fixed on the Engine. It was as though he was trying to pierce it with his vision, see through the external layers of mechanism to the interior, where resided a human being, the chess expert within this elaborate Turk.

"Mr Holmes knows I am t-telling the truth," said Quantock. "What do I have to gain at this point in the proceedings by l-lying? Our scheme stands revealed. I am making cl-claims that can be verified with little effort. The Thinking Engine is a gr-grand charade, and I am one of its architects. The other architect l-lurks within, and after all this time I think h-he would like to be f-formally reacquainted with the man who d-did his utmost to end his life but failed."

At last Holmes spoke. "Open it up."

Quantock chuckled. "There. The great consulting detective w-wants to see for himself. He knows, but knowing isn't en-enough. He will only acc-accept the evidence of his own eyes."

"Open it up," Holmes repeated, more vehemently this time. "Damn you, man, do it!"

"I c-could. Or I could simply savour the moment. I don't foresee many pleasures in my f-future, so I should t-take whatever ones I can st-still find."

Holmes lunged towards me and snatched the revolver from my pocket. He moved so fast, I could not have stopped him even if I had wanted to.

He covered the ground between him and Quantock in

three swift paces and lodged the barrel of the gun against the mathematician's head.

"Open it up or I shall open up your skull. Do not mistake that for a threat. It is a statement of fact."

"No n-need to be that way. Of c-course I shall open it for you."

"And no tricks," Holmes said as Quantock moved to the left-hand side of the Thinking Engine's front. "I wouldn't put it past you to have installed booby traps, or to have some form of weapon concealed nearby, in case of emergency."

"Then y-you have misread me, Mr Holmes. I n-never anticipated that I would be compelled to unlock the Engine. Thus I never anticipated th-that defensive measures w-would be required."

Having wrapped a handkerchief around his bloodied fingers, Quantock manipulated one of the columns of dials on the Engine. He turned them until he had lined up a set of numbers. These clearly acted like the combination on a safe, as I heard unseen bolts retract.

"The first ten primes in order," he said. "It's the most elegant and b-beautiful number sequence there is."

As the last bolt clunked back, a section of the Engine's front broke clear, swinging outward on hinges. Quantock pulled on this door, which fitted into the face of the machine like some fantastically intricate jigsaw piece. Its edges were not smooth but rather an arabesque lattice of moving parts that meshed perfectly with their neighbours when the door was shut. You would never have realised it was there unless you had known.

The opening of the door conclusively gave away the lie of the Thinking Engine, showing that what we had been led to believe was a solid block of machinery was in fact hollow. The device consisted of a shell a couple of yards thick all round, walls constructed from components that were so densely integrated one could not see through them. The Engine gave the illusion of computational activity, but an illusion was all it was. The wheels and cogs revolved at random, having no purpose other than to convey activity and make noise – the proverbial sound and fury signifying nothing.

Quantock invited Holmes to step across the threshold. I went too, as did Tomlinson.

"Be careful," I warned my friend. "If it really is Moriarty in there…"

"Regrettably, James is in no position to p-pose any direct danger to you," said Quantock. "He is no longer quite the man he w-was."

In a space no bigger than a garden shed, enclosed on all four sides by a great brass-and-steel sham, we came face to face with the Napoleon of crime.

Or rather, what was left of him.

# CHAPTER THIRTY-NINE

## A Spider Again

Up until that moment, I had never seen Professor Moriarty at close hand. As related in "The Final Problem", hitherto I had had but a single distant glimpse of him. That was when I had spied him striding along the hill path to his rendezvous with Holmes in Switzerland, a black figure outlined against the green of the Alpine landscape. At the time, I had not known who this solitary walker was, and nothing about him had struck me as incongruous or noteworthy, other than the unusual energy with which he moved. Afterwards I would realise that this had been the purposeful gait of a man who had scores to settle and murder on his mind.

Otherwise, my knowledge of Moriarty's physical appearance came solely from Holmes, who had described a high, domed forehead – not unlike his own – along with puckered, deeply sunken eyes, pale skin, and rounded shoulders. There was also the sinister detail of the reptilian manner in which Moriarty held himself, oscillating slowly from side to side as he stood, like a cobra hypnotising its prey. Sidney Paget's illustrations in *The Strand* had captured his likeness well, so Holmes told me, but could not hope to convey the aura of sheer malice he exuded. "To be in the presence of Moriarty," Holmes once said, "is to be confronted with the chilling possibility that there is no such thing as decency or humaneness. They are artificial constructs. There is only a howling pit of darkness, intrinsic to every one of us, which most do their best to disavow but which is our true nature. In Moriarty, it is not suppressed. It is not repudiated. It is given free rein."

The man seated within the Thinking Engine did not, at first sight, strike me as worthy of this reputation. For one thing there was precious little of him to look at. He lacked one arm, lost at the shoulder, and both legs from the knee down. He was fastened into a sturdy iron chair, his torso secured by leather straps. His head rested in a cradle of padded wicker which kept it upright and facing forwards. Not only was he deprived of limbs but he was quite clearly suffering from quadriplegic paralysis, mostly likely the result of a fracture of an upper cervical vertebra and the consequent severance of his spinal cord. His remaining arm displayed the flaccidity that is a common indicator of such an injury. The hand lay motionless on the arm of the chair, fingers splayed, like some hideous dead insect.

His head still had some range of motion, and as we came in he swivelled it towards us to fix us with a look. His eyes, in their wrinkled recesses, glowed like twin moons. The shape he pulled his mouth into might have been intended as a grin, an ironic gesture of welcome, but it resembled just as much the rictus of someone in dire agony.

Quantock took up position behind him, resting a hand on his shoulder. "I h-had to bring them in, James. I had no ch-choice."

Moriarty rolled his eyes up to Quantock, then back to us.

Beside me, Holmes had gone rigid, as though he was seeing a ghost. In a sense, he was. The revolver hung loose from his grasp.

He seemed to have forgotten he was holding it.

"I watched you fall," he said in hushed tones. "I overpowered you. I toppled you from the pathway and saw you strike the rocks several hundred feet below and vanish into the water. No one could have survived a fall like that. No one."

"And y-yet James did," said Quantock, patting Moriarty with a mixture of affection and veneration. "Such is his will to live. He survived when his body was so b-battered and broken, the pain alone would have killed a lesser man. Which reminds me. It's t-time for your medication, James."

There were shelves inside the Engine laden with medical paraphernalia – syringes and drugs, mostly – and also glass jars of water and tinned foodstuffs. Books sat within easy reach of the chair, works of reference such as almanacs, encyclopaedias and histories.

We watched as Quantock loaded a syringe with a quantity of morphine from a phial, then rolled up Moriarty's sleeve and turned his forearm over to expose the underside. He did this with the tenderness of a nurse dealing with a favoured patient. The skin of the arm was stippled with tiny red dots, constellations of pinpricks. Quantock was poised to administer the injection when Holmes stopped him.

"No. Stand back."

"But J-James is in constant pain. He needs relief from it."

The gun came up. "He deserves none. Step away from him."

Quantock grimaced but did as Holmes said.

Moriarty's eyes blazed.

"I would like to know how you managed it, Moriarty," Holmes said. "How you cheated death."

"Oh, I c-can tell you h-how," said Quantock.

"I want to hear it from his own lips. Can he not speak?"

"Only… with… difficulty."

It was a wisp of sound, each word pushed out on a gasping

breath with a rapid inhalation between. I added a crushed larynx to the litany of terrible injuries Moriarty had sustained. I still felt no pity for him whatsoever.

"But… I… would… prefer… to… use… the… voice… Malcolm… has… lately… given… me," he croaked. "More… articulate. Less… effort."

His hand moved. The nerve damage from the spinal break was not total and he retained some control over the appendage. It crawled to a panel mounted on the end of the chair arm. There sat a stenotype keyboard of the kind used by stenographers to record court and parliamentary proceedings. It had been cunningly modified so that it could be operated one-handed. Moriarty arranged his fingers over the spindly, fanned keys and began to tap out sentences.

Outside, the voice cabinet relayed his words, translating type to speech.

"Took precaution before departing for our assignation. Put on hidden armour of own devising. Plates of shellac reinforced with whalebone. Worn like leotard beneath clothing. To absorb blows to body."

"I did feel an unusual undergarment on your person as we fought," said Holmes. "At first I took it for a hernia truss, but then a corset seemed more likely."

Moriarty greeted the jibe with a baleful glare.

"Had we boxed rather than wrestled," my friend added, "I daresay it might have made a difference."

"Armour still served useful purpose during fall," Moriarty said. "Afforded some protection upon impact. Internal organs were undamaged. Bones not. Entered water and nearly drowned. Limbs useless. Thrown about in turbulence of whirlpool. Floated to surface eventually. Carried along by river current for some dist[ ]."

"'Dist'?" I said.

"He m-means distance," said Quantock. "Cylinder s-seventeen is missing, remember? That restricts his vocabulary. Certain syllables will inevitably drop out."

"So the Thinking Engine has a speech impediment too," said Tomlinson.

Quantock looked daggers at him.

Moriarty continued depressing the keys.

"River shallowed, flattening out. Fetched up on mud bank. Lay helpless. Stranded. Was discovered in evening by goatherd. Carried to [ ]el."

"Hovel, I think that w-word was," said Quantock.

"Goatherd and wife tended. Looked after. Money in wallet. Swiss francs. Within days, arranged to be taken to hospital in Lu[ ]."

"Lucerne," said Quantock.

"We guessed that," said Holmes tersely. "So you were saved by a goatherd and treated by Swiss doctors, who are amongst the best in the world. Your arm and legs were, I imagine, beyond salvaging."

"Twisted. Shattered. Risk of gangrene setting in. Required amputation. Recovery lasted months. Meanwhile feigned amnesia. Assumed by local authorities to be hiker who slipped and fell. Then tr[ ]ferred to sanatorium in Geneva. One whole year before healed enough to be discharged."

"By which time you had become aware that you no longer had any assets in England to speak of. Your organisation was destroyed. Everything you had built up over the course of your criminal career was now as useless to you as your body."

"Yet brain intact," Moriarty declared via the voice cabinet. "Brain the source of power. Greatest weapon in arsenal. Returned to England using contingency funds deposited in Zurich bank account. Lay low. Began to re-establish contact with few re[ ] ing associates."

"Including m-me," said Quantock. "I was the f-first he got in touch with. A b-bolt from the blue, but not an unwelcome one. I had not forgotten James. We had been so close before he l-left for London and I found a post at Oxford. I had resigned myself to life without h-him, and then all of a s-sudden he was back. How c-could I refuse his pleas for help? How could I not take c-care of him in his hour of greatest need?"

"That was nearly three years ago," Holmes said to Moriarty. "All this time you have been brooding, scheming, trying to work out how best to strike back at me."

"Not *all* that time, surely," said Tomlinson. "You were 'dead' until last year, Mr Holmes, don't forget."

"As far as the rest of the world was concerned, yes. But Moriarty would have known I was not. Watson fancied that he was the last person alive to see me before my supposed demise, but in fact that honour went to Moriarty."

"Not dead but not visible," said Moriarty's disembodied voice, which was also Quantock's voice – a weird symmetry, reflecting the weird intimacy between the two men. "Knew you were in hiding. Knew you would re-emerge sooner or later. Once you felt safe. Sherlock Holmes could not shun limelight forever. Too much the glory hound."

"And s-so we bided our time," said Quantock, "and sure enough, early last year, who sh-should prance back onto the p-public stage but the man himself?"

"Heard Mor[ ] tried to kill you in London." It seemed to frustrate Moriarty that he couldn't sound out Moran's name properly. "Informed by contacts of failed assassination bid. Reached out to Mor[ ] while in custody. Arranged escape. Reunited."

"The old firm, back together," I drawled. "With a new lackey, Quantock."

"Lackey!" the mathematician snorted. "I have been every bit as much of a p-participant in this business as James or the c-colonel."

"You've certainly fulfilled your remit as the public face of the Thinking Engine," said Holmes. "Those stunts you pulled – wandering through busy traffic on St Giles', squatting atop the clock tower of St Mary's, getting into a spat with Edward Caird – they got everyone's notice, didn't they? Now you were known to Town as well as Gown. The police had your name on their books. You even came to Tomlinson's attention."

"That was inevitable, and it s-seemed advisable to have the city's senior-most police detective right where we could see him, under our n-noses, so that we could keep an eye on the status of his in-investigations and if n-necessary make sure he d-didn't get too close to the truth. I'd heard on the gr-grapevine that he was an admirer and a correspondent of yours. The simple fact that the two of you were on c-cordial terms was, we felt, an added inducement, another reason why you would not be av-averse to travelling to Oxford."

Tomlinson clapped hand to forehead. "I was used. Oh, Mr Holmes, I am sorry! I had no idea. I would never have knowingly been a part of this intrigue. You must realise that."

"It's quite all right, inspector," said Holmes. "Knaresfield's wager alone was impetus enough to draw me here. Our pre-existing rapport made no difference in that regard."

I nearly spoke up to remind my friend that he had included Tomlinson on his list of potential suspects for Moran's master, but it did not seem appropriate at that moment. I was glad, though, that the official's innocence now lay beyond question. Tomlinson, like Knaresfield and Slater, had been peripheral to Moriarty's scheme, a satellite pulled unheedingly into the orbit of evil.

"It does seem, however," Holmes continued, "that defeating me has not been the sole object of the exercise. I put it to you, Moriarty, that you have an ulterior motive. As originally envisaged, I should by now be an abject wreck, sunk in a slough of despond, redundant, while you gallop on towards a wider, greater triumph."

"Too true," said Moriarty. "Once spider in centre of web. Destined to be spider again. In centre of much larger web."

"Yes. I see it now. This has all been about the promulgation of the Thinking Engine. You foresee a future with Thinking Engines everywhere, dozens of them, hundreds, in newspaper offices, police stations, who knows where else. A network extending to every corner of the land, apparently independent and automated but in fact artificial. All of them joined together, feeding back to you."

With a quivering forefinger Moriarty pointed to a display board mounted before him at eye level. It consisted of rows of slots, each with a letter wheel inside. The wheels currently sat so that, in order, the letters in the slots spelled out the last question which Quantock had typed in: Holmes's demand for the name of the French revolutionary.

"All enquiries from outside would appear here," he said. "Window on world."

"Enabling you to run the other Engines remotely, telegraphically," said Holmes. "It would make you the governor of police records, of news reports, of the dissemination of information. *That* has been your ambition. So much more than mere criminality."

"Circumstances altered, therefore strategy altered. Cut coat to suit cloth. Hard to run empire as before when so crippled. Multiple Thinking Engines become extensions of self. Each a branch line stemming from here, the central terminus."

"At the police stations you could wipe a crook's slate clean," said Holmes. "You could mislead investigations."

"Also stay abreast of police ac[ ]ity. Thus minimise risks to self. Cannot walk but always one step ahead."

"At the same time, access to n-newspapers would enable James to exert an influence over public per-perceptions," said Quantock.

"He could subtly sway journalists, m-manipulating reportage to his advantage. In turn, that means government policy could be his to bias. The outcome of general elections could be his to decide. That is p-power!"

"In time your Engines would become trusted as the font of all wisdom," said Holmes. "Everything they said would be regarded as gospel. I shudder to think what our world would be like with Professor Moriarty guiding it, the sole arbiter of truth."

"Truth whatever Moriarty makes it," said Moriarty. "Truth the sole province of Moriarty. Moriarty sees all. Moriarty runs all. Moriarty rules all."

"A chilling vision," I said.

"But one that shall not come to pass." Holmes levelled the revolver at Moriarty. "I can end it with just a pull of the trigger, and finish what I started at the Reichenbach Falls. It would be granting you a mercy, Moriarty, terminating this miserable half-existence of yours."

"Go ahead, Mr Holmes," said Tomlinson. "Don't let me being here stop you. If ever there was a time for a copper to turn a blind eye, this is it."

Moriarty gazed straight at the pistol, remarkably unperturbed. His hand picked out a single syllable on the stenotype keyboard.

"Ha."

He pressed his fingers down again in the same configuration. And again. And again.

"Ha. Ha."

Insistently, rhythmically, the syllable issued forth from the voice cabinet.

"Ha. Ha. Ha. Ha. Ha."

It was laughter.

The most ominous and inhuman laughter.

Moriarty repeated the sound until I felt like covering my ears and begging him to shut up. Couldn't Holmes just shoot him? End the infernal racket?

In the event, my friend slapped Moriarty's hand aside. The voice cabinet fell blessedly silent.

"You laugh as though you have won," he said. "How can you possibly think you have won, when you have quite so clearly lost?"

The hand climbed back onto the stenotype.

"When is spider most dangerous?" Moriarty asked.

"I've no patience with riddles," Holmes retorted.

"When fly lands in middle of web."

Moriarty's hand slipped to the side of the chair arm and touched something there, something that let out a sharp *click*.

Behind us, the door began to close. Tomlinson and I leapt to hold it back, but it was heavy and driven by some sort of hydraulic ram. We fought but could not prevent it from slamming shut.

Next instant, the walls around us came alive.

# CHAPTER FORTY

## Rods

Rods began shooting out horizontally. Propelled by pneumatic pistons, they jabbed and retracted, jabbed and retracted. Each was a good three feet in length and fashioned of brass a half inch in diameter, and each carried enough momentum to pierce a man's flesh, as Inspector Tomlinson discovered almost immediately, to his cost. A rod bored clean through his thigh, pulling back to leave a neat, bloody hole. As he collapsed to the floor with a bray of pain, clutching his leg, a second rod speared the meat of his shoulder from behind, its tip protruding above his collarbone before withdrawing back into the wall.

"Watson!" Holmes cried. "Duck!"

I didn't hesitate. I dipped my head, just as a rod flashed out above me. I felt it part my hair. A split second slower, a hand's-breadth lower, and it would have drilled through my cranium.

All at once, the interior of the Thinking Engine had become a scene of pain and blood and chaos. The rods spiked out here and there, apparently at random. Some were positioned high, some low. They sprang from the interstices of the machinery. There were no obvious slots or recesses, so one could not spot where any might emerge. They came thick and fast, from everywhere, so many of them, too many of them to keep track of, criss-crossing, swift, unpredictable, deadly as rapiers. One even knocked the revolver from Holmes's grasp, with an accuracy that would have seemed spiteful if it hadn't been pure chance. The gun skidded away, fetching up in the corner furthest from any of us. Whatever advantage it might have offered was lost.

We had walked into a death trap, and now every moment was a struggle for survival. We had to move and keep moving in order to steer clear of the rods. There was only one place safe from them, and that was the exact centre of the Engine where Moriarty's chair lay. Here, in this "eye of the storm", Holmes's nemesis sat serene, untouched. Quantock stood to the rear of him, pressed close to the chair's back, also out of the rods' reach, just.

The switch on the chair arm which had set the death trap going would also be the means of shutting it off. Holmes tried to get to it. The rods thwarted his efforts, however. Every time he gained ground, he had to retreat or else be impaled. It was the same for me. We were engaged in an unending dance with the rods, and any misstep could be our last.

Meanwhile Tomlinson was groaning and flailing around, stricken by his injuries. It seemed only a matter of time before another rod stabbed him, perhaps fatally. I was too busy making evasive manoeuvres of my own to go to his aid. Worse, I could feel myself tiring. It was incredibly taxing, dodging the rods. It took every ounce of strength and agility I had, and I could not afford to stop and rest for one moment. I was continually writhing, hopping, bending, recoiling, avoiding. My breath started to come in gasps and I knew I was beginning to weaken. Soon I would be exhausted, unable to carry on. I would get careless, clumsy. I would stray into the path of a rod. One was all it would take. Even if it only delivered a disabling wound, I would be left fully at the death trap's mercy.

Moriarty beheld the three of us, his hapless victims, with an imperious disdain. He had locked us inside a sophisticated modern version of an iron maiden and, unlike the torturers of old, he could actually watch us as we suffered and died in it. He had the best seat in the house.

Holmes, as far as I could tell, was tiring like me, his stamina waning. I prayed that even as he contorted himself around the rods, he was looking for a way to outwit the trap.

Finally he appeared to alight on the solution. He braced himself, then lunged for one of the reference works, a large, heavy leather-bound tome. Thanks to the rods, the book had been toppled from its perch on a lectern beside Moriarty. Holmes snatched it up and used it for a shield as he made a last-ditch desperate bid for Moriarty's chair.

He almost got there without mishap. A rod thudded against the book's thick binding, slamming it into Holmes's head. He reeled and lost his footing, but quickly he was up again and running.

All at once he had a clear view of the side of the chair where the switch was set, a simple toggle switch of the kind used to operate an electric light. Holmes hurled the book at it spine-first. Before the book struck home, a rod lashed out and caught him on the temple. It was, luckily, a glancing blow, but it tore a crease across his skin and was forceful enough to send him spinning to the floor.

The switch clicked. The rods ceased their in-and-out pulsations, shrinking back as one, vanishing from view. The walls were no longer a mass of lethal darting brass lances.

Moriarty's hand crept down to the switch to reactivate the trap. I spied the revolver some half-dozen yards from where I was crouched. I dived towards it, scurrying on hands and knees, caring little for elegance, only for speed. In one single swift motion I grabbed the gun, rolled, and took aim.

"No!"

With that cry, Quantock swung himself in front of Moriarty. I had already fired. The mathematician took the bullet square in the chest. He slumped back against his crippled confederate, stone cold dead. His head fell into the lap of the man whose life he had just saved at the expense of his own. Sightless eyes stared up. A mouth loosely lolled.

Moriarty looked down at him, then lowered his hand to Quantock's brow and gave it a brief, fond stroke. For the space of some seconds the two of them remained fixed in this tableau, the mutilated criminal mastermind and his self-sacrificing minion, like a ghastly parody of a Pietà. Then, once more, Moriarty attempted to restart the rods.

Holmes intervened, wresting Moriarty's hand away from the switch. Moriarty resisted, but it was a one-sided battle. He had neither the muscle power nor the leverage to compete with Holmes. An infant would have fared better. Holmes slid the arm inside one of the straps supporting Moriarty's torso and fastened it in place by tightening the buckle. Our captor was now our captive, helpless.

"I should like to crow over you," Holmes said. "It feels as though the moment merits it, and you would do the same were our roles reversed. However, all I see as I look at you is a pathetic wreck, a mockery of your former self. How tragic that, even after the ordeal you went through, you learned nothing. Instead you continued to pursue your mad fantasies of power. Could you not have been content as a mathematician? Your brilliance in that field is indisputable. You showed it when, as the Engine, you gave the Reverend Dodgson help with his theorem. You could have gone through life garlanded with academic laurels, earning the plaudits of your peers. Why wasn't that enough for you?"

"Money," Moriarty gasped out. "There's… little… wealth… to… be… earned… in… academe. But… also… if… the… world… rejects… you… then… you… must… teach… the… world… a… lesson."

"Rejects you?" I said.

"You… wouldn't… understand… Dr… Watson. You… have… not… been… an… outsider. You… have… not… felt… alienated… from… your… fellow… men… by… virtue… of… your… unconventional… looks… and… your… uncommon... intellect." He gazed down at Quantock's corpse. "Malcolm… understood. He… knew… how… I… feel... in... a... way... that… no… other… could. I… did… not… ask… to… be… a… pariah… but… if… I… must… be… one… then… why… not… be… the… greatest… pariah… ever?"

"Not all men who fail to fit in with society become society's enemy."

"Do… not… judge… me… by… your… own… moral… standards. I… am… not… like… other… men. I… am… Moriarty!"

"No," said Holmes. "Moriarty is dead. He has been dead for four years. All you are is his faded image, like a photograph left out in the sun. You screamed as you plummeted into the Aare Gorge. The last echoes of that scream are here with us today, and are soon to be lost."

"Gentlemen, if I may just interrupt a moment." Tomlinson beckoned with a limp hand. "I am not feeling any too clever. The attentions of a doctor wouldn't go amiss."

"Of course." I knelt by his side and examined his wounds. "No major organs have been perforated, as far as I can tell, and no arteries nicked. Still, we must bind up your leg and get you to the Radcliffe Infirmary."

"That'd be most—"

"Holmes!"

The name was bellowed from outside the Thinking Engine. The voice belonged to neither Lord Knaresfield nor Slater.

I looked at Holmes and he at me.

"Moran," we said in unison.

# CHAPTER FORTY-ONE

## The Tiger at Bay

"Holmes!" Moran bellowed again. "Come out where I can see you. I have something for you."

Moriarty put on that awful rictus smile again. "Not... quite... checkmate... yet... Mr... Holmes," he said. "I... have... one... move... left. My... knight... is... still... in... play."

"Holmes, I know you can hear me," said Moran. "There's two gents in front of me who aren't in the happiest frame of mind at present. Hardly surprising, considering how nobody much likes having a shotgun aimed at 'em."

There was the thud of a blow and a yell of pain.

"Nobody much likes getting hit around the head with a shotgun stock either," the old shikari added. "I'm giving you to the count of ten. If I don't see your fizzog by ten, one of these chaps loses a portion of his grey matter. Newspaper proprietor or journalist, nobleman or prole, I'm not bothered. Either'll do fine. One! Two!"

Holmes hastened to the door of the Thinking Engine.

"You're not seriously going to go out there," I said.

"What choice do I have?" he replied.

"But Moran will shoot you as soon as you show your face."

"And if I don't, he will shoot Knaresfield or Slater."

"Five! Six!" Moran shouted.

"Better them than you."

"You know I cannot just let them die, Watson. You know you cannot either."

"Eight! Hurry up, Holmes. What's keeping you?"

"I'm coming!" Holmes called out. "You'll have to be patient, though. There's no obvious handle on this door."

"Look for a knurled wheel, about waist height," said Moran. "One full turn of that anticlockwise releases the locking bolts."

"Thank you."

"You're welcome. Nine!"

"Watson." Holmes pulled me to his side. "We shall get only one chance at this. Don't prevaricate. The instant the door is ajar, fire. Doesn't matter where you aim as long as it is shoulder height."

"But I might not hit Moran. I might hit one of the others."

"They will be on their knees. Or lying on the floor."

"You don't know that. What if they're not?"

"Moran was a soldier. Military prisoners always are put in submissive positions, the better to subjugate and control them. Just aim high like I said. Whether you hit him or not, it'll put him on the back foot and buy me a few seconds."

"Holmes?" said Moran. "I just said 'nine'. Did you miss it? You know what number comes next and what happens after that."

"Knurled wheel," Holmes called out. "I have it. I'm turning it."

I was faced with an unenviable dilemma. Holmes was probably correct in his supposition that Moran was standing and Knaresfield and Slater were not. Shooting blind was a gamble nonetheless. I might injure one of the shikari's hostages, or worse.

The little wheel made a full revolution. The bolts clunked

back. The door began to swing open.

I sent up a small prayer to the Almighty, then thrust my revolver through the opening and fired.

"Aargh!"

I couldn't tell who I had hit, only that I had hit someone.

Holmes was through the door like a panther. I followed, to see an alarmed-looking Knaresfield on his knees, cringing, with his hands behind his head, and Slater sprawled on the floor beside him. A trickle of blood ran down Slater's neck from behind his ear, and for a moment I thought he was the one I had shot.

Then I saw Moran, and realised that fortune had smiled on us. The blood on Slater came from where Moran had thumped him with the shotgun. By some miracle my bullet had found its mark in Moran himself, catching him in the left arm. His sleeve was torn and a chunk of flesh was missing from his biceps.

That arm had been rendered useless. Moran was, however, far from incapacitated. As my friend sprang at him he raised the shotgun, preparing to fire it one-handed. I foresaw Holmes receiving a cartridge's worth of pellets full in the chest at point blank range, and my revolver barked again.

The shotgun went off a split second later. Both reports were deafening in the confines of the Thinking Engine chamber. Both shots hit their intended targets.

In Moran's case, my bullet struck his hand. In Holmes's case, Moran's shotgun blast winged him in the shoulder.

Both men were sent reeling.

My immediate thought was my friend's welfare, and I dashed over to him. He lay on his back, the shoulder-pad of his jacket shredded and speckled with blood. I ripped jacket and shirt open, to discover that the damage was not as bad as I'd feared. There were perhaps half a dozen pieces of shot embedded in him. The rest had missed entirely.

"You're lucky, old chap," I told him. "Your trapezius muscle has taken a peppering, but it's nothing a pair of tweezers and a smear of antiseptic ointment can't sort out."

"If I were truly lucky, I wouldn't have been hit at all," Holmes replied. "As it is, I have you to thank, Watson. Your marksmanship threw Moran's aim off. If you had been any less accurate, we would not be having this conversation. You are the hero of the hour. But look! The shikari stirs."

Moran was rising to his feet. He made a bid to retrieve the shotgun, which he had dropped, but Lord Knaresfield beat him to it.

"Oh no you don't, you mongrel!" his lordship cried, hefting up the gun. "You'll stay right where you are, or you'll regret it. Happens as I'm a dab hand with one of these on the grouse moors."

"You don't have the guts," Moran sneered, nursing his right hand. I was not displeased to see that I had managed to blow his index finger clean off. The big game hunter would not be pulling any triggers again with that hand.

"We'll see who has guts," Knaresfield said, pointing the gun at Moran's belly.

"The gruff, tough Yorkshireman. All bluster and wind. Go on then. I dare you. Shoot me."

"I will."

"You won't."

"Try me."

They stared at each other for a span of seconds. Neither moved.

Then, with a cluck of contempt, Moran turned on his heel and made for the exit. "It's a bit different when it's not birds, eh?" he said.

He had read Knaresfield well. The newspaper proprietor was many things, but a killer of men he was not.

"Well, go on, Watson," Holmes said. "Get after him."

"Won't you come too?"

"With this shoulder? I'd only slow you down."

I rushed off in pursuit of Moran, passing Knaresfield as I did. He had lowered the shotgun and was scowling at his own faint-heartedness. I wanted to reassure him that he had done nothing wrong. It is no mean feat, taking another's life. But there was no time for that. Moran was getting away.

I chased the shikari up the stairs to the ground floor. He was leaving a trail of blood drops behind him, the simplest of spoor to follow. He must have been in excruciating pain, and I did not think he would get far. He was unarmed, too, whereas I was not. All the same, I could not afford to be complacent. Even wounded, Moran was no pushover. He himself would doubtless have told me that the tiger is never more dangerous than when it is hurt and at bay.

He made it out of the University Galleries and down the front steps. He staggered along Beaumont Street to the corner where it met St Giles'. Sunday promenaders veered out of his path, alarmed by the sight of blood and the look of savage purposefulness on his face. Those who did not see him coming and were in his way, he shoved violently aside. One woman whom he barged into, narrowly avoided falling under the wheels of a brougham.

I gave chase doggedly, my revolver out. I knew I would corner him eventually and have a clear shot. He was losing blood. His footsteps were becoming more uneven, his gait unsteadier. He was tottering more than running.

He wove through the traffic on St Giles', crossing to a lawned island in the middle of the road. There stood the Martyrs' Memorial, the spire-like monument erected in honour of the three Anglican bishops – Latimer, Cranmer and Ridley – who had been burned at the stake in the sixteenth century for having the temerity to denounce the Church of Rome. Moran stumbled to the foot of its steps, where his legs gave way and he fell to a half-seated, half-lying position.

I closed in.

He gazed up at me, panting stertorously, his swarthy features flushed and glossy with perspiration.

"Do it then, you blackguard," he growled.

I had him utterly at my mercy, just as I had hoped I would a couple of days earlier when fetching my gun from home. My vision of Moran defenceless before me had become a reality.

It would have been such a simple thing. Aim at his forehead. Pull the trigger. One less villain walking amongst us.

"You have it in you, I know that," Moran said. "Unlike that lily-livered blowhard Knaresfield, you have the stuff. You've gone through that door, the one you can never go back out of again. Holmes too. It's how we have to be, we men of adventure, we players of the only game worth playing. We have to be prepared to go further than mere civilians. We have to do whatever is necessary to accomplish our goals."

"Don't pretend I'm like you, Moran," I said. "I am not."

"No, you're not. You're worse. I am what I am. I am nothing but what you see, nor do I claim to be. But you – you're a doctor. You save lives. Except when you do the opposite."

"There are some lives not worth saving. Yours, I reckon, is one of them."

"Then stop shilly-shallying. Damn your eyes, man, just get this over with!"

Moran's face was full of fury and defiance. He was genuinely unafraid.

I held the revolver steady.

A crowd had begun to gather around us. I was barely aware of them. I could hear a dim hubbub of voices, appalled gasps, the odd muted murmur of protest.

Moran's life hung in the balance. His fate was mine to decide, and mine alone. The presence of eyewitnesses would not deter me. Had any of them known who Moran was, they would have been cheering me on. This was my opportunity to rid the world of a scourge.

I lowered the gun.

Moran grimaced.

Then a pair of uniformed constables appeared. They were all set to arrest me – and well they might, since I looked to be the aggressor in the situation – but then one of them recognised me. It was Briggs, the policeman who had been charged by Tomlinson with escorting Holmes and me to the Grainger house in Jericho. I swiftly explained who Moran was, and added that Inspector Tomlinson lay in the University Galleries, in dire need of assistance.

Briggs and his colleague blew their whistles.

Moran laughed.

"Seems I won't be joining those martyrs after all," he said. It was hard to know if he was relieved or disappointed.

"Not today," I replied. "Not by my hand. But the hangman's noose awaits you. You and Moriarty."

"Ha! As if Sherlock Holmes will put his faith in the British justice system. I said he has the stuff, like you and me. He's willing to do what it takes. You left him with Moriarty to come after me. Go back and see how that has panned out."

# CHAPTER FORTY-TWO

## The Last Straw

I returned to the Thinking Engine chamber with Moran's words ringing in my ears. The last I saw of the shikari that day, he was handcuffed and in custody, with the burly Briggs standing guard over him.

Lord Knaresfield and Slater were still in the main part of the chamber, and Tomlinson had joined them there. While Slater gingerly probed the shape of the large bruise behind his ear, his lordship put the finishing touches to the bandage he had been applying to Tomlinson's leg. For that purpose, he had borrowed the theatre-mask tie given to Slater by his actress paramour.

Of Holmes there was no sign.

Then my friend emerged from the interior of the Thinking Engine, rubbing the palm of one hand thoughtfully with the thumb of the other. His expression was sombre, and I knew at once that Moran's prediction had been borne out. Professor Moriarty was no longer amongst the living.

"He's gone," Holmes said. "Damnedest thing. He just stopped breathing and slipped away. The final thwarting of his plans must have been too much for him. In his enfeebled condition, he couldn't take it. The last straw. His body gave out."

I drew close to him and, speaking low so that only he could hear, said, "Holmes, I don't suppose if I were to go inside the Engine I would find any indication that you had some involvement in his death."

"Moriarty is no more," Holmes stated. "That is all that needs to be said and all anyone needs to know. Feel free to go in there and see for yourself. In fact, I should be glad if you did. Official medical confirmation of expiry would be welcome."

I re-entered the Engine. There was Professor Moriarty, his head tilted back as far as the wicker cradle would allow. His arm had been unfastened from the strap and laid out as before on the chair arm. Quantock was still slumped with his head on Moriarty's lap, like some loyal supplicant.

I moved closer. Moriarty's eyes, half-lidded, stared into space. The tip of his tongue protruded between his lips. He looked, all at once, vacant and dull-witted, robbed of the intelligence which had burned fiercely within him even in his crippled state and had driven him to unconscionable deeds.

I put my ear beside his mouth. There were no breath sounds. I felt for a pulse in his neck. There was none.

His skin was cooling, gaining a waxy pallor.

I took a step back. I could see nothing to contradict Holmes's assertion that Moriarty had died of natural causes. The only thing at all suggestive of foul play was the restoring of the arm to its original position. But then, the limb could conceivably have slipped from the strap and flopped onto the chair arm of its own accord.

Holmes was right. All that needed to be said and all anyone needed to know was that Professor James Moriarty was finally, unarguably, incontrovertibly, dead.

# CHAPTER FORTY-THREE

## Shrewd People

The interview which appeared in the *Illustrated London News* a fortnight later was not the hatchet job one might have anticipated. Far from it. Archie Slater composed a balanced, broadly favourable portrait of Holmes, describing him as "enigmatic" and "quixotic" and referring to "complexities of personality" but otherwise merely quoting Holmes's answers to his questions verbatim, with next to no authorial interpolation.

By a gentlemen's agreement between Slater and Holmes, the subject of the Thinking Engine was not raised. If, from this, one were to infer that Slater's abrupt *volte-face* towards Holmes was in any way related to Holmes agreeing not to divulge the part Slater had played in the events at Oxford, one would not be far off the mark.

Lord Knaresfield's name did not crop up in the article at all. His lordship did at least honour his commitment to the wager with Holmes and privately sent my friend a cheque for £500. His public support for the Thinking Engine melted away to nothing, and his newspapers did a good job of denouncing the late Professor

Malcolm Quantock as a fraud and a charlatan who had come close to inflicting a great ill upon the world through his collaboration with the equally late Professor Moriarty. Other rival papers called the whole affair a debacle and vindictively rubbished Knaresfield. His skin, I imagine, was thick enough to withstand it. Wealth is a great insulator.

Another element missing from the article was our theft of Elias Ashmole's golden chain. Holmes had duly returned the original to its rightful place, and Inspector Tomlinson had declared himself satisfied and said there would be no prosecution. The custodians of the University Galleries remained unaware the chain had even been gone, so in that sense, could it be said that a crime was even committed?

At Holmes's request I read the interview out loud to him, while he busied himself extricating shag tobacco from the toe of the Persian slipper on the fireplace mantel at 221B and tamping it into his briar pipe, which he then lit and smoked ruminatively. When I was finished, I laid aside the copy of the *News* and enquired whether he believed Slater was done with him.

"He feels he owes us a debt of gratitude for rescuing him from Moran," Holmes said. "The sinner hath repented, as far as his dealings with me are concerned, and I doubt we shall hear anything adverse from him again."

"And Moran himself? We can expect never to hear anything from him again too?"

"If through some vagary of the law he somehow escapes execution, he will almost certainly be transported to the colonies. I consider half a world to be a safe enough distance between us. It's queer, though, Watson."

"What is?"

"Everything began with the Rubenstein Collection and dear old Pharaoh Djedhor, the unquiet mummy, in one museum. And how did it end? In another museum, with another emperor who should have been dead but was not, hidden within a different kind of sarcophagus. An intriguing symmetry there."

"Moriarty, at any rate, unlike Djedhor, will never rise from the grave again. You saw to that."

A cloud of smoke swirled about Holmes's face. He waved it away. "You cannot prove it," he said.

"Nor do I wish to. The coroner's report was unambiguous. There was a quantity of morphine in Moriarty's bloodstream but it was consistent with prolonged and repeated use of the substance. The cause of death was spontaneous respiratory failure. In a body as frail and severely impaired as Moriarty's was, that would not be unlikely. The main thing is that there were no signs of third-party involvement, such as, say, a fresh injection mark and empty phials of morphine discovered lying around at the scene."

"As if anyone would leave such obvious traces of malfeasance."

"No, a shrewd person would have injected the morphine via a pre-existing pinprick and carried the used syringe and empty phials away concealed about his body. A shrewd person would also have helped Inspector Tomlinson out of the Engine before returning on some pretext or other to administer the overdose."

"So you are happy to go along with the coroner's findings?"

"I am."

"And are you happy that you did not shoot Moran, even when you had the opportunity?"

"It is a question I have asked myself many times over these past few days," I said. "All things considered, the answer is yes. My conscience would not have let me rest if I had just gunned him down in cold blood."

"Then we are both of us shrewd people," Holmes said. "And," he added, puffing on his pipe, "both of us quite at peace with our consciences."

## Acknowledgements

I'd like to thank Nick Tucker for his support for my Holmesian endeavours and the loan of some precious bound copies of *The Strand*; Nick Landau and Vivien Cheung for being such excellent publishers; and Dr Stephen Harada DDS for being a wonderful cheerleader, even if he does occasionally send me the wrong emails.

– J.M.H.L.

## About the Author

**James Lovegrove** is the *New York Times* best-selling author of *The Age of Odin,* the third novel in his critically-acclaimed *Pantheon* military SF series. He was short-listed for the Arthur C. Clarke Award in 1998 for his novel *Days* and for the John W. Campbell Memorial Award in 2004 for his novel *Untied Kingdom*. He also reviews fiction for the *Financial Times*. He has written *Sherlock Holmes: The Stuff of Nightmares* and *Sherlock Holmes: Gods of War* for Titan Books; his new series, *The Cthulhu Casebooks*, will launch in 2016 with *Sherlock Holmes and the Shadwell Shadows.*